WILD GEESE

Lara Harte

WINDSOR
THORNDIKE

This large print book is published by BBC Audiobooks Ltd, Bath, England and by Thorndike Press, Waterville, Maine, USA.

Published in 2003 in the U.S. by arrangement with Capel & Land Limited.

U.S. Softcover ISBN 0–7862–5675–3 (General Series)
U.K. Hardcover ISBN 0–7540–1977–2 (Windsor Series)

Copyright © 2003 Lara Harte

The right of Lara Harte to be identified as the author of this work has been asserted by her in accordance with the Copyright, Designs and Patents Act 1988.

All rights reserved.

This is a work of fiction. Names, characters, places, and incidents are either the product of the author's imagination or are used fictitiously. Any resemblance to actual events or locales or persons living or dead is entirely coincidental.

The text of this Large Print edition is unabridged.
Other aspects of the book may vary from the original edition.

Set in 16 pt. New Times Roman.

Printed in Great Britain on acid-free paper.

Library of Congress Cataloging-in-Publication Data

Harte, Lara.
Wild geese / Lara Harte.
p. cm.
ISBN 0–7862–5675–3 (lg. print : sc : alk. paper)
1. France—History—Louis XVI. 1774–1793—Fiction.
2. Fathers and daughters—Fiction. 3. Dublin (Ireland)—Fiction. 4. Irish—France—Fiction. 5. Young women—Fiction.
6. Exiles—Fiction. 7. Large type books. I. Title.
PR6058.A69494W55 2003
823'.914—dc21 2003053310

WILD GEESE

For Vanya

I'd like to thank the Collège des Irlandais, Paris, for their hospitality during my time in Paris. Thanks also to the Bibliothèque Nationale de France, the Bibliothèque Historique de la Ville de Paris, the National Library of Ireland, and the University College, Dublin Library.

I'm hugely grateful to my agent Georgina Capel and Robert Caskie at Capel and Land, for their encouragement of this project over the last few years. As always, I'm also indebted to my editor, Maggie McKernan.

A very special thank you to my family and friends, especially to Michael Conlon, for lending me rare, antique books, and to my brother Vanya Harte, for many interesting historical conversations.

I

CHAPTER ONE

Inside the brick walls of a terraced Dublin house, the briskly crackling fires and luxuriously appointed rooms testified to the prosperity of Mr Reily, a merchant of late middle age. His talents were such that he had been consistently successful in business, despite the complications of international crises, trade restrictions, and his Catholic religion. Several years had now passed since the economic upheavals of the American War of Independence, and he looked to the future with confidence, now that his business had stabilised somewhat.

The mistress of the house was seated on a sofa in her boudoir. Her niece, Isabella Carroll, had just received a letter from her father in Saint-Domingue. He had also sent Mrs Reily a letter, which she continued to peruse with the utmost consideration. The girl's father wrote so seldom that one was prepared for startling news, but Mrs Reily was nonetheless unsettled by its implications.

The words were formed so small that they were scarcely legible. Isabella held the sheet to the sash window, where it caught the cool glare of the early winter sunshine. She had never known her father. But of late, circumstances had been such that her thoughts had turned to him with increasing curiosity.

In his stiff, uncertain English, he informed her of the death of her stepmother after a long illness. As he was now approaching old age, the rigours of the climate were taking their toll on him, and he planned to retire to Paris, where he had an *établissement.* By the time she received this letter he would have arrived there, and it was his wish that she should join him, so they could at last be reunited. He then concluded with a few sentences in French, which Isabella could not understand. In her excitement, she barely noticed this.

Isabella resumed her seat by the fire, consumed by an array of emotions. Relief, that a new horizon had unexpectedly opened itself to her at the very time she desired one. Anxiety, about the possible outcomes, and how her uncle would react. Her aunt saw some of this in her face, and sighed. She wondered if she was perhaps to blame. She knew she had painted a brighter picture of Peadar Carroll than she had intended throughout her niece's childhood. They had been difficult times. Her husband had been too preoccupied with his business concerns and hopes for children of his own to pay much attention to his wife's niece. Sadly, their firstborn had died in infancy, and later confinements had also ended in tragedy. Mrs Reily had taken what comfort she could in the little girl, her sister's only child, brought home from France on the death of her mother.

Mrs Reily could still remember what she herself had been like at Isabella's age. How excited she had been when she learned that her sister Marie was to marry Peadar Carroll, and that she was to travel to France with the newly-weds, so that Marie would not feel too alone in a strange country.

Carroll himself was something of a mystery, with his taciturn self-possession that could ease at will into a slightly mocking charm. On a trip to Dublin to visit some of the merchant houses there, he had met the girls' father, who had been much impressed with him, encouraging the match with his elder daughter. Day after day, Carroll had come to dine with them, recounting tales of his travels, and of his childhood in the west of Ireland. He told them how, as a penniless twelve-year-old Papist from a family long since impoverished by the strictures of the Penal Code, he had been sent by an uncle to one of the Irish merchant houses of Nantes. There, despite his lack of family connections, he had flourished, eventually becoming captain of a ship, and travelling the world from France to Africa and the Americas and back, several times over. Eventually, he amassed enough capital to become a ship-owner himself, and intended settling down to business in Nantes. Marie could not fail to notice that his time on the high seas had lent a vigour to his limbs and a spark to his eyes not often seen among the sickly, stocky young merchants' apprentices, factors, and tradesmen of her acquaintance. He in turn had been impressed by her gentle admiration and the size of her marriage portion.

The newly-weds, with the bride's sister, sailed to France at the start of a gentle summer, with pale sunshine that brought out the light blue tones of the calm sea. But the water turned grey as winter set in, and the rented house in Nantes failed to keep out the merciless winds that lashed dark waves onto the streets. Marie caught pneumonia, giving her constitution a shock from which it could not easily recover, even when the stormy rain was finally weakened by the arrival of spring. Before the new summer had ended, she was dead, leaving behind an infant daughter, whom her sister swiftly carried back to Dublin, to the comfort and shelter of their father's house.

Carroll had raised no objection. It had been his dying wife's wish that their child be raised in Dublin. It was after all a daughter, and he was still a young man. His sister-in-law suspected he would marry again without delay, and have little place for Isabella in his new household. Business affairs soon carried him to Saint-Domingue, where he settled. In time he succeeded in marrying a plantation heiress, and showed little interest in the child of his brief first marriage.

The girl's aunt had also married extremely well, taking Isabella and continuing to care for her even after her own health had been ravaged by difficult confinements and miscarriages. Eventually, her husband had also come to value Isabella as the child they could never have. The last thing they had anticipated was that Carroll would some day reclaim her. But the letter was very clear. Carroll's son by his second wife had died in infancy. Isabella was now his sole surviving child, and he had plans for her—plans he did not choose to divulge to the aunt who had raised her. It really was too provoking, thought Mrs Reily to herself. And such unfortunate timing. She regretted that Isabella had been with her in the boudoir when the letter arrived. Otherwise it might have been possible to conceal the news for a month or so. By then, she might have arranged things so that her niece's loyalties, if not her presence, remained firmly in Dublin. But it could not be helped.

'Isabella, my dear,' she said gently, 'come sit by me. You'll ruin your complexion so close to the fire.'

Isabella complied, though she would have preferred to remain where she was.

'I am sorry to learn of your father's sorrow,' her aunt continued. 'I didn't know his wife's health was so poor.'

'It is indeed sad news,' said Isabella. 'That is why he is so anxious to remove himself to

Paris, I think, to distract himself. Does he also inform you of his wish for me to join him there?'

'He does, though I do not know that we can spare you at this time,' her aunt answered thoughtfully, keeping her eyes fixed on her own letter. 'We mustn't even think of showing these letters to your uncle until the business with the Murtoghs is resolved to everyone's satisfaction.'

'I fear the business will never be resolved to everyone's satisfaction,' Isabella said with some feeling.

'My dear niece,' said the older woman sadly, 'are you still so adamant? Your obstinacy has been the source of much disappointment to your uncle, who has done so much for you.'

'I am deeply sensible of his many kindnesses to me, and would never willingly disobey him. But he chose Gregory Murtogh as my future husband while we were both children, and I firmly believe that if he had known what a drunkard and a wastrel the young Murtogh would become he would never have allowed this scheme of his to continue.'

'You judge him too harshly. Gregory's conduct can sometimes leave a lot to be desired, but he is young, and there is every chance that he will improve with age.'

'It is not a chance I am willing to take,' insisted Isabella.

'There are other considerations,' her aunt

continued. 'As you know, Gregory's father has amassed substantial capital through his success in business. You would be handsomely provided for. In addition, your uncle is attempting to persuade Mr Murtogh to invest heavily in a costly new venture of his. This would perhaps be jeopardised, if you continue to refuse.'

'Aunt,' said Isabella, shaken, 'surely Uncle's business is not at stake?' A little guiltily, Mrs Reily saw that she had succeeded in frightening her, though the girl's demeanour continued to express defiance, rather than submission. 'No child, your uncle's business is not at stake,' she admitted reluctantly. 'You must have no qualms on that score. Your uncle is far too clever to take a substantial risk on an uncertain venture.'

'But it is nonetheless a consideration,' Isabella stated thoughtfully. 'Aunt, I believe my father's letter is a godsend, and I can't understand why you don't see it as such. It gives me the opportunity to avoid this marriage by slipping quietly off to Paris. I will then ensure my absence becomes so protracted that the Murtoghs tire of waiting for me and marry their young buck to someone else without thinking ill of my uncle.'

This was precisely the scenario Aunt wished to avoid. If Isabella left under such circumstances, she would have little incentive to return and might instead remain in Paris, never to see her aunt and uncle again. It was so unfair, thought Mrs Reily: had she and her husband expended so much on the girl only to lose her so easily?

'Let's not be too hasty, my dear,' she said slowly. 'It would be foolish to leave unpleasant, unfinished business behind you. To tell the truth, I have of late had my own reservations about the match. There is the danger that a temperament like Gregory's could squander everything his father has worked so hard to achieve, and I do not like to see you unhappy. It is such a pity that there are so few eligible young Catholic men in Dublin, especially for a likely girl like you,' she sighed.

'Nevertheless, you have doubts?' asked Isabella hopefully.

'Yes, I do. But it's also unfortunate that Pamela Murtogh is to marry so well. It has only made their father more anxious to see his son settled as soon as possible. Mrs Murtogh confided in me the other day that they believe your marriage will have a calming effect on him.'

'What can we do, then? Do you think you could possibly prevail on Uncle to see this match for the folly it is?'

'I will give the matter some thought. In the meantime, I would ask you to speak no more about it. You will attend the Murtoghs' supper-party tonight with good grace, and endeavour to be pleasing to the company.'

Isabella was disgruntled by her aunt's tone.

'Do you think Uncle would object if I pleaded indisposition and remained at home?' she asked, though she anticipated her aunt's response exactly.

Mrs Reily nodded her head reprovingly. 'You know very well he would interpret it as a deliberate attempt to provoke him. But I see no reason why you should not enjoy it. I believe Mrs Murtogh has invited quite a large party, and their attention will be directed entirely on Pamela. She is a dear friend of yours, is she not? I think she will be greatly disappointed if you do not go.'

'Very well, Aunt,' said Isabella dully.

Mrs Reily's face became grave. She feared her niece was lapsing into sullenness and ingratitude. What purpose could that serve, other than to infuriate the uncle on whose good will they both depended?

'Come now, Isabella,' she coaxed. 'I promise I will do my best to help you, but you must try to shake off that ill-humour of yours. For your own sake, it is important that you look and act your best tonight.'

'And what of my father's letter? Will you also give some thought to when you can spare me?'

Mrs Reily wished she could appease her niece. It was certainly natural that she should wish to visit Paris. 'If only I had my health,' she said, more to herself than to Isabella, 'then I could travel to Paris with you, and we could all rest easy on your behalf.'

'If only it were possible,' said Isabella, with little hope. She believed her aunt's health was much improved of late, but Aunt was content to limit her exercise to a brief walk down the granite steps to a waiting sedan or Uncle's carriage. She was happy to venture no further than the chapel for Mass or the houses of other Catholic merchants for entertainment. How could such a woman be persuaded to go as far as a ship, let alone all the way to Paris?

'We could travel slowly, stopping regularly to rest,' Isabella suggested. 'It would be wonderful, would it not, to see a city as famous as Paris? Just think of it, Aunt! And then you could return home, dressed in all the latest fashions. Your wardrobe would be the talk of Dublin,' she added.

Mrs Reily smiled. For a moment, she allowed her thoughts to drift back again to her girlhood. One of the ships that sailed into Dublin, laden with the goods that made her father rich, was preparing to carry her and her sister away to a future that was surely as beautiful as the water-marked silk her sister was married in, as darkly enticing as the Bordeaux claret the new bride drank at her last meal with her father.

'No, I fear my constitution is much too delicate to undertake such a long and arduous journey,' she said, quelling her own wistfulness. 'I will conserve my strength for the

Murtoghs' supper tonight. Have you chosen a gown yet? I think you should wear the new blue silk. It is most becoming on you.'

As she spoke, a clock struck downstairs. 'Goodness, it is later than I thought,' said Aunt hurriedly. 'It will soon be time to have my hair dressed, and I have so many other things to attend to. Come with me, my dear, perhaps you can be of some assistance to me.' And she bustled her reluctant niece out of the room, thus shelving the matter for another occasion.

CHAPTER TWO

Isabella had retreated to her own room, where she was supposed to be attending to her toilette. She had spent the afternoon watching her aunt have her hair trussed up into a tall, elaborate pile of heavily powdered curls. Mrs Reily's hair had been so demanding and time-consuming that the hairdresser had had little time to devote to the niece. Fortunately, Isabella did not care to have her hair dressed so high as to impede her easy progress through doors. The hairdresser deftly pinned it up, prominently displaying her natural curls, and giving only the slightest dusting of powder so that people might think this was a deliberately simple style. As it was very becoming, Mrs Reily saw no need to berate the hairdresser for having another engagement to rush off to.

The heavy curtains had been drawn to ward off the night, which would bring a sharp frost before morning. Despite her aunt's warning, Isabella stood close by the fire, taking care only to protect her costly new silk from the flames. Aunt had been very pleased with it, and had insisted on the white lace ruffles that trimmed the sleeves and gave the underskirt its fullness. 'Look how nicely it falls,' she had exclaimed the day it was finished, pulling the wide silk overskirt this way and that so it would sit evenly over her niece's hoops. Isabella had suffered her aunt to do this because she knew she would provoke a tiff if she pulled away in irritation, and why spoil her guardian's good humour unnecessarily?

Isabella dreaded the evening's entertainment and the possible demands that might be made on her, should the Murtoghs make public their wishes for their son's future marriage. She had been chilled by her aunt's reference to Uncle's business connection with Mr Murtogh and the possible ramifications a broken match might have. After all, she thought in an ironic reflection of her aunt's words: there are so few eligible young Catholic men in Dublin. In addition, Uncle and the other merchants felt constantly stymied by the trade restrictions still inflicted by Westminster. They were always beset by insecurity, no matter how successful they became, and there was an ever-lurking fear of bankruptcy and ruination.

Exasperated, Isabella turned her attention back to the small notebook she was reading by firelight. It had been written in hand especially for her by Miss Doyle, the elderly spinster who had educated her before dying of pneumonia the winter Isabella was sixteen. A lively storyteller who had been to France, Miss Doyle had responded to Isabella's fascination with history by setting down in writing the story of the Wild Geese, the dispossessed Irish who had spread their wings and flown away to the Catholic countries of Europe. Isabella treasured this memento, and knew by heart Miss Doyle's account of how Ireland's hope had died with the defeat of the Catholic King James 11 in 1691, how many of his Irish followers had followed him to France, brave soldiers who entered the service of King Louis XIV, itching for an opportunity to return to Ireland and avenge its fate.

The feats of the Irish Brigades were enthusiastically extolled, especially the Battle of Fontenoy in 1745, when they unleashed their fury on the troops of the English King, George 11, but what had always interested Isabella most was how, generation after generation, young Irishmen had continued to cross the sea to France in search of a better life: soldiers, merchants' apprentices like her father, and students like Miss Doyle's brother, who were denied an education at home.

Isabella's favourite part was the end, where Miss Doyle described her own adventures in Paris as a young girl, visiting her brother. In Paris, the possibilities were endless, Miss Doyle wrote, and Isabella had always longed to go there. Now the father she had always longed to meet was also there . . .

Isabella heard the slow, heavy rustle of her aunt's skirts approaching the room. Hastily, she put the notebook away with the books, pamphlets and newspapers she had accumulated over the years. Then she went to the looking-glass, beside which the candles had burned right down some time ago. The darkened reflection reminded her that she had neglected to tighten her stays and fix her overskirt evenly over her petticoat. At this precise moment her aunt entered the room, her hair elaborately piled up and freshly powdered, pendant diamonds gleaming proudly at her throat.

'Isabella!' exclaimed her aunt in exaggerated horror. This is completely unacceptable, thought Mrs Reily as she silently pulled at the hems of Isabella's skirts so that her petticoat was not hanging down. She then ushered her down to the hall, where Mr Reily was waiting, stout in a new frock coat. His sharp eyes ran appreciatively over his wife's and niece's appearances, assessing how well they would look beside the other women tonight. They really were a credit to him, he thought, as they stepped into the carriage, carefully arranging their skirts before sitting down.

It was a cold, sharply crisp night. The stars were so clearly delineated against the sky that Isabella neglected to watch her more immediate surroundings. Instead, she contemplated the moon as they drove through several poorly lit streets, many of whose occupants were ill clad to withstand the harshness of a night that did not offer a single cloud as protection against a sunless sky. Their carriage then took them through a clean, well laid-out square, where her aunt drew her attention to several ladies who were descending a smoothly carved granite step to a magnificent carriage bearing the livery of one of the country's most prominent Protestant families.

'I imagine they're attending tonight's entertainment at the Castle,' said Mrs Reily, straining to see what she could of their attire, which was concealed under long, luxuriant pelisses. She comforted herself with the thought that she and Isabella looked every bit as fine as they did, even if their family was excluded from the Castle.

A short time later, they arrived at the Murtoghs'. Isabella discovered, to her great relief, that Gregory Murtogh would not be present at the supper. Pamela Murtogh whispered to her that he had expressly disobeyed his father's orders by going to the play. There was even the possibility that he might not return at all.

It was a curiously imbalanced company that assembled to drink Mr Murtogh's finest champagne and be served delicacies from silver tureens. What was most striking to all was the absence of O'Beirne, Pamela's betrothed. He had promised her most particularly that he would do his utmost to be present, but he had had to return home to make some arrangements for the marriage. Nevertheless, the conversation revolved around what a social coup this marriage would be for the Murtoghs. The O'Beirnes were an old Irish family, whose lands had been held for them by a neighbouring Protestant family throughout a century of penal oppression. After the Relief Act of 1782 they had bought back these lands, and their status had consequently soared. It was quite a dazzling connection for a merchant's daughter. Still, Isabella wondered if O'Beirne's absence on an occasion like this suggested a certain contempt for the Murtoghs, even if their financial status had proved tempting. She found this ironic, considering that trade had been one of the few professions permitted to Catholics, scorned as it was by the Protestant ruling class, who considered it beneath them.

The Murtoghs were nonetheless able to take consolation in the presence of Mr M'Guire, a connection of the O'Beirnes. They assured themselves that he could not fail to be impressed by the lavishness of the supper: three courses, including calf's head, venison and roasted birds, as well as potato and vegetable dishes and an unending flow of fine French claret from one of Mr Murtogh's correspondents abroad. Mr M'Guire was a brewer, and the elder merchants present were somewhat in awe of his achievements. Despite the industrial strife and upheavals of recent years, he had maintained a steady equilibrium in business, and his family had provided him with capital whenever the need arose. As he took precedence among the guests, Isabella was thankfully able to escape notice, though she did not have another opportunity to speak to her friend Pamela until the female company had retired upstairs to the drawing room.

The drawing-room carpets had been rolled up for the dancing that would soon take place. Pamela drew Isabella aside to show her friend a recently commissioned portrait of her soon-to-be husband. Isabella saw a stocky young man, standing in formal dress against a dark, indistinct background. She had met him in the flesh only once, and too briefly to form an opinion of him. But, she thought it showed considerable bad manners on his part, to be absent on such an occasion, though she judged it wise not to say so to her friend.

'It's a very good likeness,' remarked Isabella. 'How fortunate you are to have it.'

'Yes. It was painted at his home in the

country,' Pamela replied, tracing the heavy gilt frame with her hand. 'We are to live there, you know.'

'My aunt told me,' Isabella smiled. 'I've heard that Galway is very beautiful. I imagine it will be very refreshing to you, to breathe pure air.'

'I suppose so, though it will be quite a change for me. The O'Beirnes say I'll even have to learn Irish, in order to speak with the tenants, and I'll be very sorry to leave you all.'

Pamela looked longingly around the drawing room, with its wine damask wall-hangings and sparkling chandelier, and the delicate flower and bird motif of the ceiling cornice she was so much attached to. She was a very young girl, and had never been away from home before.

The two Misses O'Brien sat together on a sofa, whispering together and narrowly observing the company. Their father had suffered huge losses during the American War, having been heavily dependent on the export of linen to this market, and his fortunes not yet having recovered, their own expectations were not what they should be. They were both resentful of Pamela Murtogh's dazzling match and anxious to ingratiate themselves with her, in case it should prove to be to their advantage. Having caught her eye as it sought to memorise her home, they rose hastily, balancing uneasily in their high-heeled faded satin slippers.

'My dear Pamela, you are the most fortunate girl in the whole of Dublin!' enthused the younger sister.

'Is it true that your father is sparing no expense with your clothes?' the other sister asked. 'I heard he ordered all the latest cloths from London. Are you really to have fifty pairs of silk stockings, each in a different colour?'

As always, Pamela was somewhat taken aback by the combined onslaught of the O'Briens. 'It is my father's wish that I be dressed in a manner befitting a lady of the first fashion,' she replied.

'I am sure it is,' agreed Miss O'Brien. 'After all, the O'Beirnes would expect nothing less of you. We have heard the house is very beautiful.'

'Yes, I believe it is. I would be very glad to receive you there, should you ever wish to see it,' she offered, extending the invitation more out of nervousness than a liking for the O'Briens.

'That is most kind of you,' said the elder O'Brien, concealing her surprise. 'We would be most happy to visit you there in time, though I imagine the country is very dull at this time of year, with endless rain, and cold draughty rooms, and no company for miles around.'

Pamela's face darkened and she looked away.

'In that case,' said Isabella sharply, 'you will have to forgo the pleasure of having everyone see on what intimate terms you are with Mrs O'Beirne.'

Both O'Briens stared back at Isabella, unabashed. 'And when are we to have the pleasure of addressing you as Mrs Murtogh?' the younger sister inquired.

'I notice your beau is not among us tonight,' the elder continued. 'How are we to interpret this?'

Although addressed to Isabella, this was also aimed at Pamela, and it struck home. Mrs Reily had heard some of the exchange from her position at the card table. Frowning over her cards, she thought how unfortunate it was that those O'Brien girls were here. It was true that there were very few girls who were suitable to be invited to such an occasion, but the sisters had a vindictive streak that served only to sharpen Isabella's tongue, and her niece did not need sharpening tonight.

'Miss O'Brien,' called Mrs Reily sweetly. 'Your mother tells me you have a wonderful new music master, and I'm simply longing to hear you play.'

Isabella winced at the thought, but her aunt was gratified to see her smile with relief as both sisters moved towards the pianoforte.

'I am only too happy to oblige,' said Miss O'Brien, seating herself at the instrument. 'I flatter myself that I have improved immeasurably under my new master. He is newly arrived from London, you know, and worth every penny of his exorbitant fees.'

It was not an idle boast: although not particularly accomplished, Miss O'Brien's playing had improved dramatically since the last time they had heard her. But Isabella's thoughts were elsewhere. She beckoned Pamela towards the door, and they slipped out. They heard voices wafting up the stairs. There would be little time for conversation before Uncle and the others appeared in the drawing room.

'I received a letter from my father today,' said Isabella quickly, holding the door shut. 'He has gone to Paris, and wishes me to join him there.'

'Paris!' Pamela was suitably impressed. 'But that's wonderful news! Surely you will not now be obliged to marry my brother?'

'That I do not know. My aunt has promised to speak to my uncle, but she believes it may take some time to persuade him to part with me. She says that Paris is so very far away.'

'Forgive the intrusion,' said Mr M'Guire, who came on them rather more suddenly than anticipated. 'I couldn't help but overhear part of your conversation. Am I to understand that your father is now in Paris?'

'He is,' answered Isabella politely, wondering how much he had heard.

'I am not personally acquainted with him,'

continued Mr M'Guire, 'but I have connections in the West Indies who have spoken very highly of him in their letters.' Opening the door, he ushered them back into the drawing room. 'I was very sorry to learn of his bereavement. Please accept my most sincere condolences,' he said, looking at Isabella with interest now that she was clearly illuminated by the chandelier and the generous clusters of candles. He had often admired Miss Carroll, who was looking particularly well tonight in a new silk which must have cost her uncle quite a consideration. But while her uncle's fortune was certainly attractive, it had never been quite sufficient to entice Mr M'Guire fully. However, her prospects had now improved immeasurably. As long as her father remained unmarried, she also stood to inherit those Saint-Domingue plantations. This invitation to Paris suggested that, at the very least, her father took a keen interest in her future and would pay a substantial marriage portion.

'You are most kind,' said Isabella warily, wondering why he was gazing at her so fixedly. 'I trust all is well with you?'

'Indeed it is. Business is more than satisfactory, and cannot but continue to improve. As you are perhaps aware, some of the more galling trade restrictions have recently been removed by the Parliament in London, and it is only a matter of time before these measures are implemented here.'

'Do you really think so?' she asked with interest. 'Will there then be a further relaxation of the Popery Laws? It would be truly wonderful, would it not, if Catholics were finally allowed to practise law, and vote, and enter Parliament as MPs in their own right?'

'I believe it will come to pass sooner or later, and not before time, too. As you can imagine, it is both troublesome, and dare I say costly, constantly having to prevail on my Protestant friends to look after my interests both inside and outside the Parliament,' he said, with an air of taking her into his confidence.

The O'Brien sisters were viewing his attentions to Miss Carroll with some alarm. They now decided to act.

'Mr M'Guire!' said the younger O'Brien, her skirts pushing Isabella aside. 'My sister is undecided what to play next, and wishes you to assist her in her choice of music.' Isabella was amused to see him so adroitly manoeuvred towards the pianoforte.

Seeing her alone, her uncle approached her and drew her aside. Speaking in a low voice, he said: 'Mr Murtogh assures me his son will be home presently. He seems to have been unavoidably detained on business of some kind, but I am sure he is aware what a momentous occasion this is.' Mr Reily nodded significantly, before moving away to rejoin Mr

Murtogh.

Feeling riled, Isabella returned to her place near Pamela. Can Uncle ever be persuaded to give up this cherished scheme of his? she wondered.

Pamela smiled at her thoughtfully. 'Mr M'Guire has shown you marked favour of late,' she said. 'I wonder what it signifies.'

Isabella laughed dismissively. 'What can it possibly signify, when the Misses O'Brien are so anxious to keep him and his companion by the pianoforte all night?'

'You mean Doctor Connor,' said Pamela, glancing at the group in question.

'Is he a doctor?' asked Isabella, observing that he looked slightly ill-at-ease.

'Don't you remember?' asked Pamela, surprised. 'You were introduced to him at supper.'

Isabella had been too preoccupied at supper to pay much attention to the proceedings, but she now vaguely recollected that he had been introduced to her as a physician. 'Is he newly arrived in Dublin?' she asked.

'I believe he may have been here a year, but he has already earned a considerable reputation for his skill. My mother tells me he has entirely cured her heart palpitations.'

'He is very young to have established such a reputation,' said Isabella, studying him more closely. 'Though it is clearly his youth that appeals to Miss O'Brien.'

'I would be inclined to attribute it to his having distinguished himself in his studies at the University of Paris,' laughed Pamela.

'Did he?' asked Isabella with admiration. It signified little that the Dublin doors of the Royal College of Surgeons had been closed to Catholics for so long when Paris-trained doctors were considered to be infinitely superior.

The drawing-room door was flung open. The long-awaited Gregory Murtogh stumbled in, intoxicated and accompanied by an elegantly dressed lady, whose finery dazzled the practised eye of the assembled company. Even her headdress was adorned with brilliantly set jewels, and her hoops were so wide that Isabella and Pamela had to step aside to let her pass into the centre of the room. But not even a skirt fuller than the current fashion dictated could conceal her condition: this lady was heavy with child, and her *accouchement* would soon come to pass.

'Mr Murtogh,' she exclaimed, addressing her companion, 'you did not lead me to expect such a fine entertainment.'

'It is exactly as I promised you: a small family gathering to celebrate the imminent marriages of my sister and myself. Allow me to present to you my father,' he said, turning to greet this parent, who was just as infuriated as might have been expected. 'Father, this is Mrs Mahon. Is she not every bit as beautiful as I raved in my enraptured descriptions?'

Gregory's speech was slurred, but he had deliberately spoken sufficiently loud to break all the little conversations among the company. Miss O'Brien's fingers crashed on the piano in a screeching wail, and then there was a silence in the room. Mr Murtogh had been standing by the fire, intent in conversation with Isabella's uncle. Now, he indicated to his wife to remain where she was at the card table, and came forward to take Mrs Mahon's arm and pull her towards the door.

'Mrs Mahon, as my son seems determined to force the connection on me, I cannot but acknowledge your presence, but as this is not the occasion for it, I would ask my son to remove both your presences until a more suitable opportunity arises.'

'But there can hardly be a more appropriate time than this?' asked Gregory, feigning surprise and roughly pulling her away from his father. 'Surely you cannot wish our friends to continue under the misapprehension that it is Miss Carroll I intend to marry?'

Isabella almost laughed aloud. How refreshing to discover that he was as opposed to the match as she was! Her aunt came to her side and took her arm, anxious to keep her niece from participating unfavourably in such a scene. Taking his cue from his wife, Mr Reily stood up and said: 'Mr Murtogh, I cannot remain here to have my niece insulted in such a manner.'

Were they really to drag her away, Isabella wondered, anxious to witness the outcome. She stole another look at Gregory and his companion as her aunt ushered her towards the door. Mrs Mahon remained standing in the middle of the floor. Her stillness was almost glacially composed, but her very isolation and lack of focus seemed to suggest some bewilderment and confusion. Isabella pitied her, thinking she had been very badly used by Gregory.

'Poor dear Isabella,' the elder O'Brien whispered audibly to her sister. 'To be passed over in favour of such a woman! In which lodging-house do you suppose he found her?'

Ironically, this seemed to serve as the ammunition Mrs Mahon had been waiting for. Her hand went momentarily to her throat, as if to reassure herself that the jewels nestling there shone brighter than anything else in the room. She examined her designated rival with what Isabella interpreted as a mixture of scorn, pity and curiosity. Then Mrs Mahon cast a composed eye over Miss O'Brien's attire.

'Judging by the state of your petticoat,' she said coolly, 'I daresay my lodgings are better than yours.' Then she turned to Mr Murtogh. 'I thank you for your kind hospitality. It is late, and I must retire now, but I feel sure your son will be only too delighted to remain and titillate your company to their utmost gratification.'

Mrs Reily dragged Isabella and Mr Reily out. 'My poor Isabella,' she said, bustling protectively around her niece in the hallway, 'I would not have you remain here a moment longer.'

'We have little choice, Aunt. The carriage is not due for at least another hour.' Isabella strained her ears: the others were still in the drawing room. What was being said in there?

'Your uncle will go find a hackney. But hurry!' she said, dispatching her husband and glancing nervously at the staircase they had just descended. 'It is not so very cold, come outside and wait on the steps.'

Isabella found it bitterly cold, and clutched her new velvet pelisse tightly around her. From inside came the sound of raised voices. Isabella identified them as Gregory's and his father's, but was unable to hear what was being said. Then Mrs Mahon emerged, pushing by them fast, like a bolting horse, and rushing out alone onto the dark street. The door opened again, but this time it was the young physician who emerged. Turning to see where their eyes were fixed, he too saw Mrs Mahon as she collided with a passing group and fell. Isabella started forward, but her aunt's grip tightened on her arm. She watched as the doctor went to the woman's assistance. He spoke a few words to her, then they turned the corner together, as if he had offered to take her home. Isabella turned to her aunt, but Mrs Reily's eyes had narrowed.

'There is your uncle,' she said with relief, as a shabby, jerky hackney-coach approached. 'Let us go immediately.'

'My poor niece,' she added, as soon as they were safely driving away. 'To have been insulted in such a manner! That Murtogh boy was made for mischief and will come to no good, though I am equally vexed with his father. To think that Mr Murtogh actually knew of the connection!'

'I agree,' said Uncle, exasperated. 'I was led to believe that Gregory's bad conduct was confined to an excessive taste for taverns and the play. I was unaware he frequented such low society.'

'But Mrs Mahon was well-spoken, and exceedingly well attired,' Isabella pointed out.

'My dear child,' said Aunt, shaking her head. 'How do you suppose a woman of her kind came by such jewels? Mrs Mahon indeed! The presumption of it! I don't know what that young doctor was thinking of, offering such courtesy to her.'

He showed presence of mind, Isabella reflected, and was the only one of the company to have shown any consideration of the woman. She remembered the look Mrs Mahon had given her and was filled with distaste, for herself, and for all the Murtoghs and O'Briens who could not look beyond their own selfish preoccupations to proffer some kind of sympathy to a woman soon to be delivered of a child sired by Gregory Murtogh, of all people. All they could think of was the social disgrace her position implied.

'You are quiet, Isabella,' noted her uncle. 'I hope you have not been too grieved by the events of the night. I daresay we can find you a better husband than that rakish good-for-nothing.'

'Uncle,' said Isabella, trying not to sound too pleased, 'does this mean I am released from my engagement?' She sank back into her seat with relief.

CHAPTER THREE

Isabella rose early the next day, feeling completely refreshed. Surely her uncle would now welcome the opportunity for her to leave Dublin long enough for the whole business with the Murtoghs to blow over? Her aunt would not rise till noon, as was her habit after such a late night. Her uncle, however, was preparing to leave to attend to some business. Once Isabella had made it clear that she wanted most particularly to speak with him, he agreed that she could accompany him.

Isabella had always loved walking along the

quays with her uncle. On a dry winter's morning, the air would be cold, clean and crisp, no matter how congested the Liffey became with ships. That morning, Mr Reily intended overseeing the unloading of one of his ships at the Custom House, as he had of late been disputing some of the calculations made by the officials.

'I imagine you wish to speak to me about young Murtogh,' he said. 'Words cannot describe how sorely he has disappointed me. I can assure you, my dear, that I was completely unaware of the connection. I will be speaking to Mr Murtogh as soon as possible, and again I assure you, strong words will be exchanged.'

'Thank you, Uncle, but I wished to broach quite a different subject,' she said. 'We did not have an opportunity to inform you, but Aunt and I received a letter from my father yesterday.'

'A letter from your father? What a rare and unsought delight.' His conciliatory tone remained unchanged, but she did not read delight in his face.

'Yes, I was pleased, though the contents were for the most part sad.' She wondered whether or not to continue, as her uncle now appeared preoccupied with the sight of a ship being loaded. 'Uncle, he writes about a very important matter.'

'I do not doubt it. He writes only to inform us of the momentous events in his life: the occasion of his second marriage, the birth of his son, the death of said son in infancy . . . He then rustles up a general inquiry after your health, several lines of best wishes, and you are consigned to oblivion for a few years more.'

Isabella felt the harshness of his words. Had he anticipated her father's request and already resolved to oppose it? 'You are right to maintain that my father has taken little or no interest in me, while you and Aunt have cared for me all my life. But Saint-Domingue is so very far away. Surely anyone who has lived there for so long could be forgiven for neglecting their family ties in Ireland?'

'Let's not be too forgiving,' said Uncle. 'I imagine he is in constant contact with France for trade and business purposes. There is also the issue of your deceased brother. If he had lived, he would certainly have been sent to Paris for his education. Do you think your father would have spared any pains in following his progress there?'

'Perhaps not, but . . .' Isabella knew how much her uncle had wanted a son. She was also uncomfortably aware that he would not have taken such an interest in her if his wish had been granted. 'His son was born in Saint-Domingue,' she said. 'I imagine that would have etched him more sharply on my father's memory, whereas I belonged to another life, almost. There is surely something dreamlike about such a connection. At least, that is how I have always seen him, as a mirage of fleeting impressions, conjured up by my aunt's stories.'

Uncle seemed quite amused by this. 'What then, does this phantom write of?'

'My stepmother has died, and he has left Saint-Domingue and set himself up in Paris, where he wishes me to join him. I've always longed to see Paris, and I've often wondered what it would be like to be reunited with my father . . .'

'My poor Isabella,' said Uncle, on reflection. 'You have been wounded by the events of last night, and wish to heal your wounds somewhere far away from the prying eyes of Dublin's scandal-mongers. It is entirely understandable that you see this invitation as heaven-sent, but I do not think running away is the answer. Moreover, I am concerned for your aunt's health, and she would not want to be parted from you at this time.'

'My aunt's health? But I believe her to be much improved of late.'

'You are mistaken, my dear. In fact, I fear she may have caught a chill last night, while waiting for the hackney. Winter is a dangerous time for a weakened constitution. It would be better if you stayed with her, at least until the spring. She cannot do without you, you know.'

'Yes, but I'm sure she understands how much I want to see my father, and as for Paris . . .'

'Don't be so glum, Isabella. I'm sure we can

make it up to you somehow! But we could not have you embark on such an unpleasant and hazardous journey at this time of the year. Best to wait for more clement weather.'

'Is that your final word?' Isabella asked.

'I can see how acute your disappointment is, and I promise to bear it in mind. Meanwhile, you must excuse me. I have some business to attend to. You should return home now, and see to your aunt.'

Isabella was dismissed. They retraced their steps, Uncle escorting her back as far as the front door before setting off again. If Aunt were really ill, thought Isabella angrily, why did she go into company last night at all? It was surely an excuse, but if he simply did not wish her to go to Paris, why did he not say so outright?

'Your aunt wishes you to go to her immediately,' Molly the maidservant informed her on opening the door.

'Isabella! Where have you been all this time?' Aunt called as her niece crossed the landing into her chamber. 'I've been lying here all morning in considerable discomfort. I caught a chill last night, and I'm exceedingly feverish, and I've had to rely on that useless girl to do my bidding and take care of me.'

Isabella turned inquiringly to the 'useless girl,' who told her: 'I've filled the bedwarmer with hot coals, like she asked me to, and the fire's been lit all morning.' Aunt's peevishness had clearly soured Molly's temper beyond all redemption.

'Thank you,' said Isabella. 'I'll look after her now.' Her aunt had barely been out of doors for ten minutes last night, if even that. Isabella felt there might be a simpler explanation: after large entertainments, she had noticed that her aunt was inclined to be bad-humoured and to magnify minor complaints into serious illnesses that demanded everyone's attention. Her ill-health would generally last until there was the prospect of another entertainment.

'What can I do for you?' Isabella asked after Molly had gone.

Her aunt appeared to give the matter some thought. 'I should like to send for that new physician, but I don't know how appropriate it would be,' she said finally.

Isabella did not want her aunt's indisposition to be considered sufficiently serious to justify a physician's services, especially when she suspected that her aunt was merely seeking to distract herself. 'There is no need to send for him. I can care for you perfectly well,' she said.

'Oh, no, you must send for him. My usual physician can't seem to do anything for me, and Mrs Murtogh swears this new one has entirely cured her heart palpitations! Besides, I didn't think badly of him. I was merely expressing my reservations about a young man who would willingly venture to escort . . . Last night's circumstances were surely such . . . But I should like to have him attend me, and I will own to having some curiosity about him. So I would be very much obliged, my dear niece, if you would go to my writing desk. I believe you will find his address there. Mrs Murtogh was kind enough to furnish me with it, in the days before . . .'

'Very well, Aunt. You should try and rest now,' said Isabella.

'Oh, and before you go, could you bring over the looking-glass? I'm sure I look an absolute fright.'

It was hardly surprising that last night's coiffure had not survived well. All the trussed-up powdered curls had been aggravated overnight into a dirty, tangled mess. Aunt groaned and hid the disaster as best she could under a clean cap.

'Now,' she said, 'I am fit to receive the young doctor.'

Isabella wrote a brief note, outlining her aunt's complaint, then sealed and directed it. After dispatching their manservant John, who always ran their errands, in search of the physician, Isabella was free to do as she pleased. She went to her own room, where she took out her father's letter and re-read it. The light was so dull that the characters appeared indistinct in places, making the invitation to Paris seem a lot further away than it had yesterday. She put the letter away and took out the gown she had worn last night. When she had returned home, she had noticed that she had caught her heel in the back of the skirt and torn the hem. She knew her aunt would be furious if she saw this: 'Isabella! How could you be so careless! Imagine ruining such a costly gown the first time you wore it!' As she was wiser than to reply: 'I'm sorry, Aunt, but you were so zealous about concealing my petticoat that you pulled the overskirt down far lower than was necessary, so it is hardly surprising I should trip on it!', Isabella fetched a needle and thread and sat down to darn it so that her aunt need never see it.

CHAPTER FOUR

That morning, in his sparsely furnished rooms in a narrow street near the quays, Dr Connor had received an urgent summons from Mrs Murtogh. He had thought twice about going there, immediately assuming that this request for professional service was but a guise for interrogating him in a reproachful manner, and he had absolutely no desire to become involved in a 'situation'. Moreover, he had had little sleep and would not be able to muster up the verbal dexterity required to avoid any barbed questions or assertions with politeness. On the other hand, he had attended Mrs

Murtogh a number of times before, and he had to rely on these wealthy merchant families for his livelihood. The letter specifically stated that she was unwell. He was a physician, after all. Wearily, he made preparations to leave.

Outside, in the crowded and filthy streets, the doctor's mood darkened. To have spent so many years working towards his doctorate, only to know that he was powerless to alleviate the suffering of those around him! He knew that their suffering was caused in the most part by poverty, misery and unsanitary living conditions. Only the most radical reform could ever hope to cure it. But what use dreaming of reform when even the rising Catholic merchant class, of which he had initially had such hopes, chose to bury themselves in luxury and ignore the plight of their fellow-countrymen only to occupy themselves instead with mindless imitation of London fashions, affectations, and petty obsessions about their own little social hierarchies? His student years in Paris seemed so far away, as if they had equipped him only with a supply of Four Thieves' Vinegar to ward off the infection in the streets.

On arriving at the Murtoghs, he was informed that Mrs Murtogh's malady was a nervous one. She was in a highly agitated state, claiming that the shock and the anxiety had brought her palpitations back.

'I honestly don't understand my son,

Doctor. I just don't understand him. Why would he do such a thing? And in front of all our company! What was he thinking of?'

It was perfectly obvious to the doctor what Gregory Murtogh had been thinking of. His father had gone to such lengths to break the connection that Gregory, in a fit of rash bravado brought on by heavily intoxicating liquor, had thought his harebrained scheme would successfully oppose him. But Dr Connor knew better than to explain this, and remained silent as he felt Mrs Murtogh's pulse and observed that she was only marginally more flushed in colour than she had been the previous night.

'I daresay she's quite a bewitching creature, after a fashion,' continued Mrs Murtogh. 'But how could he possibly favour her over Isabella Carroll? Did you not remark on how well she looked last night? Her toilette was so exquisite, and her hair! It was dressed in the style of a London actress who played a triumphant season here several winters ago. What was her name? I cannot quite recall it . . . can you recall it, Doctor?'

Dr Connor was momentarily confused. What precisely was he being asked to recall? Miss Carroll's hair? 'Oh. The name of the actress? I cannot, Mrs Murtogh. I imagine I was still in Paris at the time,' he answered, wondering that she could be so inanely trivial in such a situation.

'Of course you were, Doctor. You must forgive me. I really am not myself today. Is there anything you can do for me?'

He had come to the conclusion that there was very little wrong with Mrs Murtogh today. But from previous experience, he knew his reassurances would be greeted with disbelief, his prescription of regimen, air, exercise, and diet ignored. She insisted she had a nervous complaint, and certainly her agitation was real. She should be treated accordingly.

He affected an air of grave reflection: 'The delicate fibre of your nerves has been attacked by a nervous disease: a condition of hysteria for which there are a number of remedies. The consumption of soap can have a calming effect, though in a case as serious as this, I believe I would prefer you to take a strong dose of soluble tartar.'

'Tartar, Doctor?' asked Mrs Murtogh with outright revulsion. 'Are you certain it is as serious as all that? Perhaps you should reconsider. Some other remedy, perhaps?'

He nodded with sagacity, went to the door and whispered some instruction to the maidservant outside. 'There is indeed something else,' he confirmed, returning to his patient's bedside. 'Simple, but highly effective.' On hearing a loud banging noise directly outside the room, he then went to the assistance of a young male servant, who had been instructed to bring in a large, rarely used tin bath.

'What is this?' asked Mrs Murtogh with dismay as her maidservant re-appeared with a large jug of water.

'A French doctor, whose theories I much admire, recommends that hysterical patients be immersed suddenly and repeatedly in ice-cold water. I believe you will find it most beneficial, though I should warn you that you may initially be surprised by the violence and force of the plunging.'

It was at this moment that Pamela entered hesitantly, clutching the note from Isabella, which she had just received from John. 'I apologise for the interruption,' she said, addressing her mother, 'but I have just received this note from Miss Carroll. It seems Mrs Reily is also indisposed. Perhaps you are both suffering from the same malady?'

This sent the patient into a fresh fluster, though she seemed somewhat relieved by the distraction.

'She insists that you attend her,' said Pamela, offering the doctor Isabella's note. More casualties from last night's entertainment, he thought wryly. But curiously, it seemed to be the aunt who was afflicted, not the jilted niece.

'Poor Mrs Reily! This mess has evidently taken its toll! I really feel quite responsible. You will go to her at once, won't you, Doctor? I am not so gravely afflicted. There is really no need for ice-cold baths.'

Dr Connor hesitated. He was not acquainted even with the Reilys, let alone the niece who was at the centre of this fuss. But Dublin was quite a small place, really, and he was bound to encounter them sooner or later. Better to do so in a professional, civilised fashion.

'Very well, Mrs Murtogh,' he said. 'I shall postpone your treatment and go there directly.'

Judging himself fortunate to have escaped so lightly, he and John set off together. The cold air revived him somewhat, but he could not shake off the sense of suffocating frustration that enveloped him. Was it for this I left Paris? he wondered as he hastened towards yet another case of Dublin's mildly ailing ladies, hopefully one who would not drive him to seek desperate remedies for his own nerves.

Fortunately for the doctor's nerves, Mrs Reily had to be roused from a deep slumber when he arrived, and its heavy, numbing quality extended to her tongue. She did not speak of either the Murtoghs or 'the creature', confining her remarks to her indisposition.

Isabella was waiting for him in the next room. Noting that she showed no obvious signs of emotion, he judged her to be in a fit state to be entrusted with the care of her aunt, who was feverish, but suffering only from a cold. She listened to him calmly and attentively.

'Her condition is not grave, then?'

'Not in the slightest. I imagine she will have recovered within a week.'

'Thank you, Doctor. I have been invited to spend some time in Paris, but if my aunt's malady were to persist . . .'

'Your aunt's constitution need not detain you,' he assured her, his interest sparked. 'It is not as robust as yours, clearly, but I very much doubt she is any serious danger. You should seize any opportunity you can to visit Paris.'

'I shall try to convince my uncle of that. He is anxious that I should stay with my aunt,' she said. 'You studied in Paris, did you not?'

'Yes, I arrived here less than a year ago. Though it sometimes seems much longer ago than that.'

'Was it wonderful?' she asked curiously.

'I thought so,' he replied. 'The university, my friends, my rooms near the Seine . . .'

'Then you were happier there than you are here?' Isabella wondered, struck by his tone.

'I'm sorry,' he said, embarrassed. 'I didn't mean to suggest . . .'

'No, it is I who should apologise. I imagine last night painted us all in a very bad light. It was thoughtless and selfish of Gregory to act as he did, but I believe we were all equally remiss in our lack of consideration.'

'You should not blame yourself,' he said, surprised. 'I am sure it came as a great shock to you to discover that . . .'

He trailed off in such a manner as led Isabella to understand that even the physician knew she had been intended for Gregory Murtogh. 'Mrs Mahon's attachment to him was very evidently stronger than mine. Was she very distressed at her reception by the Murtoghs?'

'I believe so. I really don't know what he was thinking! Such self-dramatisation is all very well in the tavern or at the play, but when it comes to pleading one's cause with an unsympathetic father . . . It seems to have been a measure of last resort, but . . .'

'Surely there are more tactful measures of last resort?' she suggested.

'Quite,' he said hastily, recollecting himself 'You must forgive me, I have spoken more frankly than I intended. Your aunt will soon recover, but I have assured her I will return tomorrow.'

Isabella showed him out, reflecting on what a singular individual he was. She would welcome an opportunity to speak longer with him, though preferably one that was not related to her aunt's ailments. Seize any opportunity to visit Paris, he had told her. It would be no small feat to persuade Uncle that Aunt was in no grave danger, but perhaps she would succeed, and then she too would be free to leave.

This reverie was interrupted by the return of her uncle.

'Isabella, my dear, I have just been with your aunt. She tells me you had to send for a physician! Was it only this morning we spoke about what a great anxiety her health is? It is such a great relief to me that you were here to care for her.'

'Thank you, Uncle, but I did very little really, and I hope she will soon recover.'

'I hope so too, but . . .' He shook his head in despair. 'You will of course write to your father, if you have not done so already, informing him that we cannot possibly spare you at this time.'

This was no more than she had been expecting, but she was nonetheless exasperated. 'Uncle, I took the liberty of discussing the matter with Doctor Connor, and he sees no reason for real anxiety.'

'Hmm,' said Uncle, acting as if he had just been struck by something entirely different. 'I do have some reservations about this physician, though they may be unjustified . . . I will make inquiries about him, and perhaps invite him to dine with us, in order to form a better opinion of him.'

'I should like him to dine with us,' said Isabella, though she was resentfully aware that her wishes would not be taken into consideration.

Her uncle looked closely at her, as if attempting to gauge her mood. 'I have spoken with Mr Murtogh,' he said in a low tone. 'I will not relate the particulars, as they will serve only to distress you. Suffice it to say that there will be no more talk of your marrying Gregory Murtogh. Other than that, we shall proceed as if last night never happened,' he concluded, nodding his head significantly.

Were they also to proceed as if her father's letter had never happened? she wondered as he left. Disheartened, she tidied away her sewing, hiding the mended skirt behind her other clothes. The fire had burned low, and Isabella built it up again. The rekindled flames lit up the rose-coloured wallpaper which had been chosen, like everything else, by her aunt, who was noted for her taste. At least she was no longer intended for Gregory Murtogh, she tried to console herself. But this did not produce the desired relief.

Well, it could not be helped. If Uncle intended to ignore her father's letter, then she would simply have to ignore his request for her to write to her father declining his invitation. This small act of rebellion, minuscule as it was, infinitely improved her mood.

CHAPTER FIVE

Mrs Reily's illness dragged on for the best part of a week. As the weather was wet and stormy, Isabella was compelled to remain indoors with her aunt. Due to the lingering awkwardness with the Murtoghs, she was even advised by her uncle against going to visit her friend Pamela at this particular time. This was hard, given that Pamela would soon be married and living in some far-flung corner of the country. However, Isabella's uncle soon gave her some small consolation. Having made some inquiries and having ascertained that there was nothing objectionable in the doctor's conduct as a rule, he had invited him to dinner in a week's time.

Dr Connor arrived punctually on the appointed day. Isabella had just unlocked the silver in the dining room, thinking to herself that this custom of keeping valuables under lock and key did little for the maid's humour and less for her own, when she was called upon to greet him. The responsibility had fallen to her today because her aunt was still too weak to come downstairs. Unfortunately, Aunt's illness didn't prevent her from overseeing her niece's toilette from her sick-bed, much to Isabella's irritation. Nevertheless, they both agreed that the plain velvet became her very well.

Her uncle arrived home immediately after the doctor, and took to questioning him closely once they were at table and had been served with some fine claret. This new physician really was a curious sort. There was something not quite right about him, Mr Reily thought, though he couldn't put his finger on it. Certainly his medical reputation was well deserved—his wife was constantly singing the young man's praises. But, in Mr Reily's experience, young men who had been educated in France acquired a certain level of . . . finesse. *Politesse* and worldliness aside, they also dressed in the latest Parisian fashions, which were far more elaborate than the Irish styles, and they peppered their speech with French words and phrases, which of course made their conversations difficult to understand if one was not fully cognisant of the French language. But this particular young man spoke little at all, and when he did it was in plain, simple English. He also lacked a certain polish, even though his youth and professional manner were clearly set to make him all the rage with the Dublin ladies.

For his part, Dr Connor thought the merchant's appearance ridiculous. Apart from the ill-fitting wig, the waistcoat was nothing short of gaudy—red silk, with heavy green and gold embroidery. He was wearied already, and he had only just finished answering inquiries about his family. Isabella had been very interested to learn that he was the younger son of a middleman. From reading her uncle's newspapers and pamphlets, she had gathered that they were particularly ruthless individuals, managing country estates to their own advantage by exploiting both tenants and absentee landlords.

'And you never thought of apprenticing yourself to a merchant house?' her uncle asked, mentally reviewing the limited openings for ambitious young Catholic men.

'No, sir. I was intended for the medical profession from a very young age. The family physician took an interest in me, and gave me a rudimentary introduction to his skill. Both he and the priest who educated me recommended that I be sent to Paris to study.'

'Indeed? At that age I imagine you were a lively country lad, who would have preferred the adventure of a commission in the Irish Brigades to years of study?' Mr Reily was trying to picture the situation.

'That would not have been to my taste,' answered Dr Connor. 'I have no desire to serve such a King as Louis . . .' He could have elaborated on this, but clearly judged it more prudent not to, much to Isabella's disappointment.

'Indeed?' remarked Uncle. 'Well, I suppose that's as good an objection as any, though I understand the pay is not good, and the uniform rather costly.'

'My distaste has nothing to do with financial considerations,' said Dr Connor, feeling a little riled by his host's manner.

'Oh? And yet you were hardly the type to study for the priesthood in one of the Irish Colleges?' asked Mr Reily, smiling to himself as he wondered what the physician's predominantly female patients would make of this idea.

'No, I have no desire to serve the Catholic Church either,' the doctor answered tersely.

'But you are a Catholic, and one who chose to practise his profession among Catholics,' Isabella pointed out, intrigued.

'Well, having studied in a Catholic country which denies Protestants many rights, including the right to practise medicine, I thought for contrast to practise under a Protestant legislation that denies Catholics the most fundamental of political rights,' he replied with some irony, before clearing his throat awkwardly. 'I also thought it would be interesting to come to Dublin in the wake of all the changes that have taken place in the last few years,' he said, addressing Isabella's uncle.

'These are certainly interesting times,' Mr Reily agreed tentatively. 'Though I could wish for more stability. My business is good at the moment, but others are in immense difficulty . . . Nevertheless, now that the American war is behind us, and we have free trade . . .'

At that moment, Isabella heard the sound of someone arriving. She hoped that they wouldn't be interrupted—she was always longing to hear about her uncle's business, and he spoke about important matters so seldom. Molly the maidservant entered with a note. Uncle quickly read it.

'You will have to excuse me,' he said. 'It seems I have another guest, one I must speak with in private.'

This was quite a fortuitous turn of events for Isabella. She seized the opportunity to have the doctor explain himself.

'So,' she said curiously, 'you find Dublin considerably less fascinating than you had expected?'

'On the contrary,' he replied. 'It never ceases to amaze me.'

'What, then, is the source of your frustration?'

He sighed, wondering just how sympathetic she really was. 'Miss Carroll, what do you know of the history and present situation of this country?'

'Just what I learn from newspapers, though I read them at every opportunity. Miss Doyle, who educated me, used to tell the most horrific tales about Cromwell. Then, because I was born in France, she would tell me about King James and the Jacobites and how the Wild Geese followed him to France. I've also picked up a certain amount from my uncle, but

I suspect this is coloured by his own concerns—which I have been discovering may not be my concerns.'

'Really?' he asked, surprised. 'In that case, you are exceptional. I hope you're not offended, but most girls in your position desire nothing more than a rich husband, and an extravagant trousseau, shipped from London. Take the Misses O'Brien, for instance . . .'

Is that how he sees me? Isabella thought sadly. 'The Misses O'Brien, Doctor?' she asked. 'I must say, you did seem rather taken by their musical abilities.'

'Of course,' he said, pretending to be serious. 'Their music master does charge the highest fees in Dublin, you know.'

'And what about your fees, Doctor? Do your patients not reward you handsomely for your services?'

'I didn't mean to imply that one doesn't need money. What I dispute is the pursuit of money at the expense of everything else. The American war was caused by grievances similar to your uncle's: a colony's frustration at English trade restrictions. But I feel certain that, like all Irish merchants, he was furious when it erupted, because of the trade embargoes and because France was effectively cut off to him. Then again, he would have been relieved when Westminster restored the woollen trade in an attempt to soothe Irish grievances, and as for the Catholic Relief

Acts . . .'

'Uncle would have welcomed them from purely financial considerations, you are right,' she said eagerly, her voice encouraging him to continue.

'Men like your uncle have limited vision. They rail against the legislation that keeps Catholics out of Parliament, but primarily because seats in Parliament would enable them to further their financial interests, not because they have any interest in reform. It is ironic that it is a group of Protestant patriot MPs who wish for further separation of Ireland from England. Your uncle would be horrified by such an ambition, because any political upheaval would disrupt business.'

'But my uncle is a prominent member of the Catholic Committee,' she pointed out, thinking she had been disloyal enough.

Dr Connor laughed scornfully at the mention of the Catholic Committee. 'Their policy has always been to be as conciliatory as possible to the British Parliament and King.' He struck the pose of a middle-class merchant addressing a meeting, full of his own pomp and self-importance: '"My friends, let us all sign a petition showing how loyal we are to the King, how much we support him during this trying time!"'

'But the Irish Parliament *is* corrupt: it's controlled by Dublin Castle and government-owned boroughs,' said Isabella, remembering fragments of what she had heard her uncle say.

'You can be sure that parliamentary reform is far from your uncle's mind,' insisted Dr Connor. 'He objects to the corruption only because it functions against him.'

'Perhaps so,' she said thoughtfully. 'Why on earth did you come to Dublin, Doctor Connor?'

He shrugged. 'I had taken my medical degree, after some wonderful years in Paris, where my head was filled with all manner of new ideas. There I was, a middleman's son, from an oppressed part of an oppressed country in which my father had preyed on the peasants and manipulated the landlord to his own profit and gain. Somehow, I had been saved from all that. A French-educated physician had shown me a nobler way to earn a living, a French-educated priest had opened my eyes to the world of learning, and then I too had been sent to Paris. There I met others who shared my views, and I thought, what better way to give something back to my country than to return, to practise in Dublin.'

'Coming back must have been a great disappointment,' remarked Isabella. 'But I envy you. This past while, I've been longing to escape to Paris. I long to see if it is different from here, and now you describe it exactly as I thought it would be. Surely that is enough for you? To have experienced that? Why are you so frustrated here?'

'Meeting the same kind of people over and over, listening to constant talk of business . . . It wearies me, and I fall into a melancholy frame of mind. Then, when I am drawn into a *débâcle* like the Murtoghs', I really feel that my situation is intolerable.'

Were their situations so very different, Isabella wondered, thinking at the same time that the Murtogh *débâcle* had offered her a measure of freedom. 'Do you consider becoming involved in politics?' she asked. 'Do not look at me so, I haven't forgotten that Catholics are forbidden to stand. I merely meant to suggest an association like the Catholic Committee. From what you've told me, I understand it consists of men like my uncle, who are hopelessly tame. Nonetheless, it would be a start, would it not?'

Dr Connor thought about it, then shook his head. 'It's difficult to explain,' he said. 'I feel jaded, as if all the ideas I once had have died, as if they had never even existed, and I can't seem to find a way of rekindling them.'

Isabella was both amazed and amused by this. 'Come now, I hardly think the situation is as desperate as all that. You have no idea how fortunate you are! You had the opportunity to spend years in Paris, whereas my uncle forbids me even to visit it to meet a father I have never known.'

'Paris is not *all* wonderful,' he said gently. 'The King is corrupt, as kings tend to be.

Furthermore, though the French bourgeoisie are pressing for reform and the abolition of excessive taxes, it is only because they envy the nobles, who are exempt from the *taille.* It is not because they care about the suffering of the poor.'

'Is that really so?'

'I regret that it is, though I must say that even the streets of Paris are not quite as shocking as those of Dublin. I have never seen such filth and misery as I have here. I have tried to alleviate some suffering by lending my services to the Charitable Hospital, but there are so many in need of them that there is little I can do. It is most discouraging. The real key to improvement lies in political and economic reform, and employment.' On this note, he began to grow animated again.

'But you can see all this because of your Paris education,' marvelled Isabella. 'Surely that is all you need: to hold the memory of a time and place in your mind and make it live again.'

They were both so absorbed that they failed to notice Mr Reily come back into the dining room, accompanied by Mr M'Guire.

'My dear, we have a visitor,' Mr Reily said, flustered.

'How do you do?' said Isabella politely, too vexed at the interruption and at seeing Mr M'Guire to wonder what he was doing there.

'And of course you are acquainted with

Doctor Connor,' continued her uncle.

'How do you do?' responded the doctor. Both Mr Reily and Mr M'Guire then sat down at table, though the food had by now grown cold. Isabella and Dr Connor had long since finished eating. The conversation turned to the weather and other dull topics for what remained of the meal.

Afterwards, Mr M'Guire did not leave the room with Mr Reily and Dr Connor. Isabella was very surprised by this, and did not know what to think. Mr M'Guire cleared his throat awkwardly. He was always at a loss for words with this Miss Carroll. She didn't encourage conversation the way the Misses O'Brien did, for instance. However, he had just seen her *tête-à-tête* with that physician, who had been in Dublin barely a year and had already succeeded in taking the place over.

'I hear your aunt is unwell,' he said finally.

'She is greatly improved, thanks to Doctor Connor.'

'Indeed,' he remarked. There was an awkward lull in the conversation. She didn't seem to notice it, but he did. 'And you're keeping well yourself?' he added. 'Yes, you looked very well the other night.'

Isabella looked at him warily, wondering if he remembered what she had told Pamela about her father. He interpreted this as a sign of displeasure that he should speak so openly about an evening that had surely caused her pain.

'I must apologise,' he said. 'I do not mean to distress you. Quite the opposite, in fact. Gregory Murtogh is an absolute scoundrel, if I may say so, and it is a blessing that this came to light sooner rather than later.'

'I am grateful for your kindness,' she responded, rather distantly, he thought.

'I have taken the liberty of discussing the matter with your uncle,' he continued, 'and I know that he considers this to be an opportunity to plan a far more illustrious future for you.'

'I'm sorry?' she asked, confused.

He cleared his throat. 'Surely you have given some thought to your marriage prospects now?'

Isabella looked at him, amazed. There was a certain expectancy tinged with hesitancy in his manner that was more than a little discomfiting. 'On the contrary,' she replied. 'I have given them no thought at all. Nor do I intend to for the time being.'

Mr Reily, who had delayed his return as long as possible, came back into the dining room. 'Uncle!' exclaimed Isabella, seeing her way to a temporary escape. 'I'm afraid I'm feeling a little unwell—my head aches. So if you'll both excuse me . . .'

'Mr M'Guire wanted particularly to speak with you,' he said, unsure how to interpret the situation. He glanced inquiringly at their guest.

'That's quite all right,' answered Mr M'Guire, as if he was trying to make up his mind about something. 'Another time, perhaps.'

Isabella left immediately, her hand to her head. For heaven's sake, she thought, I do hope this doesn't mean what I think it does. She went directly to her chamber. If Mr M'Guire wanted to make a proposal, then he would lose no time in doing so. He had obviously already spoken to Uncle and obtained his consent. Where on earth had all this come from?

The fire had burned right down to a few skeletal grey coals, about to collapse into ashes, but there was still some warmth. Isabella stretched her hands over the embers. She would just have to send Mr M'Guire away, and that was all there was to it. She rubbed her eyes. Where was Dr Connor now, she wondered. At least he didn't have to contend with the Mr M'Guires of this world.

CHAPTER SIX

The next morning, Isabella was called to breakfast with her uncle. As she usually ate with her aunt in her boudoir, she could only assume that he wished to speak with her. She feared she had a good idea upon what subject.

'I trust you have recovered?' he inquired as soon as they were at table.

Isabella debated how useful it might be to prolong or exaggerate her headache. This deliberation was rendered futile when her uncle continued without waiting for her reply.

'Any remaining indisposition will be eradicated by the rather astonishing news I have to impart. Congratulate yourself, my dear, you are the most fortunate girl in Dublin.'

'How so?' she asked faintly, thinking he was wasting very little time in coming to the point.

He seemed too full of eagerness and awe to procrastinate. 'Do you consider yourself sufficiently recovered from your disappointment over Gregory Murtogh to think of your future?'

'I have been thinking of it for some time now,' she replied.

'In that case, prepare yourself for a far more illustrious match. Mr M'Guire came to speak at length with me yesterday, and I must say, your good fortune has left me speechless ever since.'

'Uncle,' she said slowly, 'surely you cannot mean to marry me so readily to Mr M'Guire? I do not believe you are all that closely acquainted with him, and I know scarcely anything about him, other than that he has an enormously prosperous business.'

'His connections speak for themselves,' he said dismissively. 'I will make some inquiries, if you wish, but I would not fret unduly.'

'I can assure you, Uncle, I am not worrying unduly. You may find him unobjectionable, but our tastes may prove completely dissimilar. I have scarcely ever spoken to Mr M'Guire. I cannot contemplate a marriage with him, and I am utterly amazed he would even think of me, knowing so little about me as he does.'

'Do not distress yourself, my dear,' her uncle said, astonished. 'I will give you some time to calm your fears and accustom you to the idea and to him.'

Molly the maidservant knocked and entered. The look she gave Isabella made her realise that she must have overheard them.

'Please excuse me, Uncle,' said Isabella. 'My head continues to ache unabated.'

'Isabella!' Mr Reily called after her as she made her way upstairs. 'Mr M'Guire will be returning this afternoon, and you will be civil to him.'

'Isabella, is that you?' her aunt's voice wafted from her boudoir. 'Come in and shut the door—I'm sitting in the most terrible draught.'

Why did you leave the door open then? Isabella wondered to herself with exasperation.

Dressed in a morning gown, Aunt was seated in an armchair, drinking tea from the delicately painted china set she kept in the boudoir for her own use. She appeared to have recovered completely.

'You were rather a long time at breakfast,' she said. 'What did you and your uncle speak of?'

Isabella was infuriated by her aunt's tone. It was perfectly obvious that she knew exactly what had been said. 'Has Uncle not spoken to you? He means to marry me to Mr M'Guire. What does it matter that we scarcely know each other, when he's wealthy, well-connected, and will serve the useful purpose of keeping me in Dublin?'

'Don't take on so,' said her aunt in dismay. 'You'll spoil everything before you've had the opportunity to think it through carefully. Honestly, my dear, you look at things blindly, and you fly off the handle at the slightest provocation without considering that there are usually wider issues at stake. I will concede that your uncle erred in speaking to you so soon and perhaps too bluntly, but surely you are sensible of the great compliment you have been paid?'

'I am only too sensible of it. What a triumph over the Murtoghs! What signifies it that Gregory behaved so badly when we could secure a catch who dare I say rivals Pamela's?'

'You laugh now, but you will not laugh when you want for the necessaries of life. Your uncle has always provided for you, but he will not live for ever, and what then? A match like this is a gift of fortune. That he should also be Catholic is a heaven-sent blessing!'

'Oh Aunt, those are hardly the only qualities to seek in a husband!' Isabella exclaimed. 'How can you value people solely for their success in business and their connections?'

Aunt looked at her sharply. 'You're not in love with some unsuitable young man, are you?'

Isabella almost laughed. 'Don't be ridiculous, Aunt. Why must you dismiss everything I say as the whim of a foolish child? I am no longer a child, and I hope I'm not a fool.'

'You are becoming unreasonable,' her aunt said. 'I was prepared to accept your distaste for Gregory Murtogh, but really, Isabella, you have gone too far this time. And after all we've done for you! How could I have raised such an ungrateful niece?'

'I am not ungrateful, Aunt,' Isabella said more calmly. 'Nor do I wish to cause you distress.'

'In that case, I suggest you occupy yourself in a useful manner for the rest of the morning. Perhaps you could trim my new bonnet—that should compose you sufficiently for Mr M'Guire's visit this afternoon.'

CHAPTER SEVEN

It is debatable whether the morning's occupation had the desired effect on Isabella. It did succeed in straining her eyes as she struggled to see her handiwork by the winter light, and so she was wearily taciturn when her aunt came to release her, carrying one of her best gowns.

'Listen to me, Isabella. Mr M'Guire is waiting with your uncle in the drawing room. You must compose yourself before you go down to him. You must not make matters worse. Your uncle is most distraught at your behaviour as it is.'

Under her aunt's critical gaze, Isabella paid the most perfunctory attention to her toilette, before allowing herself to be led to the drawing room.

'Good afternoon, Uncle,' said Isabella. But her best efforts couldn't rise to greeting Mr M'Guire, and so she sat on a chair at some distance from them.

'Well now, isn't that fortunate, you arrived just before the rain,' said Aunt pleasantly to Mr M'Guire.

'Yes indeed,' he replied, a little awkward now that Isabella was present. Perhaps he had been unwise to insist on seeing her right away, particularly as her uncle had just cautioned him that she had not quite recovered from Gregory Murtogh and was understandably reluctant to contemplate another match so soon. The silence was loaded. Uncle looked to Aunt for guidance on how to handle the situation. He had blundered this morning.

'Isabella,' said Aunt, 'why don't you play for us?' hoping that some music might drown out the tension in the room.

'I think not,' Isabella replied, reluctant to be put on display. 'I play *very* badly,' she said, addressing Mr M'Guire.

Aunt sighed. Nevertheless, her niece was sitting there in a reasonably docile fashion. 'Isabella, you do look tired,' she said. 'You must forgive me, I hadn't noticed. Why don't you take a little claret? It might restore your spirits.' She busied herself serving the wine.

Isabella drank gratefully from one of her aunt's best crystal glasses. The wine tasted warm, and restorative. There was a knock on the door.

'I beg your pardon, Mr Reily, but your presence is required downstairs,' Molly said smugly, her eyes darting briefly towards Isabella.

Aunt threw a glance at her husband, indicating to him that they should both excuse themselves. And so it was that Isabella found herself alone with Mr M'Guire. This really is too much, she thought, staring fixedly at the carpet.

'Mr M'Guire,' she said at last, emboldened by the wine, which she had drunk rather fast. 'I am sure you're aware that my uncle has spoken to me already, so there's really no need to say whatever it is you're intending to say. I thank you for thinking of me, but I must decline your kind offer.'

'You speak as though it were some ominous portent of disaster, and I can hardly blame you for that. But I am not Gregory Murtogh, and I can assure you, Miss Carroll, there are no skeletons in my closet.'

'I do not mean to offend you,' she insisted. 'But we are barely acquainted, and we have scarcely ever exchanged any more than a few polite words of conversation. You must see what a surprise it is that you should suddenly come to speak to my uncle on such a matter.'

'It may seem sudden to you, but I have held you in esteem for quite some time now. It was only that you were so obviously destined for Murtogh.'

'I'm sorry,' she said. 'I was completely unaware.'

'Yes,' he said. 'I can see that I have been too hasty, but it could not be helped. I was anxious to speak to your uncle before anyone else did.'

'That was quite unnecessary! It's not as if I'm being inundated with offers every day of the week.'

'Perhaps not, but I'm sure that will soon change.'

'Oh?' she inquired with curiosity. 'Why?'

He hesitated. 'You will forgive me, I'm sure, if I refer so bluntly to what I overheard between you and Miss Murtogh. The fact is, I know quite a lot about your father from my connections in the West Indies, and it would appear that you now stand to inherit his fortune. This makes you a very attractive matrimonial proposition. Your uncle is a merchant of comfortable circumstances, and he has promised to provide handsomely for you, but your father's Saint-Domingue plantations place you in quite a different league.'

'I don't understand,' she said, startled. 'Why then was it my uncle you spoke to?'

'I would welcome an opportunity to speak with your father. As I told you, my connections have spoken very highly of him, and I am sure they will recommend me to him. I even thought we could pay him a visit—if I remember correctly, this was the wish you expressed so fervently to your friend.'

These were far from the circumstances I had in mind, she thought to herself. 'You seem to have given this a lot of thought,' she said. 'I'm not surprised Uncle is so in awe of your business achievements. I only wonder that you could succeed in recommending yourself to others by speaking in such crude terms.'

'I see I have wounded your delicacy, and I apologise for that. I have little experience in these matters, and should have proceeded more cautiously. I have clearly neglected to plead my own cause.'

'Allow me to,' said Isabella. 'You are a very wealthy man, with some degree of power through the influence you claim to exert on certain MPs and other well-placed Protestant friends. However, as I recall, such connections come at a high price, and my apparent fortune would relieve you of some of the financial pressure your ambitions entail.'

'You are quite the pessimist,' he said with surprise. 'Credit me with at least a little more imagination than that, and think of the possibilities of the match. You speak as if I were motivated solely by a need to guard myself against the most basic of Catholic fears, like your uncle, who has spent his entire life attempting to predict the vagaries of trade and increase his capital without ruffling the feathers of the Establishment, hiding the opulence of his furnishings behind the unremarkable exterior of his house, concealing the silks he dresses his womenfolk in from the eyes of all but his fellow Catholic merchants.'

'You speak plainly, Mr M'Guire, but I cannot quite fathom your meaning. First you appear to mock my uncle for failing to oppose all the restrictions that weigh so heavily on this country, but then it seems you are mocking him solely for the exterior of the house, which is surely infinitely superior to most people's.'

'I was simply attempting to illustrate the difference between your uncle's objectives and my own. Your uncle seeks to bury himself in as splendid a hole as possible. I, on the other hand, have already raised my head above the parapet, and seek to explore what I see as best I can.'

'I understand. It might surprise you to learn that I too wish to raise my head above my existing circumstances. However, yours is a prospect I do not wish to share, nor do I envisage your wishing to share mine.'

'Do not be hasty, I am sure you will come to think differently in time,' he reassured her confidently.

Was there to be no escape? thought an exasperated Isabella. 'You must excuse me now,' she said. 'I am feeling overwhelmed. I cannot quite accustom myself to my new status as plantation heiress. You have been most enlightening, Mr M'Guire.'

'As you wish,' he said, rising to his feet. 'But let me assure you, Miss Carroll, I shan't relinquish my suit so easily. Nor will your uncle and aunt, I imagine.'

CHAPTER EIGHT

When Isabella heard her aunt call for the physician to be sent for, she at first thought it was the last straw. Then she decided to turn it to her own advantage by insisting on going to fetch him herself in the carriage. She was longing to escape the house, and even hoped to steal a few moments to confide something of her trouble to the physician. He had struck her as unusually resourceful, despite his self-proclaimed malaise, and when he had related his impressions of Dublin life, it was as if he had articulated the very source of her own unrest.

It was such a wet day that Aunt could not possibly imagine Isabella intended to profit by enjoying it as an excursion in itself. Hoping to impress on her niece the consequences of her ingratitude, and having endured all the heated exchanges she could bear for one day, she dispatched the girl in the now drizzling rain, accompanied by Molly. The maidservant really could not be spared, but nor could Isabella go alone, particularly in these circumstances.

Now that Isabella was away from the house, her anger grew more distant. As it did so, she became reflective and began to be truly shaken by the events of the day. There had been such a curious tone to their response, as if they were merely marking time until she began to conduct herself as a dutiful niece. She wondered what Molly made of all this. It still rankled with her how Uncle had arranged for Molly to call him away, and so she confined her remarks to general inquiries on household matters.

The driver had reached the doctor's address. It was a small house, but in a respectable area. The door was eventually answered by an older woman, who Isabella correctly took to be his landlady. She stared long and hard at Isabella—was this another of Dr Connor's patients? The girl didn't look in the slightest bit ailing.

'The doctor's not here at present,' she announced.

'Would you mind if I were to wait for him?'

An overtly speculative look came over the landlady's face. 'As you wish,' she replied. 'Are you a patient?'

'Not at present. My aunt is,' she volunteered, but did not choose to divulge any more, thinking that should be quite enough to satisfy her, though the landlady's eyes were drifting towards the carriage. Isabella told the driver that they would have to wait, but as the rain seemed to have finally cleared, he didn't seem to mind. Isabella stepped inside, followed closely by Molly.

'I imagine he'll return shortly,' said the landlady, leading them up a dark stairway.

'Perhaps you'd care to wait in here?'

She showed Isabella and Molly into what appeared to be a study. Then, to Isabella's great relief, the landlady offered tea, and prevailed on Molly to assist her. She presumably intends to pump Molly in the kitchen, thought Isabella, but she welcomed the opportunity to spend a few moments alone.

Looking around her, she was astounded by the quantity of books, having never seen so many before. She found on inspection that many of them seemed to be concerned with physic, surgery and science, and were written in Latin and French. There were other books too, but again they were written in French, and the names of the authors meant nothing to her. There was a stack of pamphlets, many in French, but some of them from Dublin, and there was an assortment of Irish newspapers. The desk near the window was strewn with papers, pamphlets and hand-written sheets, but it showed such obvious signs of recent work that she thought it better not to disturb it, and sat down to wait.

Eventually, she heard voices outside. The landlady was saying: 'She said she wasn't a patient, but she wanted particularly to see you, so I thought it might be of a *personal* nature, and I showed her in there.'

She is very forward, thought Isabella, feeling awkward now that the doctor had returned. The tea appears to have been forgotten, which would indicate that she finds Molly's conversation far more interesting. I wonder what the girl is telling her? This train of thought was interrupted by the physician.

'Miss Carroll,' he said, surprised. 'Is your aunt unwell?'

'She claims to be suffering from a complaint which I have inflicted on her,' she replied dryly. Half-regretting her bluntness, she looked away. 'I've been admiring your books,' she said. 'I have never seen so many before.'

'There aren't all that many,' he told her, wondering what had happened.

'You only think that because there are so few books in the houses of your uncle and his friends.'

'Perhaps so. I don't wonder that you can speak with such eloquence and authority on a variety of subjects when you have so much to refer to.'

'You are too kind. Unfortunately, they can also carry distinct disadvantages. I am going away very soon, and there are far too many to bring with me. I shall simply have to store them in a trunk and trust to my landlady's safe-keeping.'

'Going away? What new project is this?' asked Isabella, both disappointed and envious.

He sank into the chair near the desk with an air of fatigue. 'I have been with Mrs Mahon all day,' he said. 'She was thrown from a Noddy, causing the child to be born before its time. She insisted on my being sent for, but there was nothing I or the midwife or the other physician could do—the child was dead and the mother distraught.'

'I am very sorry,' said Isabella, searching in vain for appropriate expressions. 'Is Gregory with her?'

'I'm told she has refused to see him of late. Apparently, she has returned to the protection of the gentleman who sent for me.'

'Another gentleman?'

'Yes. He did show some concern for her well-being, and I suggested she be removed to the countryside, where the clean air and change of scene should hasten her recovery.'

If only she too could slip from her predicament with the ease of a Mrs Mahon who had been offered such ready sanctuary by another, Isabella thought, even though it had been often enough impressed upon her that the ultimate fate of the Mrs Mahons of this world was poverty and desolation. And yet, Mrs Mahon had seen fit to spurn Gregory Murtogh.

The physician was at a loss to interpret Isabella's thoughtful silence. Recollecting himself, he said: 'I apologise if I have insulted your sense of delicacy, or whatever you choose to call it, by speaking so openly of her circumstances—I understood you interested yourself in her?'

'I do not take offence so easily, Doctor, though I trust your absence will not be caused by your accompanying her to her country retreat?'

'On the contrary, I intend to take up a friend of mine on a long-standing invitation to visit him at home in Paris. I have been reluctant to do so, because his living quarters are not all that extensive, and his wife has lately been delivered of a son. But I long for a rest, and to see him again, and so . . .'

'Even the anticipation of it has vastly improved your spirits,' Isabella observed with a touch of dejection. 'You are lucky. Would that I could simply set sail for Paris.'

'You sound sombre,' remarked the doctor. 'Might I be so bold as to inquire the reason for your aunt's new indisposition?'

'I would not presume to trouble you with my woes,' she said tentatively. 'Nonetheless, as my aunt is waiting for you on her sickbed, you might find it useful to know that my reluctance to be married to Mr M'Guire has been a profound shock to her nerves.'

'Mr M'Guire? There has clearly been little time lost!' He pondered this for a moment. 'It is not for me to interfere, but from the little I know of you, I can hardly imagine it an ideal match.'

Her eyes darkened. 'I find myself in an intolerable situation. If only my uncle had not forbidden me to go to Paris, I feel sure I could have prevailed on my father to oppose the match. But he is not even aware that I have no means of joining him.'

'In that case, you should appeal to him,' said Dr Connor thoughtfully. 'Write a letter detailing all recent developments, and I will deliver it to him in person. If he is as eager to be reunited with you as he claims to be, then I imagine he will send someone for you immediately. He may even come for you himself, and the whole matter will be resolved to your satisfaction.'

Isabella knew this was the most appropriate step to take. She balked at it only because it required an inordinate amount of waiting for an answer of some kind. She felt that her patience had already been tested to its limit. How could she placate her aunt and uncle and delay any marriage settlements with Mr M'Guire? She would have to resort to duplicity and feign some degree of willingness to consider him favourably if she hoped to secure that vital extra time.

'That is very generous of you,' she told the doctor, even as all the implied constraints of his suggestion weighed so heavily on her. 'Should I write now, before we leave?'

He cleared a space for her at his desk and provided her with fresh writing materials. 'Dear Father,' she wrote hesitantly. There was so much to be conveyed. How could she write such a letter when she had never even seen a likeness of him? 'I was deeply saddened to learn of your recent sorrow, and equally moved by the wish you expressed to have me come to you in Paris. I can only regret that circumstances have conspired so cunningly to confine me here in Dublin.' Feeling the physician's gaze on her, she hastened to complete her entreaty.

'I am greatly indebted to you,' she said, handing him the letter once it was sealed and directed. 'I am only too aware of the imposition I have made on you, particularly as you are also attending my aunt.'

He seemed discomfited by this and unsure how to respond. 'For my part, I am only too aware of how little I can help you,' he said finally. 'I wish you well, Miss Carroll. Would that you had not been compelled to come here on such an errand.'

Reluctantly, she fastened her pelisse. Her aunt would be impatient. Dr Connor hastily scrawled something on a sheet of paper.

'My address in Paris, and the time the packet leaves for England, should you need to contact me before I leave,' he said.

Isabella carefully folded his note and concealed it in her deep pocket. Molly was then retrieved from the kitchen, where she had been passing the time pleasantly gossiping with the landlady. However, time had not flown all that fast: they had both noticed just how long the doctor had spent alone with Miss Carroll.

Molly's eye lit up with a knowing glint that was completely lost on Isabella.

The carriage hurriedly jerked and jolted them back to the house, where Isabella was permitted to retire for the night while Dr Connor went to her aunt.

'Mrs Reily,' he said wearily. 'I understand you have been beset by some new and troubling symptoms. Could you perhaps describe them to me?'

He listened to her account of anxiety and agitation, and found himself wearily thinking of Mrs Murtogh the morning after her disastrous entertainment. One woman with a disobedient son, the other with a disobedient niece, both hiding under the bedclothes from the genuine sickness of the society they perpetuated.

But he would soon be far away from here! On returning home from Mrs Mahon's ill-fated confinement, he had found a letter from his friend Bernard, full of concern about Connor's low spirits, prescribing travel and a restorative trip to Paris. Even the thought of it had lifted him from the despondency of his reflections on Ireland and given him a rush of freedom, an urge to flight which he seized after only the most cursory consideration of his practice.

Meanwhile, there was Mrs Reily to be dealt with. He decided to prescribe opium: it would tranquillise her nerves sufficiently to give her poor niece some respite, even if only temporary.

CHAPTER NINE

Having confined herself again to her boudoir, Aunt grew increasingly petulant over the next few days, despite the soporific administrations of a heavy opiate. She sent for Isabella. Her niece was to supervise Molly cleaning the silver and not take her eyes off her for even a moment, because the maidservant was even more useless than usual today. Despite feeling that her aunt was being unnecessarily harsh, Isabella had to admit that Molly seemed preoccupied and subdued.

'Is anything the matter?' she asked, after Molly had taken several items from her with an unusual roughness.

Molly looked at her, as if trying to gauge her reaction. 'Our youngest has been taken bad with the cold, and we're all driven mad with worry.'

'Molly, I'm so very sorry. Why didn't you say? I'm sure my aunt will do all in her power to assist you.'

'The mistress is angry with me for breaking one of her good china cups yesterday, and she's stopping it out of my wages. In any case, we don't need to consult the wisdom of your fine Doctor Connor to know what sickness and misery a hard winter can bring.' She seemed to break off here, as if she was struggling to hold something back.

'What's on your mind?' Isabella asked, studying the maid closely. 'Speak as frankly as you wish, I shan't hold it against you.'

'Oh it's nothing. You wouldn't be interested in any of my troubles, I'm sure of it.'

'Don't be silly! If something's troubling you, I'd much rather you told me about it instead of bottling it all up inside. Especially in a situation like this.'

'What do you want to know, then? What it's like for my family, huddled together in one stinking, icy room? What it's like for me, seeing in this house all the things we need but can't afford? I don't imagine you are capable of persuading your uncle to lower the price of his coal, but have you any idea of the suffering caused when people cannot afford it, how many people die from the cold?'

'Is my uncle's coal so exorbitantly expensive?' Isabella wondered uneasily, realising she did not know the current price. She was aware that he bought it from ships that came from Newcastle, and that it was often a source of frustration to him, as it arrived at such irregular intervals. Sometimes nothing for months, then a whole fleet of ships together. They generally came during the summer, when there was no demand, and so the coal had to be stored in warehouses until the winter came. Isabella knew that the coal could be bought quite cheaply in summer, and that it was general practice amongst merchants to sell it at a higher price in winter—there were storage costs and other expenses. But Molly's words made it seem as if he were almost preying on the poor.

'It pains me to see how unsparingly it is used here,' replied Molly.

Isabella locked away the silver. 'Come upstairs with me, and wait outside the boudoir until I call you,' she said.

Isabella found her aunt now occupied with some embroidery. She was seated quite close to the fire, with the screen positioned to protect her complexion.

'Molly's family require your urgent assistance: the youngest has been gravely affected by the cold, and they cannot afford to purchase the coal to keep her warm.'

'Is that the reason for her clumsiness? Why did she not come to me herself?' Aunt asked in exasperation, putting down her needlework 'Send for her immediately.'

Isabella brought Molly in.

'Molly, you must always inform me of your troubles—how else can I be expected to make due allowances for your behaviour? Now, I shall send John round immediately with some coal, and I'll see what we can spare from the pantry.' She crossed the room, and unlocked a box. 'If I give you this gold sovereign, do you promise to spend it on victuals and clothing for the child? I shall send some brandy for medicinal purposes, but not a penny of that sovereign must be squandered on bad spirits in some cheap tavern.'

Isabella winced at her aunt's implication, but Molly meekly accepted the sovereign and carefully put it in her pocket. After dispatching John, and personally making up a basket of vegetables, meat and cakes, Aunt allowed Molly the day off. The girl seemed both surprised and gratified.

'I do hope the child's health recovers soon, and may our maid's humour recover with it!' said Aunt, much taken with the notion of her own generosity.

They were standing in the kitchen, where the remains of what food had not gone in the basket lay scattered around the large table. Isabella uneasily tidied together some of the vegetables. 'Aunt, I am a little troubled by something Molly said in passing. Is it true that Uncle, and all the other merchants too, exact so heavy a price for coal that it is beyond the means of many, and they perish as a result?'

'Is that what she told you?' her aunt was affronted. 'Well, and I was so good to her too! I suppose it must be beyond the means of the beggars on the street, but I am sure that if the price were too high, it wouldn't be bought at all.'

'But surely one has no choice but to try to meet the cost of something so vital,' Isabella persisted. 'Surely it is not right to profit at the expense of families like Molly's?'

'It is hardly your uncle's fault that this country is in such a deplorable state. You know very well about the trade restrictions, about how crippled we've been until so very recently . . . You should thank your good fortune that you have been prevented from sharing the fate of so many of your fellow Catholics by the efforts of your uncle, who you can be sure works a great deal harder than any of Molly's family ever will.'

Isabella spoke no more on the subject, but as they returned upstairs, it was quite plain to her aunt that it continued to weigh on her. Exasperated, Mrs Reily decided she would exchange a few words in private with her husband when he came home.

Her niece was obviously still in such a pet about Mr M'Guire that she was ready to find fault with anything.

Isabella was thinking how different things must be in Paris. Her aunt and uncle were so preoccupied with maintaining the shaky position they had attained that they had become incapable of looking beyond their own success. But from what Dr Connor had told her, there seemed to be room in Paris to voice an uneasiness with society, and her mind seized on this idea to such an extent, she failed to realise that her aunt's rushed conversation with her uncle, just behind the door, pertained to the morning's events.

'What new foolishness is this?' her uncle asked once they were at table. 'Your aunt tells me you've been asking about the price of coal. Surely you cannot believe me indifferent to the misery I see on the streets every day? But I cannot be held responsible—if you must find culprits, look to London and the yoke of legislation which has only been partially lifted. It was not me who brought this country to its knees. I must struggle to stay afloat like the others of my class. Why should I not be rewarded for my efforts?'

What kind of class saw misery as its reward? thought Isabella. Her mind turned again to Paris. How could she remain in Dublin any longer when every warm fire would serve as a constant reminder of Molly's family and her uncle's business practices? Of course there was truth in what her uncle said about how he had struggled against the odds to establish himself, but what use was that knowledge when she also remembered Mr M'Guire's words, and how he would use any further repeal in the present laws only to advance his own worldly position, as if the hoarding of position and possessions were all that mattered. Why should she remain here, only to be forced into marriage, possibly before her father could intervene?

If only she too could leave for Paris, fly away from this accursed country like all the Wild Geese before her. The physician had promised to deliver her letter to her father, but that would take too long. If only she could leave on the same packet as Dr Connor. It was very hard that she could not simply travel alone and as she pleased.

But why shouldn't she? Isabella almost choked on her food at the thought, but it seemed to open up a wondrous vista inside her head, and suddenly all manner of ideas and possibilities began to whirl around.

This is madness, she thought. She did not even possess the necessary funds to undertake such a journey—her aunt settled all her expenses with bills of credit and IOUs, and that box of gold sovereigns in the boudoir was very likely to remain locked against a disobedient, ungrateful niece for the foreseeable future.

But a little ingenuity might advance her cause. Isabella thought it probable that Pamela would have access to a ready store of gold—the wedding preparations were lavish, and the date was so soon that her father would very likely have provided her with some money as a comfortable cushion with which to begin married life. Why not appeal to Pamela? Why ever not? She looked across the table at her aunt, and then at her uncle, as if they were already distant objects.

'Uncle,' she said, sweetening her voice as

best she could, 'how much longer must we wait before we resume friendly relations with the Murtoghs? Pamela is to be married very soon, and I do not know when I may see her again. Might I not arrange to take a walk with her in the Rotunda Gardens? Or even to visit a silk mercer? Then I could avoid encountering all the others by calling for her in the carriage without being obliged to enter the house.'

Her aunt was inclined to agree. It was certainly hard on both girls that they were deprived of a confidante at such a time. And she herself was longing for the sympathetic ear of Mrs Murtogh—it was really too provoking that her dear friend was the least appropriate person to hear of Isabella's ingratitude, not while Gregory's actions lay so fresh in their minds. But Pamela was such a good girl, and had never caused an ounce of trouble. Her future husband was also known to be a connection of Mr M'Guire. Surely that alone would make her amenable to the match. Pamela might talk sense into Isabella. At worst, she could hardly fail to express some form of reproof and disapproval.

'It is a very great favour to ask,' Aunt urged her husband. 'Nevertheless, some pleasant distraction might coax Isabella into a better frame of mind.'

'Very well,' said her uncle. 'You may write to her, if you wish. I may even send John directly and have him wait for an answer, despite the fact that your aunt must already make do without Molly today. But I hope you appreciate the extent of my kindness in granting you such a favour at a time like this.'

Isabella's heart beat fast, as if her scheme had already been put into action. 'Thank you, Uncle,' she said. 'I am indeed grateful.'

CHAPTER TEN

It was clearly a kindness Aunt did not wish denied herself, for the next day, Isabella found her preparing to go out. 'I thought it would perhaps be more appropriate if I were to accompany you. Once Mrs Murtogh has been made aware of my presence, she may even judge it proper to join us on our little excursion.'

Isabella concealed her frustration as best she could, assuring herself that she would find some pretext to speak with Pamela alone. On arriving, they were shown in to Mrs Murtogh immediately, whose face lit up at the sight of her old friend. But the raw winter sunshine failed to entice her out, for she remained indisposed. However, as Mrs Reily had troubled herself to come so far, could she be prevailed upon to stay, despite what had happened? Mrs Reily was only too willing.

This rapprochement gave Isabella the

opportunity to ask Pamela to show her the wedding trousseau before they left for their walk. After a hasty look at her mother for approval, Pamela brought Isabella to an upstairs chamber, where an astonishing array of morning gowns, formal dress, underskirts, bodices, lace, caps, headdresses, stockings, and capes were neatly packed away in trunks. Conscious of the pride Pamela took in these garments, which were made of the most costly fabrics, Isabella attempted a show of delight. And in fact, she was overwhelmed by the beauty of the colours, the delicacy of the lace, and the magnificence of the brocades, but they made her dwell too deeply on Mr M'Guire's proposal, and her thoughts grew darker and more distant as Pamela listed the precise number of garments, and their cost.

'You grow pensive,' remarked Pamela. 'Do you think of your own marriage? I was told in confidence that Mr M'Guire had made you an offer.'

Isabella saw how her friend's face filled with admiration at the very name 'Mr M'Guire', and she wondered how she could ever hope to convey the truth of her own feelings.

'Pamela, I came here to ask a very great favour of you. Could you lend me a sum of money? It is not a great deal, but it is nonetheless more than I can secure without suspicion.'

Pamela's face grew grave, but she unlocked

a box from which she filled a bag with coins. Isabella buried the bag deep in the pocket of her skirt, as grateful and relieved as Molly had been to receive her aunt's gold sovereign, she thought.

She reserved her confidences for when she and Pamela were safely caught up in the bustle of strangers outside and away from the Murtogh house.

'But why must you object so to Mr M'Guire?' Pamela asked in dismay. 'Mr O'Beirne speaks very highly of him. If you were married, we would be able to see each other often—you could even come to stay with us in the country.' She hesitated before adding quietly: 'I fear I shall be lonely in the country.'

This was not the first time Isabella had sensed the gentle sadness underlying her friend's wedding preparations. But she also knew that Pamela accepted without question that this marriage was in her best interests, and after all, she and Pamela were so very different.

'Perhaps you will find the change refreshing,' she said hopefully. 'There is such a harsh air in this city. The Mr M'Guires of our class seem casually to dismiss the slums as evidence of bad government, while seeking at the same time to ingratiate themselves at all costs with those responsible. Do you never wonder what it would be like to wake up in a city where considerations of religion and history do not weigh so heavily upon you?'

Pamela smiled, but did not answer.

'Of course not. All you can think of is the country,' said Isabella, glancing at her friend. 'Does Mr O'Beirne know of your anxieties?'

'He tells me I worry unnecessarily. His mother and sisters get along very well there, and we will be visiting Dublin from time to time, but . . .'

'Still, you worry, as I would in your place. Even so, I don't suppose you'd consider leaving it all behind and coming to Paris with me?'

'What nonsense you talk!' Pamela exclaimed. 'At the very least, you have a father awaiting you there. Can you imagine what foolishness it would be for me to go too? Paris indeed! And it's a great deal further away than the country, you know.'

On this note, they went into the packet office, where Isabella booked her passage. Was it really that simple? she asked herself, astonished. She had paid the sum to travel, and all she had to do was present herself at the point of embarkation on that date, where a vessel would be waiting to carry her, the mail, and all her fellow-passengers to Holyhead in Wales. Unless, of course, there was a contrary wind, or a storm, in which case they would not be able to sail . . . She would simply have to pray for a good wind, and hope that she could endure the long journey by land through Wales and England.

'I will send the money to you,' she promised Pamela as they returned to the Murtoghs' house, hoping that this would not compromise her friend. Isabella was now troubled by the thought that her uncle would probably pester Pamela when he discovered her gone to Paris.

'If my uncle comes to you, answer his questions in whatever manner you see fit. Do not spare me in any way,' she said, as they paused on the threshold.

'Do not be anxious on my account, though I shall certainly be on yours. You must remember that your father is a stranger to you. It is we who are your friends, Isabella.'

Isabella and her aunt drove away in the carriage. Mrs Murtogh and Mrs Reily had comforted each other so well that Aunt's spirits were greatly soothed. This produced a lull in her disappointment.

'My dear Isabella,' she said. 'Must we quarrel so? I brought you here from France when you were a new-born infant, and I nursed you so carefully when no one else interested themselves in you. Surely you cannot doubt that I want only what's best for you?'

Isabella felt a twinge of guilt. There was so much truth in her aunt's words. She had been shown nothing but kindness by her dead mother's sister. She knew she owed her aunt so much, but she never could accept that genuine gratitude should oblige her to marry some odious husband. As they approached the house, she had the sensation of observing both herself and her home from a distance. Because she was so much at odds with her designated role of merchant's niece, she felt almost as if she had become a ghost, as if her morning gown and pelisse clung tightly to a dressmaker's dummy, awaiting the obedient, unthinking Miss Carroll they had been made for. Nevertheless, those skirts and petticoats were carefully lifted to follow Aunt across the threshold.

Knowing that the packet would sail in a few days, Isabella began at once to make preparations. Of immediate importance was to find an excuse that would allow her to slip away on the day. She knew she would be able to take very little with her, just the bare necessities for her journey. Her eye fell on the silk gown she had worn to the Murtoghs' ill-fated evening. She remembered how it had been made especially for that occasion, and how her aunt had insisted on the heavy lace ruffles, and the ornate embroidery. She fingered the miniature of her aunt, which hung from a heavy gold chain around her neck. It was a good likeness, though several years old. Isabella decided to keep it on. Then, conscious that the gold might attract the attention of undesirables on her travels, she concealed it about her person, before adding her old governess's tale of the Wild Geese to her bag.

All this was done by flickering candlelight. The contours of the chamber seemed indistinct, as if it were slowly fading away into blackness and would be gone by morning. Outside the night was clear and mild, and though she could not judge the wind, she saw no reason why the packet should not sail. Goodbye, thought Isabella. Whatever path I took, I could not have remained longer. Dutiful or undutiful, I was destined to leave this home on bad terms. After comparing Mr M'Guire to Paris, can I really be blamed for seeking the latter?

CHAPTER ELEVEN

Dr Connor had risen early. He had made all the necessary arrangements the night before, and in the morning the hackney-coach was waiting outside with his luggage. He had bidden a final farewell to his landlady, who was reluctant to see him go as he had been so good and quiet, and made him promise several times that he would return. This exasperated him, as he was keeping the rooms, had paid for them, and had left his books and papers in her care, locked securely in a heavy trunk. She knew that he would have to return for them, that he was even taking something of a risk, entrusting them to her. As soon as she had parted from him, and he was about to step into the coach, he was hailed by Gregory Murtogh, who was looking rather the worse for wear, as if he had not yet been to bed.

'I must speak with you,' he said. 'Can't you spare me a few moments?'

The doctor hesitated. 'I mustn't tarry here any longer or I'll miss my packet,' he prevaricated, with an idea of Gregory's purpose.

'Are you leaving us, Doctor?' asked Gregory, surprised. 'In that case, you must allow me to accompany you as far as the ship. I have urgent business with you.'

'I think not,' insisted Dr Connor. 'The coachman will be driving the horses as fast as he can—it will make for a bumpy ride.'

'Such things mean nothing to me,' declared Gregory. 'Please Doctor, you cannot turn me away.'

Not wanting to waste any more time, Dr Connor allowed Gregory to join him. The horses set off at a brisk pace. Gregory slouched back into the seat and turned his bloodshot eyes on the physician.

'Mrs Mahon has disappeared, and I am driven to distraction looking for her,' said Gregory. 'Won't you tell me where she is?'

Dr Connor sighed, having anticipated this question. 'I don't know where she is at the moment, and I suggest you be patient. If she wishes to contact you, then I am sure she will.'

'How can you be so lacking in compassion?' demanded Gregory, dismayed. 'She sent me a note, so brief and spiritless, informing me of her accident and tragic confinement. Yet still she refused to see me. I succeeded at least in learning that you had attended her. Surely you cannot refuse to aid such a miserable wretch as me?'

'I recommended she remove to the country for the sake of her health,' said Dr Connor uneasily. 'I do not know where she chose to go.'

'But if she were to write, you would inform me directly?' he pressed.

Again, Dr Connor hesitated uncomfortably. The feckless Gregory Murtogh had clearly been deeply affected by recent events, but Dr Connor did not wish to be implicated any further in his affairs. He also felt an obligation to Mrs Mahon.

'I see a marked reluctance in your face,' Gregory said at last. 'It is curious that you should maintain such a loyalty towards Mrs Mahon when I believe you have also been attending my mother. How do you reconcile such a conflict, Doctor?'

'I take my responsibilities as a physician seriously,' Dr Connor replied. His voice was calmer than Gregory had expected.

'Indeed,' remarked Gregory. 'Do you then tend to their ailments without passing the slightest judgement on their conduct? My, what a paragon you are.'

This time, the physician chose not to answer. There was a lot he could have said, and in some ways it would have been a relief to do so. But why complicate the situation any further when he was so close to his destination?

Despite his frustration, Gregory realised there was nothing to be gained from further antagonising the doctor. 'Forgive my ill-temper,' he said. 'I had rather a lot to drink last night. I forget myself.'

'Perhaps you should not drink so much. It has a bad effect on both your conduct and your constitution.'

'I take it you are alluding to my bringing Mrs Mahon home that night. All I can offer in my defence is that despair at my circumstances led me on my course of dissipation.'

'Then I can only regret that you have dragged others down in your wake,' said Dr Connor.

Gregory felt a strong stirring of resentment. Who was this physician to lecture him? What did he know of Gregory's circumstances? Gregory always felt it hard that others should condemn him for a lack of steadiness—it was hardly his fault that his father refused to allow him to marry Mrs Mahon, and as for his lack of income, well, again he could not be blamed for his dependence. After all, he was the only son, and he had neither talent nor taste for business.

The hackney-coach stopped. 'Goodbye, Mr Murtogh,' said Dr Connor, extending his hand. 'May we meet again on better terms.'

Dr Connor paid the coachman, who then handed him his luggage. The quay was crowded with people—clearly the packet was going to be very full. The weather had been so unsettled lately that half of Dublin seemed to have decided to take advantage of the clear skies and travel now. A considerable number of passengers' carriages were also being loaded onto the ship.

'Where to now, sir?' the coachman asked Gregory, who had remained in the hackney.

The truth was, Gregory Murtogh had no place to go. He had of late been living in lodgings, but he could not return there, as he was in some financial embarrassment and had failed to persuade any of his friends to advance him more than the smallest of sums. In addition, his father had instructed the merchants and business people of his acquaintance not to issue his son with any more credit. Under these circumstances, Gregory had no desire to return home. He judged himself capable of cajoling his mother into relenting somewhat, but he was in no condition to face his father.

'Wait here, driver,' he said, proffering his few remaining coins. 'I should like to take the sea air for a little while. The breeze will soothe my head.'

He strolled down towards the point of embarkation, where he noticed that the doctor and a woman were involved in a heated dispute with some ragamuffin over a piece of baggage. His curiosity aroused, he decided to take a closer look.

'I really must insist on seeing to it myself,' the woman was saying. 'As I said, it is but a small bag, and there is no need for you to carry it on board.'

'Leave us,' said the Doctor, dismissing the boy and retrieving the bag.

Suddenly Gregory caught sight of the young woman's face. His long-suffering head reeled with speculation and his eyes lit up with surprise and vindication as he recognised Isabella Carroll. No wonder the doctor had been so reluctant to have his company! He was clearly eloping with the Reilys' niece.

'Miss Carroll,' said Gregory, announcing his presence with relish. 'I am glad to see you did not wait long for consolation. Doctor, I congratulate you. But is such a flight advisable? Consider your reputation.'

'You are mistaken, I assure you,' said the doctor angrily. 'I merely happened to come upon Miss Carroll here, and it is fortunate that I did so, as she was in danger of having her belongings snatched from her.'

'What say you, Miss Carroll?' Gregory

asked slyly.

Isabella was at a loss for an answer. She could not allow him to think she was eloping with the physician—she cared little for Gregory's personal opinion of her, but she knew how easily he could cause a scandal, even if his own reputation had been discredited. Much as she was reluctant to tell him the truth, she felt it might be wiser to do so. Surely there was little he could do now to stop her boarding the packet, and once it had set sail, it would be too late for him to fetch her uncle.

'It is not your affair,' she told him. 'But as you have so falsely accused us, I feel obliged to inform you that I am going to Paris to join my father. Now, if you would be so kind as to let me pass.'

'But of course, Miss Carroll,' said Gregory mischievously. 'Allow me to escort you to your companions. I consider it remiss of them to have left you waiting here alone all this time.'

By now, most of the passengers had boarded, and there was very little activity on shore. Last calls were being made for the few remaining travellers, and it was quite obvious that there was nobody seeking Isabella. Nevertheless, she led Gregory towards the point of embarkation, followed by the doctor. Once her foot was firmly placed on the plank, she turned to Gregory nervously and said: 'Thank you for your concern. I believe they have boarded already. I shall find them myself.'

'However,' said Gregory smugly, 'I shall feel uneasy about your safety. Allow me at least to satisfy myself by seeing you safely into your friends' hands. When next I see your uncle and aunt, I would like to be able to assure them that I left you safe and well . . .'

The idea of Gregory Murtogh pretending superiority to her was really too much. 'Very well,' she said angrily. 'You force me to admit that I am travelling alone, unknown to my aunt and uncle. But it is hardly my fault if I have to resort to such measures merely to obey my father's wishes. You are in no position to judge me, Mr Murtogh.'

'Travelling alone!' cried the doctor, who had been taken aback by the exchange. 'It is not safe for a young woman to travel alone.'

'But she is not alone,' remarked Gregory. 'You cannot expect me to believe it a mere coincidence that you should both set off for Paris on the same day? Neither, I imagine, will your friends. If you wish to save your reputation, Miss Carroll, allow me to return you to your uncle's house. Otherwise, I will have no choice but to inform him of what I have seen. Unless, of course, the good doctor feels able to furnish me with the information I require.'

The ship's crew were becoming impatient. They had been waiting several days for a wind as favourable as this. 'Are you boarding or not?' the steward asked.

'Perhaps you had better return home,' Dr Connor told Isabella. 'I don't have the information he wants, and I shudder to think of the damage he could do to your good name.'

Isabella looked at the doctor in disbelief. She knew there was truth in what he said, yet somehow she would have expected more of him. She struggled to find words to express the significance of her actions, the effort it had taken to leave her uncle's house, the measures to which she had had to resort in order even to reach the packet. Failing in this, she turned from them, and quickly lost herself amongst the crowds that thronged the decks. Dr Connor boarded hastily, but could not see her anywhere. The ship started to move away from shore.

'I never suspected she possessed such spirit,' Gregory called out. 'I imagine she'll be quite a handful, Doctor. I only hope she's worth it.'

Gregory strolled back to the awaiting hackney-coach. Now he knew where to go. It only remained to speculate on the possible reasons for an elopement. Surely the physician would have made a reasonable match? Granted, he was in the early stages of his profession, but he already had a few wealthy patrons, and respectable Papists were rather thin on the ground. Why would the Reilys have objected to him as a suitor for their niece?

Gregory sank back into his seat as the quays faded away behind them. He imagined he would soon find out.

CHAPTER TWELVE

Dr Connor eventually found Isabella. Like most of the other passengers, she was standing on deck, watching the shore grow smaller and more distant. All around her, voices grumbled about the discomfort of the vessel's accommodation, and the suffering that lay ahead of them on the journey, but what Isabella felt most was an overwhelming sense of freedom as Ireland began to disappear behind an expanse of dull grey waves.

'Doctor Connor,' she said. 'I must apologise. I had not bargained on Gregory Murtogh. When foreseeing all possible pitfalls, it never occurred to me that your name would be slurred in such a manner.'

'Perhaps it would be wiser if we persuaded the captain to put you to shore before it's too late,' he said uneasily. 'Murtogh has a talent for mischief, if nothing else, and he could make it difficult for you to return to Dublin at a later date.'

Isabella was silent as the consequences of her actions sank in. She had been fully aware of the disapproval she risked in secretly quitting her uncle's house, but because she had assumed they would realise she had gone to Paris, she had hoped that they would cover up the irregularity of her departure by informing their friends that they had made all the necessary arrangements for her. It was quite natural that a girl should visit her father, and although they would be angry with her, she had imagined they would not wish to be implicated in her disgrace. But now they would receive a completely different interpretation from Gregory. How could they not form a poor opinion of her?

'I had not expected my departure to be so final,' she said at last. 'But I could not have remained in Dublin much longer. I found myself too much at odds with my aunt and uncle's society to want to be married into it.'

'Your sentiments are admirable, but we must look to more practical considerations now,' he said briskly. 'I need hardly remind you that the journey to Paris is beset with perils for a young woman travelling alone, especially one dressed so fashionably, and it would be quite inappropriate for you to travel with me.'

Isabella wished he had not come upon her struggling to retrieve her bag from that boy. He must think her utterly helpless. She had taken care to dress as simply as possible, but her aunt had seen to it that her clothes were made of the finest materials, and the gown was new, even if it was not as widely hooped as some of the other passengers' skirts. Perhaps she would invite attention, but that could not be helped now. In any case, surely it was better to have a warm, serviceable pelisse than none at all? The wind was cold and sharp, and the ship was beginning to roll in a way that she found disorienting, this being her first time at sea.

'I am sorry,' she said simply. 'I chose to travel by this packet because I was anxious to leave as soon as possible. And you had given me the details of this one. I was hoping to join a suitable party on board, but most of these seem to be bound only as far as London. However, it does not signify. I can travel to London, and then seek new travelling companions.'

'It need not come to that,' he said, anxious not to place her entirely in the hands of strangers. 'I will make inquiries—there may well be others for Paris, and if they are willing to serve as chaperones, it might be possible for us all to proceed together. We will in any case be travelling by public mail coach . . .'

'Chaperones?' Isabella was amused despite her mounting discomfort. 'You intrigue me, Doctor. You condemn society for its pettiness and corruption, and then you are even more scrupulous about appearances than my aunt!'

'We must think of how you will be viewed in the eyes of the world.'

'I fear it may be too late,' she said, leaning unsteadily against one of the carriages that had been fastened on to the deck. Isabella was not the only one to succumb to seasickness. But the doctor was a more seasoned traveller, and after tending to her and guiding her to a berth, he judged it best to make his inquiries now, before the sea exacted a heavier toll and the majority of passengers took to their cabins. He encountered a variety of travellers: a young English family returning home after the husband had attended to some business in Ireland, Ascendancy types of all ages, seeking the pleasure and dissipation of the London season . . . he even spoke to an earnest young man of his own religion, who was being sent by a wealthy uncle to study law in the Temple in London.

Wincing at the moans and wails of the horses, which had all been shut up together and were also suffering the effects of the sea, Dr Connor returned to the deck. There he saw a stout priest whom he recognised from his time in Paris. They had never actually spoken before, though Connor had known him by sight, and he did appear to be the only traveller bound for Paris. Would an elderly priest be considered appropriate to guard a young woman on such a hazardous trip? Her aunt was a devout Catholic, and he had never heard any aspersions cast on this particular priest. There was a huge respect for French-educated priests in Ireland, some of it justified. Moreover, he didn't imagine very many in Ireland would have read the lascivious satires of the clergy published clandestinely in France, explicitly dramatising their supposed licentiousness while acting as confessors to innocent young females.

Dr Connor decided to approach him, thinking ruefully of the lengths one must sometimes go to when aspiring to be correct. His friend Bernard and his wife Julie would greet this bizarre tale with much hilarity when he related it to them.

'Good day to you, Father. You are the Abbé O'Donnell, are you not?'

'I am, and trusting to the will of God that I may survive the rolling of this vessel at my advanced age. And who might you be, my child?'

'Doctor Connor, bound for Paris,' he said hastily. 'Monsieur l'Abbé, I have by coincidence encountered a young woman of my acquaintance on board, who is in great need of your assistance. She is travelling to Paris alone, where she hopes to be reunited with her father, but I hardly think it wise for her to continue alone, so could I possibly prevail on you to speak to her? Perhaps you might offer her your protection for the duration of the journey?'

'What role have you in all this?' the priest asked with a mixture of reluctance and suspicion.

'I am physician to her aunt in Dublin. It seems that the uncle objected to her leaving his home, and she decided to leave in secret rather than disobey her father's wishes. I am travelling to Paris to visit some friends, and have already had the misfortune to be mistaken by her former fiancé as the instigator of an elopement. I would therefore be exceedingly grateful if you were to intervene—I do not wish her to travel alone or with strangers, but it would be imprudent for me to continue with her without the presence of a third party who could vouch for her conduct.'

The priest's eyes had glazed over long before Dr Connor had finished. 'This all seems highly irregular,' he said vaguely. 'You are travelling together, but not as man and wife, and you require the word of a man of God to assure the world that there is nothing untoward in all this? If her uncle prevented her departure, then surely it was her father's place to make satisfactory arrangements for her safety? I am tired, Monsieur, and my constitution is weak. I will count myself blessed if I reach Paris at all.'

'I am sorry to hear it. I am a physician, as I say, and could perhaps be of some assistance to you during the journey.'

'A physician.' The priest's clouded eyes sharpened. 'But you are too young to be fully versed in the skills of your profession.'

‘I assure you, Monsieur l’Abbé, I received my doctorate from the University of Paris.’

‘Then I offer you my congratulations,’ he said, turning his head to look out at the waves, which had grown progressively greyer as the sky darkened, threatening bad weather and a rough crossing.

‘I beg you to reconsider,’ said Dr Connor, attempting to control his anger. ‘I understand the young lady’s father is a man of considerable wealth, and would be keen to make his gratitude felt.’

‘Is that why you are so eager to safeguard her passage?’

The doctor did not answer. Having been forced to resort to a tactic he thought crude but effective, he could hardly take offence when the priest tarred him with his own brush.

‘Well, it is an unfortunate situation, but I imagine we will hardly be able to avoid one another completely on a journey by public coach. Is she an obliging sort of girl?’

‘If you mean will she do your bidding and attend to your comforts, then I believe she will,’ said Dr Connor, seething underneath. ‘Particularly if she has secured your word that you will write to her uncle, absolving her of any undue impropriety.’

‘Highly irregular of course, and I cannot see that I will succeed in salvaging the young lady’s reputation. However, if she is determined to continue on this blind course of action, then my guidance may at least serve to restrain her from committing even graver errors.'

After further deliberation and persuasion, Dr Connor succeeded in coaxing the priest to the cabin where he had left Isabella. The bargaining session had left a very bad taste in his mouth, but her green-tinged pallor gave him immediate cause for concern.

'Perhaps you should loosen your stays, in order to breathe more freely,' Dr Connor suggested. 'Tight corsets are veritable instruments of torture.'

'It's unnecessary,' Isabella insisted. 'I am not inclined to lace tightly—even my aunt has an aversion to boned bodices, formal occasions excepting.'

'Then you are at least fortunate in that.'

The abbé cleared his throat. 'You comment very freely on the tightness or otherwise of the young lady's dress.'

'I am her physician, Father,' said Dr Connor shortly. 'Miss Carroll, this is the Abbé O'Donnell. He has very kindly agreed to see you safely to Paris.'

'Father, I am greatly indebted to you,' she said, as she succumbed to another bout of sickness.

The Abbé O'Donnell looked as if he already regretted his decision, but to give him his due, he didn't retract it.

CHAPTER THIRTEEN

Despite the roughness of the sea and the rolling of the boat, the wind remained favourable for the first four hours of the crossing, spiriting them away from the Irish coast in the direction of Holyhead before tiring of that and beginning to blow them off course. The sails fought valiantly against this new inclination, but it was a full twenty-two hours before they sighted their destination. The seasick passengers emerged from the precarious shelter of their cabins only to find that they had to be carried to shore in flimsy boats rowed by weather-toughened Welshmen, who very capably deposited the shaky, legless travellers on dry and reassuringly stable land. Even the doctor had been weakened by the length of time spent on board, and it took all his remaining resources to get the dreadfully ill Isabella and the equally indisposed abbé through their luggage inspection. Thankfully, they were unencumbered by trunks, carriages and exceedingly disturbed horses, so he was able to secure them rooms in the better of Holyhead's two inns ahead of all the others.

Once her stomach had settled a little, Isabella slept soundly until early morning, when she was woken by voices outside her door. It took her a moment to realise where she was, as she looked around the small, plainly furnished room, before identifying one of the voices as Dr Connor's. The other belonged, she guessed, to the innkeeper's wife. From what she overheard, she gathered that her own fitness to travel was their concern.

'The weather looks set to stay wretched, you think,' she heard Dr Connor say. 'Can she travel today?'

'Of course I can,' she said, shivering with the cold of the sea-wind draught as she stepped out to join them, having dressed hastily. 'I am ready to leave as soon as you please.'

He looked at her, still pale and sickly, and shook his head. 'You do not know what lies ahead of you,' he said. 'There have been storms lately, and the road is likely to be bad. This is difficult country . . .'

'But I would feel easier if we did not tarry here any longer than necessary.'

'In that case, I'll serve you breakfast,' said the innkeeper's wife, anxious to be about her morning chores.

'Perhaps you're right,' said Dr Connor doubtfully, once she had left them. 'I do not think any other vessel would make the crossing in this wind, but it might be for the best if we did leave by the morning's mail-coach, though it really is an arduous journey.'

Isabella's thoughts had been so consumed by the idea of Paris, and the packet that would carry her away from Dublin, that she had scarcely stopped to consider the entire land mass of Wales and England. A regular mail-coach now carried letters and passengers along a turnpike road, the entire two hundred and sixty miles from Holyhead to London, but conditions were often treacherous, especially in winter. It was only after they had left the island of Anglesey that Isabella realised the enormity of their journey, as the coach slowly attempted to pick its way over mountains taller than anything she had ever seen before, heights dizzier than anything she had ever known. It soon began to rain, and though the horses kept to their route, they were reduced to crawling at a rate of a few miles an hour, and once when the coach's wheels had become stuck in thick mud, she felt them stumble. She counted her blessings that the coach reached the next stage intact, and that the good, plain food of the inn warmed her and took the raw, acidic taste out of her mouth.

By next morning, all the travellers were beginning to feel better, though even the beauty of the scenery could not entirely distract them from the jolting of the coach. Their fellow-passengers were an English couple of middle-age, who spoke little, regarding the Irish trio with thinly-veiled suspicion and distancing themselves from them as much as the cramped space allowed. As she was not accustomed to such long spells of travelling, Isabella's bones ached painfully, and each night's rest provided little respite. Dr Connor was also fatigued, but suffered the demands of the querulous abbé as best he could. The old priest expected to be waited on hand and foot, and complained loudly about everything, from the draughty cold of the mailcoach to the poor quality of the food in the inns.

His constant presence also meant that Isabella could not speak as freely to the physician as she would have liked. There was so much she wanted to explain: all that had led her to leave Dublin, the gratitude she felt for his assistance, and the awkwardness of knowing what position she put him in. But Dr Connor seemed to have responded to the situation by retreating into a moody self-preoccupation, and did not seem inclined for conversation.

Eventually, the mountains softened into gentler hills as the mail-coach began to leave Wales and make its way towards the agricultural lowlands of the south-east. The road became easier to navigate, and the horses picked up pace, bringing them into London a week after they had left Holyhead.

'London, where all roads lead, sooner or later,' remarked Dr Connor. 'Inescapable, and magnificent in its way.'

So this was London, where every aspect of her country's fate was decided. Isabella thought it singular that she should encounter it so, as a mere stop on their itinerary at an hour so advanced in the evening that she could see little of it but crowds and indistinct buildings.

'I had a large purse of money stolen from me in an inn here once,' said the abbé sourly. 'Let us delay here no longer than necessary to get ourselves in to the next mail for Dover.'

They therefore continued along their way, reaching Dover without incident two days later. Fortunately, the weather in the south had been fair for the past few days, and they were able to board a packet for France the day after their arrival. Isabella had been dreading the rolling of the ship and another bout of seasickness, but the waves were calmer, the journey shorter, and the thought of finally being close to France so thrilling that she did not suffer half as badly as she had feared. Instead, she positioned herself on deck long before Calais was due to come into sight, and found herself wondering about her mother, and how she had come to France only to die within a year . . . What had *her* expectations been as she waited to catch her first glimpse of Nantes, and was Calais in any way like Nantes? Seagulls cut roughly through the sky above the Irish girl's head, and her imagination turned to all the Wild Geese who had landed on these shores, and the different fates that had awaited them there.

'You seem to have weathered this crossing

better than the last one,' Dr Connor remarked, joining her as the harbour began to come into view.

'Yes, I must have found my sea-legs. My father was a ship's captain before he married my mother. Perhaps it's in my blood.'

'Perhaps,' he smiled, fastening his *surtout* against the knife-sharp wind. 'Well, I'm glad. We've been travelling at such a relentless pace, and with so little rest, I was afraid you might not make it to Paris in one piece, particularly since we face yet another journey once we land.'

And perhaps I'm made of sterner stuff than you thought, smiled Isabella to herself 'What then? Will we proceed by mailcoach?'

He shook his head. 'Travelling in France is very different,' he said. 'If I were alone, I would simply take the *diligence*—which is essentially three coaches stuck together—but it is so slow and awkward that under the circumstances, I think it safer, and indeed swifter, to take the more expensive step of hiring a carriage and travelling by post.'

'You mean we would have our own carriage, and then change horses and driver at every post?' asked Isabella, the idea appealing to her after all the discomforts of the previous journey.

'A very wise plan,' said the abbé, coming on deck.

To have finally arrived! The moment Isabella put foot on dry land, she was filled with wonder at the scene around her, the voices and the people which were so different to those she had left behind her. Even the long, maddening customs inspection, where everything they possessed was turned inside out, upside down, and thrown about by surly officials, failed to dampen her good humour, though she was relieved she had taken only one bag with her, seeing the delay caused to other passengers by their large trunks.

'Well, Mademoiselle,' said the abbé when they were finally free to walk through the streets of Calais, which though ugly, filled Isabella with an immense curiosity. 'How does it feel to be but two or three days from Paris, if we are fortunate?'

Two or three days! And Paris was nearing all the time, for after seeing Isabella and the abbé to the inn of the abbé's choice, Dr Connor left them long enough to change money, hire a carriage and make the arrangements for them to travel the following morning. That night, they were served with a wide array of dishes, all unfamiliar to Isabella, but as her stomach was still weak from the rolling of the ship, she confined herself to a ragout, deliciously seasoned with herbs. The abbé drank his fill, loudly announcing how much he had missed French wine, and how good it was to taste it again. Isabella hoped it might put him in better humour for the remainder of the journey, while Dr Connor hoped it wouldn't give him such an aching head as to render him unbearable in the morning. Isabella found her bedchamber dirtier than those she had been given in England, but the bed was so comfortable she immediately fell into a sound sleep.

Early the next morning, they left Calais in a tolerably comfortable carriage, driven by a French *postillion* whose extraordinarily large jackboots fascinated Isabella. Soon they found themselves in softly rolling countryside. Despite her fatigue, the excitement of being close to her destination acted as a keen stimulant, and Isabella examined her surroundings alertly.

'The roads are unusually good,' she exclaimed.

'Yes, we have the *corvée* to thank for that,' said Dr Connor ironically. 'That charming system whereby the poor farmers and peasants, who cannot afford to pay the King that tax he demands as his God-given due, must instead toil and sweat to keep his roads in a fitting manner.'

The abbé glared at him, but did not choose to comment, and fell a few moments later into a loud sleep. Isabella turned with new eyes to the road, and watched the farmers go about their work in nearby fields.

They took advantage of the dry weather to proceed as far as they could, through Boulogne, and flat country, making their way towards Abbeville, where they stopped the following day for a late dinner. As they were too tired to go any further before nightfall, they elected to stay, Isabella and the abbé remaining in the inn, while Dr Connor went to a nearby coffee-house in search of recent newspapers. On his return to the inn, he found Isabella downstairs by the fire, in conversation with the innkeeper, who spoke a little English. He was telling her about the cathedral at Amiens, where his mother had been born. It was *vraiment magnifique*, he said proudly, a fit home for the relics of Saint John the Baptist.

'Of Saint John the Baptist?'

'His head is the most precious of all,' the innkeeper beamed. 'My mother would pray to him in time of trouble, because she always said his head protected the people of Amiens from harm. Once a year, there is a special pilgrimage, and then they display the head, and she would make her supplications to him then.'

'Of course,' said Dr Connor ironically. 'Why direct our thoughts on the incompetence of the King and his government, when we have faith that the real head of John the Baptist lies deep in the heart of the cathedral, protecting us from harm? I bid you good night, Monsieur, we have a long road ahead of us tomorrow. Miss Carroll, do not let these colourful tales keep you up too late.'

But Isabella's imagination had been captured. The head of John the Baptist, delivered on a platter to a spoilt princess, had somehow found its way to the north of France, where a cathedral had been built for it. She was even more impressed once she realised it was a Catholic cathedral. She was accustomed solely to the back-street chapels of Dublin, and the innkeeper's descriptions of its splendour, its domination of an entire city, gave her a curious sense of liberty.

She was not disappointed: they stopped at an inn within view of the gothic cathedral, which was every bit as imposing as she had imagined. The abbé was gratified by her awe, which had the effect of softening his mood as they three surveyed the magnificence of the entrance: the *grand portail*, with three porches, glorifying Jesus Christ, the Virgin Mary, and the local saints.

'The men who built this have my deepest admiration,' remarked Dr Connor. 'They really did know how best to create the illusion of divine power and mystical intervention. No wonder the local people believe whatever the Church chooses to have them believe.'

'What is this nonsense?' snapped their companion, good humour dispelled.

'Nonsense indeed, Abbé,' replied Dr Connor dryly. 'Nonsense to believe that what await you inside really are the remains of John the Baptist, let alone that they possess any so-called divine attributes.'

Dr Connor thus quit their presence, and

angrily wandered the streets around the cathedral, returning to the inn only when he judged it time for supper. Isabella had been much taken with the relics in the cathedral, but thought it best to avoid the subject at table.

'Is it true that there are many beautiful churches in Paris?' she eventually asked, her mind nonetheless distracted by the view of the cathedral from the window.

'Yes, but I would not grow too enamoured of the French Church,' said Dr Connor shortly. 'All her property and wealth have been amassed at the expense of the people, who are overburdened by excessive taxation.'

Isabella was surprised. Did this mean that the Catholic Church employed the same dubious means as the landowners in Ireland, or indeed her merchant uncle in Dublin?

'Do my ears deceive me?' the abbé asked disapprovingly, much taken aback by Dr Connor's words.

'I mean no disrespect, Abbé,' said Dr Connor, weary of constantly having to bite his tongue. 'I was educated in Ireland by a priest, and I have great admiration for institutions like the Irish Colleges, the one in Paris in particular. Sadly, it is my belief that such instances of great learning and benevolence are few and far between, and the abuse of power is widespread.'

'You led me to believe you adhered to the Church of Rome,' said the priest, observing him narrowly. 'Are you not ashamed to mock the ancient and noble traditions of a country known as *la fille aînée de l'Eglise,* a country that offered us sanctuary when we were driven out of our own land?'

La fille aînée de l'Eglise. The eldest daughter of the Church, Isabella translated to herself. Her knowledge of French was confined to such phrases, and she was anxious to learn the language as soon as possible.

'You mistake him, Abbé,' she said, hoping to make peace. 'Dr Connor has an interest in political thought, and he concerns himself solely with possible forms of more equitable government.'

'My child, do you seek to excuse him?' The abbé was again astonished.

'She overstates the case,' said Dr Connor hastily. 'I apologise wholeheartedly, Monsieur l'Abbé. Would you be so good as to forgive me?'

The abbé looked as if he detected an underlying insolence here, but as it was time for supper, no more was said about it until after Grace, when the abbé asked the Lord to bless the godless sinner he beheld before him.

'There are some enlightened men of the cloth who share my views,' said Dr Connor, now at the end of his tether. 'I am personally acquainted with a few of them.'

'Enlightened, you say? Then they have clearly exercised a most detrimental influence on you, though the prevailing Protestant order in our oppressed land may already have led you astray.'

'I should not think so,' replied Dr Connor. 'The Church of Ireland cannot be remarked upon for a proselytising zeal. Rather than share their spoils with new converts to their faith, they seem content to allow us Catholics to wallow in godless savagery. Of course, I should add that the Presbyterians have been persecuted every bit as much as we have. Then there are the Quakers, whom Cromwell banished to Ireland for being too radical even for his tastes. Though I must admit, they did attempt to convince as many new Friends as possible, even if most of their potential Irish Friends were massacred, transplanted or transported by the time Cromwell had finished with us.'

'Am I to infer from your blasphemy that you belong to the Society of Friends?' said the abbé, now well and truly baffled.

'He is merely expressing a belief that the Catholic Church in France is as capable of abuse as the Established Church of Ireland,' said Isabella doubtfully.

'I was perhaps unnecessarily flippant,' Dr Connor conceded. 'But truly, Abbé, have you never been struck by the capacity of the prevailing orders of Protestant England and Catholic France to stain their hands with the same blood, despite their mutual antagonism? Look at the persecution of the Huguenots, for example.'

The abbé angrily rose to his feet and removed his heavily laden supper plate to the furthest end of the table, where he was welcomed by a matronly lady and her maid, both dressed in mourning. Angrily, Dr Connor continued his speech in a voice just loud enough to penetrate the outer reaches of the table.

'Catholic France drives the Huguenots out of her land, thus ruining the French silk industry in the process. Some of them then bring their silk-weaving skills to Ireland, where they develop a high-quality industry, only to be ruined again, this time by Protestant London, which decides to destroy their trade simply to protect England's industries at the expense of her colonies. It beggars belief, does it not? But then, why should we feign surprise, or expect logic and consistency from Kings and Parliaments, when the poor in London feel the cold every bit as much as the poor in Dublin, or the poor in Paris, for that matter?'

Having vented his spleen, Dr Connor then dropped his voice. 'I apologise, Miss Carroll. I fear I have completely alienated our travelling companion.'

'It could not be helped,' she replied, despite her anxiety. 'It is always refreshing to hear you speak your mind so clearly,' she added, though she understood now why he felt it necessary to assume such a quiet, overly decorous manner in most company.

Dr Connor glanced down the table at the elderly Irishman, who was imbibing large quantities of claret. 'Look what solace he takes in the company of that worthy *dame*, who is only too happy to seek consolation for her bereavement in the words of a priest. I cannot imagine he has ever been troubled by questions of conscience or history, or finds any difficulty in reconciling religious belief with the abuses of the Catholic Church.' Conscious that he was becoming overheated again, he attempted to compose himself 'I rant and rave. I sincerely hope I regain some semblance of sanity in Paris.'

'Do all your friends think as you do?' Isabella wondered.

'My thoughts are my own, though they have been coloured by those I have encountered. I do not share the vehement anticlericalism of some individuals, though I agree with them in sentiment. I also admire those who have rejected the constraints of Christianity and all its vying sects in favour of a form of Deism which they can adapt to their own beliefs. But I fear, Miss Carroll, that you will find in me a poor guide to French society. Such sentiments are hardly widespread, although it is fashionable in some circles to hold salons in which to discuss the ideas of the *philosophes.*'

'Did you frequent such salons with the friends you are going to visit?' asked Isabella.

Dr Connor smiled. 'My good friend Bernard was a fellow student at the University of Paris. It was he who first lent me his pamphlets and *nouvelles à main*, and introduced me to the most interesting booksellers in Paris. There was such an astonishing array of material published, much of it illegally, from serious works of history and philosophy to hugely amusing satires of the King and clergy. I wonder if our travelling companion is familiar with any of the adventures of the fornicating Jesuits which have much tickled the public's fancy?'

The abbé returned to their end of the table with his black-garbed supper companion in tow. Her lace headdress was encrusted with stale powder and dirt, and a foul odour emanated from her person.

'Miss Carroll, we are quitting the company of this odious young man and we are continuing to Paris with Madame Dupont. I have just learned that she is a near relation of some of my most devoted congregation. Consider yourself fortunate that she has agreed to take you into her care.'

Isabella examined her new travelling companion with dismay. Madame returned her gaze with a scathing glare, and barked out a swift, peremptory stream of French.

'Out of consideration for your safety, she says you may share her bed, provided you make yourself useful to her between here and

Paris,' Dr Connor translated. He then whispered: 'You see how foolish it can be to speak one's mind in certain company?'

There was no need for him to impress upon her the consequences of his falling out with the abbé. She was only thankful that they had the bulk of their journey behind them.

'Must we part, then?' she said regretfully, despite the abbé's frowning presence and her consciousness that he would be sending her aunt a full account of her conduct.

After a sidelong glance at the abbé, Dr Connor leaned across the table and continued in a low tone. 'Loth as I am to admit it, it would be infinitely more prudent for you to travel with a woman of her age and character, though her manner is rather forbidding. *Au revoir*, Miss Carroll, I wish you as pleasant a journey as possible. May you find Paris to be all that you hope it will be.'

Wondering if she would ever see him again, Isabella was drawn away by Madame Dupont. She knew him sufficiently well to judge that he would not dream of resuming the connection until her father had dealt with all the awkward repercussions arising from her travelling circumstances. But perhaps 'connection' was too strong a word, she thought. She had prevailed on him enough. It was time now for him to join his friends, unhindered. It was time for her thoughts to turn towards what lay in store for her in Paris.

II

CHAPTER ONE

Madame Dupont's carriage was considerably more comfortable than a mail-coach or hired conveyance. The cushions and blankets that lay around smelled stale, but this was offset by the draughts that poured in around the window and the edges of the door. Isabella was more than happy to be ignored as she fixed her gaze on the woods and fields of the countryside, thinking about all that Dr Connor had told her as a means of distracting herself from her worsening backache.

The abbé was clearly so peeved by last night's altercation that he did not address Isabella once during the entire journey, until they reached the point where the Paris road began to cross the Prince de Condé's forest around Chantilly, when he loudly declared in English that if he was to suffer the deprivation of daylight for the sake of ten miles of magnificent wilderness, he was at least blessed in having been relieved of the presence of the odious young blasphemer. Isabella gritted her teeth, but as she had never been in a forest before, she soon forgot herself in wonder at the height of the trees, the birds that circled them, and the little squirrels and animals that ran out onto the road before disappearing into the thick undergrowth beyond.

A little over two weeks had passed since they had left Dublin when Madame Dupont's carriage finally approached the gates of Paris. After remarking on the already late hour, she asked Isabella for her father's address, but was then quite clearly impressed when she heard it, looking at Isabella with a new respect.

'The Faubourg Saint-Germain,' Madame repeated, with a significant glance at the abbé. 'I had not realised that he lived there.'

'Yes, her father is obviously all that I had been led to believe he was,' the abbé replied. He looked as though he might continue, but was interrupted by Madame, who announced in broken English that it was at least convenient for her to go there, as the abbé lived in the nearby Saint-Germain des Prés. '*Dommage* that first we cross this entire ugly part of the city,' she added, as she banged on the roof of the carriage for the *cocher* to drive faster. 'We are lucky it is dark, so we do not have to look at it.'

The *cocher*, who had slowed down on entering the narrow streets of northern Paris, obliged by forcing his way through the crowds at a furious pace. Isabella was horrified to see how the horses almost trampled several people, as they jumped aside to escape the onslaught. She noticed how the carriage took up most of the width of the street, leaving very little room for the pedestrians. Her heart was in her mouth as they crossed the river to the

Rive Gauche, when the carriage finally dropped back to a more leisurely pace.

'The Faubourg Saint-Germain,' sighed the abbé with an air of relief, squinting out of his window. 'Finally, we near the end.'

Here the streets were wider, emptier, more tranquil, with beautiful pale buildings, their elegance faintly discernible against the night sky.

'It's lovely,' exclaimed Isabella.

'But of course,' replied the abbé. 'All the best houses, the grandest *hôtels* of Paris are here. The air is better than anywhere else, and the nobility find it the most convenient *quartier* to reach from Versailles.'

Despite these words, Isabella was nonetheless unprepared for her father's house, which stood alone on a corner, surrounded by a garden. It seemed to be a great deal more imposing than her uncle's, and at least as large as some of the most talked-about residences in Dublin. Perhaps it is not really so, she told herself as she approached the front entrance with some trepidation, accompanied by the abbé. Perhaps it is the suggestive power of darkness. Could my father really have risen so high?

After a long interval, the door was opened by a French servant. Isabella asked to see Monsieur Carroll in clear but poorly accented French. The servant said something that Isabella could not understand, and made as if to shut the door on them.

The abbé stood forward. '*Il est son père*,' he announced.

Still the servant affected not to understand, but he opened the door again, assessing Isabella in an overtly insolent manner. '*Irlandaise?*' he eventually asked, as if something was dawning on him.

'*Oui*,' Isabella answered, wishing she had been taught more than a few phrases of French.

'*Alors, attendez s'il vous plaît*,' he said, before slamming the wide, heavy door in her face.

Isabella furiously knocked again, but the servant didn't return. This is really too much, she thought. I never once imagined I should get so far, only to be turned away at the threshold by a servant. She glanced awkwardly at the abbé, hoping she would not have to prevail any further on him or Madame Dupont, who was watching them from her carriage window.

As she was considering her options, the door was reopened by a girl dressed in black, whom Isabella judged to be perhaps a year younger than herself. She wondered who she was, noting the intricately dressed hair was at odds with the plain gown before remembering uneasily that the household might still be in mourning for the deceased stepmother who had failed to make it as far as Paris.

'You wish to see Monsieur Carroll?' the girl

asked in carefully pronounced English with just a touch of an unidentifiable brogue.

'Yes,' replied Isabella gratefully. 'I believe he has been expecting me, though I arrive unannounced: I am his daughter.'

The girl looked stunned for a moment. She then concealed her surprise as best she could. 'You must forgive us. We were not expecting you,' she said.

'I left Dublin so hastily, I was unable to notify him of my travel arrangements,' Isabella said as smoothly as she could. Her eyes attempted to penetrate past the girl into the indistinct hallway. 'Is my father at home?' she asked.

'Not at present.' The girl took Isabella's bag and placed it inside the door, motioning Isabella to follow her into the *vestibule*.

The abbé cleared his throat. 'In that case, I'll take my leave of you,' he said. 'I will of course write to both your father and your family in Dublin, letting them know that you came to no harm while in my care.'

'Thank you,' Isabella smiled. 'I'm so grateful to you.'

The abbé rejoined Madame Dupont in her carriage, and Isabella waved them off before turning to follow the other girl inside.

'You must have had a long and tiring journey,' she remarked, closing the door behind them.

Isabella heard strains of music, soft lulling

sounds that intensified her weariness. 'Is that a harp?' she asked.

The girl smiled and opened a door into a wood-panelled salon, its pale pink and white décor lit with cool brilliance by a crystal chandelier, a myriad of diamond icicles encasing clusters of candles. Isabella saw an older woman of slight build bent over a harp.

'*Seo chugainn a iníon*,' the girl told the woman.

The woman rose from her instrument. The grey silk gown, closed at the back and trimmed with almost insubstantial lace ruffles, served to emphasise a figure whose frailty was strangely offset by a commanding presence. She responded to the girl in words that Isabella again failed to understand. These words were then addressed to Isabella.

'You do not speak the Gaelic tongue,' the woman said finally in English.

'No.'

'You have lived in Dublin all your life, then?'

Isabella smiled, a little bewildered. She took off her pelisse, realising that the room was intensely hot, despite the barely perceptible glow of the fire, the barely discernible sound of fuel burning. The woman took her pelisse and gave it to the girl, again issuing instructions in Irish. The girl left, and the woman indicated to Isabella to sit beside her on a pink-upholstered sofa. Isabella saw that she had a beautiful face, though her skin looked old and dried out.

'My daughter is seeing to it that a room is prepared for you directly,' she said. 'We always speak Gaelic between ourselves,' she added, as if it were an afterthought.

'I believe my father is not at home?' Isabella inquired, wondering that the two Irishwomen had not yet seen fit to enlighten her as to their identities.

'Not at present,' she replied, echoing her daughter a few minutes earlier. 'I shall have one of the servants send a note to him, and I imagine he will return tomorrow morning.' After a pause, during which she thoroughly examined every aspect of Isabella's appearance and clothing, she continued: 'You seem weary and dishevelled. The journey has clearly taken such a toll on you that I shall resist inquiring into the particulars, my dear Isabella. I may call you Isabella, may I not?'

'And what may I call you?' Isabella asked.

The woman looked surprised. 'You may call me Cousin, if you wish. Your father and I are cousins. He invited us to live with him some years ago. He is very fond of music,' she added, as if it were an explanation.

'Your playing is very beautiful,' said Isabella, although she was taken aback. Her new cousin saw this, and folded her hands, as if an unpleasant fact had been confirmed.

'He did not mention this in his letters, then?'

'My father writes so seldom.'

'Does he?' her cousin asked, as if this were a new, important matter, also to be considered.

At that point, the younger woman returned. 'Your bed will be ready soon,' she said.

'Thank you,' said Isabella uncertainly. 'Are you newly arrived in Paris?' she asked this other cousin.

The girl smiled stiffly and evasively. 'No. But my mother is only recently arrived from Saint-Domingue,' she said.

'Our position in this household is somewhat special,' her mother added.

Isabella guessed they were dependent on her father's kindness, but they were so unforthcoming that she was disinclined to pursue the exact relationship any further tonight. She would wait until she saw her father.

'I think I'd like to go to bed now,' she said finally.

'Of course,' said her father's cousin, rising from the sofa. 'I believe you'll find a supper tray awaiting you?' she said, addressing her daughter.

The girl smiled, and led Isabella down a passageway and upstairs. 'I imagine this is the apartment your father intended you to have,' she said. 'The furnishings are a little *démodés*, and I heard him speak of changing them, but I believe you will be tolerably comfortable, at least for tonight.'

'You are too kind,' Isabella answered. 'I am accustomed to much smaller living quarters than these.'

Her companion absorbed this information, but made no comment. Isabella noticed a faint, musty smell, as if the chamber had not been slept in for a while. Perhaps the house had lain unoccupied for a considerable period before her father's arrival. She wondered when, and in what circumstances, it had passed into his deceased wife's hands. She lifted the cover of the silver tray and sipped the glass of wine, which struck her as particularly good. The chicken was cold, but it too was very appetising.

'I'll leave you to your supper, then,' her cousin said, moving towards the door. 'We'll speak tomorrow.'

'We haven't been properly introduced yet,' Isabella smiled, hoping to learn at least this new cousin's name before morning.

It was a simple inquiry, and yet the girl hesitated before responding. Eventually, she said: 'When we speak together in Irish, my mother calls me Eibhlín, and I was always Eibhlín in Ireland. But in the convent, the nuns called me Hélène, as it was the closest French equivalent, and I have grown accustomed to hearing myself referred to as Hélène. I'm not quite sure what an English speaker from Dublin would choose to call me.'

'Whichever you prefer,' said Isabella, both

amused by this spiel and curious to learn more.

'You are in Paris now,' said her cousin after some consideration. 'Perhaps you had better call me Hélène.'

'Very well, then. And I am Isabella. Good night, Hélène.'

Hélène smiled, before making her way back to the salon.

'*An bhfuil sí in a codladh?*' her mother asked when she entered, in case a servant overheard them.

Hélène shrugged. 'She's not sleeping yet, but she soon will be.'

'He neglected to tell me he had sent for her, though I suppose it was to be expected,' her mother continued.

'There was something furtive about her arrival, though,' said Hélène thoughtfully. 'She simply appeared at the front door, with one small bag and an old abbé in tow, asking to see her father.'

'Yes, I feel certain there's something not quite right about her, though her manner is too natural for an adventurer. Neither is she sufficiently ingratiating for me to take her for an impostor.'

'I should never have suspected that,' said Hélène slowly.

'No? But as I have told you time and time again, it is wise to be constantly on your guard. One never knows what to expect in the world.

He may well have sent for her, like she said. When he returns tomorrow, he will do as he sees fit. We shall simply bide our time, and . . .'

Hélène anxiously waited for her mother to conclude. So many times, the precariousness of their situation had been impressed on her, how easily they could lose the tenuous foothold they had gained in this household and find themselves out on the streets. Hélène did not particularly care for ignominy, but she sometimes secretly thought that, if they were really to be abandoned to fate, she would not mind, as long as it was in the shadow of the Connaught mountains where she had been born. Often in the cloistered prison of the convent, she had dreamed of the savage, rain-fuelled wind. But it cost money to return to Ireland, and that was so long ago now. Why not try her luck in Paris, this city that had for so long lain unseen beyond the convent walls, so near and yet so far?

'We must try to find out as much as possible about her,' her mother continued. 'Perhaps it might work to our advantage that you two are so close in age. I'm sure you can gain her confidence, discover her weaknesses?'

'Her weaknesses?' Hélène almost laughed. 'She has so many advantages that any weaknesses she has will always be easily accommodated.'

'Precisely. She has surely become so accustomed to being indulged that she may not notice the distinction between accommodation and exploitation.' Her mother gazed significantly at her.

'I don't understand,' said Hélène, though she understood more than she cared to admit. 'You speak as though she were at our mercy, when it is we who are at hers, or her father's.'

'Eibhlín, if you look at it in that light, then your circumstances will never change. To succeed in the world, you need the means to do so. As you do not yet have those means, you must wait and watch for an opportunity to attain them.'

'Was it for that you left me so long shut up in that convent?' Hélène asked.

'It may have been hard for you,' her mother acknowledged. 'But I do not believe my cousin would have placed you in such a costly convent if he did not have plans for you—it was such an opportunity, to be educated with the daughters of some of Paris's best families. Surely you employed your time to your advantage, as I counselled you in my letters?'

Hélène traced the flower marquetry of the harpsichord. 'You know the difficulties I encountered. It would have been easier had our cousin revealed his intentions then.'

'Perhaps it is better that he did not. Isabella is his sole surviving child, and yet it is you who were educated in Paris at his expense. If you play your cards right, who knows what might happen?'

Who knows indeed, thought Hélène, wearied and anxious.

CHAPTER ELEVEN

After her mother had retired for the night, Hélène remained in the empty salon. She had not been prepared for the arrival of Isabella, and needed some time to gather her thoughts. She paced the parquet floor, watching her reflection appear in the different looking-glasses—mirrors had been forbidden in the convent, and so this was still something of a novelty to her. Then she touched the keys of the harpsichord before finding in favour of the catgut strings of her viola da gamba.

Hélène possessed only a little of her mother's hardness. Her life had been such that she sometimes saw this trait as one to be admired and cultivated within herself, even though she resented the unfortunate impact her mother's driving characteristic had often had on her own fate. Her mother Brighid was a cousin of Carroll's on her father's side. Brighid's mother belonged to one of those ancient and noble Gaelic families that had been dispossessed and reduced within a few generations to the grinding poverty of peasantry. However, the family had managed to keep alive some of their old traditions. They had once been famed for their musical skills, and their ability to write in the technically demanding forms of classical Irish poetry. All of this was passed *ó ghlúin go glúin*: from generation to generation, and finally on to Brighid in a bare cabin with a smoking fire.

This in itself was quite a feat. Many West of Ireland peasants claimed to be the remnants of the old Gaelic aristocracy, completely worn down by the unremitting hardship of scraping what little sustenance they could from a hard and barren landscape, fighting the knife-sharp sea wind with the nourishment of the potato and the numbing, incapacitating warmth of poitín. But against the stark, harsh beauty of such roughly hewn country, Brighid learned what she could until cold and disease had carried off what remained of her family.

Brighid was blessed with good health, the fresh pallor of an Irish complexion, and a rich shade of dark auburn hair. She seemed to need as little protection from the unforgiving Atlantic wind as the mountainous rocks, and succeeded in marrying a man who rented a respectable-sized farm. In his two-storey farmhouse with glass windows, she bore him one child, her daughter Eibhlín, whom she rigorously invested with classical Irish poetry and music and all the old dreams of her people. However, Eibhlín was often more comfortable in the softer, less exacting company of her quiet father. As he went about the farm, whistling his own tunes, and entertaining his daughter with funny stories, Eibhlín was content and at ease with herself, sitting on the rock that she loved so much. But her father died of consumption when she was fifteen years old, leaving Eibhlín and her mother destitute.

Brighid was shrewd and highly resourceful, considering her situation without panic or despair. It was known to her that her older cousin Carroll, who had been lucky enough as a youth to secure an apprenticeship in one of the Nantes merchant houses, had risen in the world. He was now a property owner in Saint-Domingue, possibly too wealthy to remember how his family had once prided themselves on their connection to her mother's people, how they would gather with eager awe in the smoking cabin to listen to their tales, poetry and songs. Perhaps it was all too long ago, but he might remember. So despite her own pride, which balked at the step she was about to take, she wrote to him in Saint-Domingue, hoping that he might offer assistance of some kind.

The American war had just ended. Nevertheless, it took some months for a reply to reach the West of Ireland, despite Carroll's prompt response. The last of Brighid's saved pennies had been eked out, and they were in very real danger of starvation. They had been forced to leave their stone farmhouse for a cabin which the land agent had lent them on sufferance only because of Brighid's assurances that she was in a position to pay. But the letter that came afforded them some surprise.

> My dear Cousin (he wrote), I write in English as I would prefer not to inflict on you what ill-phrased, badly-remembered fragments of the Gaelic tongue I still possess, and I do not think you understand French.
>
> I am deeply sorry for your trouble and propose to do what lies in my power to alleviate your distress. The situation is this: I am intending to return to France and settle in Paris, but because my wife is too ill to travel, we are obliged to remain in Saint-Domingue for some time. Perhaps it is because I am getting older, but of late my thoughts have often turned to my early years in Ireland, and I have a certain wish to hear again the music of my native land. Though you were a child when last I saw you, I remember your beautiful, gifted mother swearing to make you the best harpist in Ireland . . . If you have lived up to your early promise, it might be very interesting indeed to meet again . . .
>
> On a more mundane note, we are badly in need of a housekeeper, and if you agree to join us in this capacity, both

you and your daughter will be provided for. I do not recommend that your daughter accompany you to Saint-Domingue. The climate is cruel, and many parents prefer that their children remain in Europe while they are in the colonies. I have written to my Paris agent, who will arrange for her to stay in a convent of the first order until such time as we return from Saint-Domingue. I do not envisage a long separation, perhaps a year at the utmost, and the arrangement will prove to your advantage. You may then decide whether you wish to remain in Paris, or return to Ireland.

I leave the matter in your hands, but I would urge you not to delay: it is a long voyage to Saint-Domingue, and who knows how fate will intervene in the meantime. I enclose a Bill of Exchange, which you can draw on at a house in Galway—the sum should prove sufficient for your expenses.

I remain, your cousin,
Peadar Carroll

They set off for Galway that very day. Brighid could not afford the luxury of reflection. She knew there was nothing for them in Ireland. It had been different while her husband was alive: the demands of the house and the farm had kept her from brooding too much on the legacy of all those poems and songs she knew by heart. Like others of her kin, she knew that if she were ever to reclaim the position she felt she was entitled to, she would have to go elsewhere, like all the Wild Geese before her. Now that her husband was dead, why not aim to achieve this in France, where her cousin Carroll had reaped such rewards? Still in her early thirties, her health was as good as it had ever been, and she saw no reason why she should not live for years to come.

So Brighid and Eibhlín set sail for France in a smuggler's ship, this being the most immediate and convenient way of travelling. Aside from the captain and his crew, whose purpose was the clandestine purchase of French brandy, wine and silk, their companions were a few young men, intending to join the Irish Brigades or pursue their educations, and some others travelling to France for various reasons of their own. But the two women were too absorbed by sea-sickness and anxiety for the future to pay them much attention. Arriving in Paris somewhat the worse for wear, they placed themselves in the hands of Carroll's Paris agent, who drove them to the convent where Brighid bade farewell to her daughter.

Still grief-stricken by the loss of her father and homesick, Eibhlín found herself alone in this cold dark building, where the parlour and the grilles were to be her only link with the outside world until her mother's return. The nuns took her, dressed her in the black gown of the convent, concealed her hair under a cap, and left her to find her way without a single word of French.

Once the novelty of having a new girl among them had worn off, the other girls began to make fun of her accent and lack of words. It was unfortunate that the most malicious of these, Elisabeth, slept in the next bed to the newly named Hélène. A Parisian banker's daughter, Elisabeth would entertain herself and the other girls by mislaying or soiling Hélène's bed-linen and petticoats. The French girls would then stifle their laughter as best they could while the uncomprehending Hélène was severely chastised and punished *en français* by Soeur Jeanne.

Hélène found herself frequently reduced to tears, and retreated for consolation into memories of her father and the hope that her mother would soon return to take her away. But it was some weeks before she received a letter from her, and even this held little consolation: Saint-Domingue was not quite how she had imagined it, Brighid wrote. Nevertheless, she was getting along as best she could, and Eibhlín would have to do the same. It would only be for a year, she hoped.

A whole year in this place? Hélène was devastated. Nevertheless, she had inherited her mother's musical ear and ready facility with language, so she soon picked up enough French to communicate passably with the other girls and the nuns, although she continued to find herself totally at sea in the classes. They seemed to lack the thorough, systematic approach of her mother's lessons. Why was she noticing so many different spellings of the one word, and why was she being given such conflicting instructions on the same points of grammar?

Despairing of ever escaping the tag *la bête Irlandaise*, she was rescued some months later by the music lessons that her unknown but pervasive cousin Carroll arranged by letter from Saint-Domingue. It was the family wish that she continue her musical instruction to the highest possible standard, he wrote, and so the Paris agent procured a music master who came highly recommended, and the nuns allowed him into the convent several times a week, despite the fact that he was considerably younger than the elderly and partially deaf tutor who came for the other girls.

Monsieur Beaufils had some talent but little success as a composer. Disenchantment and contempt for the world had seeped into his fine intellect and soured his sensibilities, and he expected little from his new pupil but vexation and headache, to be suffered in return for a rather handsome payment. But he was surprised by her cool manner, free of the affected coyness of her fellow inmates, who were bred to believe a husband and worldly admiration were their God-given rights. He also found himself fascinated by those strange but curiously affecting airs and melodies of her native land, and the artistry of her interpretation.

'You are one of the most accomplished young ladies I have ever encountered,' he said with astonishment when he heard her play. 'All that remains is for me to introduce you to the French style, with which you are as yet unfamiliar.'

Hélène smiled with a mixture of sadness and emotion aroused by the songs she had been playing. He saw the melancholy, and was struck by the flavour it lent to her countenance.

'You are too kind,' she said. 'I fear you will find me as awkward and clumsy as all the others.'

He urged her to tell her story, which she did, despite her faltering French. Once he had identified the source of her predicament, Beaufils resolved to equip her with his own armour.

'You have been very carefully educated, but you have not been nurtured to any particular purpose,' he mused. 'The romance of your mother's noble kin, coupled with the beauty of your accomplishments, is deeply affecting, but it will not serve to advance your cause unless you use it very carefully.'

'I do not understand you,' she said. 'Everyone here seems to act in accordance with some unspoken rule, and they greet my ignorance with scorn.'

'You attribute to them faculties they do not possess,' he said bitterly, feeling his own grievances welling up inside.

Under her music master's guidance, Hélène began to notice a few interesting facts. Elisabeth, for example, chose to torment only those whose purses were less plentiful than hers, reserving her smiles and platitudes for those who had rooms and personal servants of their own, like Émilie, who was good-natured but slow-wilted. Émilie was to marry some duke who was quite a favourite at court, so she was never accused of *bêtises* in the classroom, or subjected to pranks. Beaufils whispered tales of the Duke's mistresses into Hélène's ear.

As she began to understand, Hélène began to drop a few hints about her own noble ancestry to the other girls, intimating mysteriously that old wrongs would be set aright in France. As her French improved, she even translated some of her family's verses, lamenting the lost splendour of a castle destroyed long before her birth. She consciously played on the imaginative susceptibilities of the cloistered girls, whose image of the outside world was sustained only by their own memories. They devoured her tales with fascination, and called on her to entertain them many a long, weary night. But because of all Beaufils had told her, and because she saw them as responding only to techniques he had taught her to employ, Hélène never relaxed her guard sufficiently to form any lasting friendships with these girls.

Meanwhile her music master, who had seemed so weary of the world, discovered that he did not find it so objectionable after all: at the end of her second year, he left to marry a young widow with a large fortune and was replaced by a proficient but duller older man. Hélène began to apprehend with dread stories she had been told of girls left for up to ten years while their parents were detained in Saint-Domingue or Martinique. Would her mother ever return, she wondered, studying the curious letters written in a mixture of Irish and English. She traced her name, *Eibhlín.* It was beginning to seem distant and unreal, as if it might never be her name again. In anxiety, she wrote a long letter to her mother, dutifully alternating between languages, pleading with her to speak plainly: what was the situation in Saint-Domingue? Would they ever return to Ireland?

It was three full years after her arrival that Hélène was finally called to the parlour to be taken away by her mother. Brighid had aged considerably in the years apart, but her new frailty belied a hardened character. As the carriage pulled away from the grey stone walls, Brighid said little of her time in Saint-Domingue, other than to indicate, in quietly bitter terms, that Carroll's entire fortune would not adequately compensate her for all that she had endured. But it was the very least that she deserved.

CHAPTER THREE

Carroll returned home early the next morning. When he heard of his daughter's arrival, he asked Brighid to wake her so that he might speak with her before breakfast. The journey had exhausted Isabella, and it took both cousins some considerable effort to rouse her. She had barely time to make a hasty toilette and to lament the sorry state of her polonaise before being ushered through the large dark doors of her father's library.

He stood up to meet her—a tall man, not as stout as her uncle, but just as ostentatiously dressed. She knew he was in his mid- to late forties, but he seemed somehow older, despite the vigour of his movements. Perhaps it was his complexion that aged him—what had once been fair, freckled Irish skin had been long since stripped raw by the Saint-Domingue sun.

'You look so much like your mother,' he

exclaimed. He spoke as if he were a Frenchman, trying to translate his words into the correct English phrases. This surprised Isabella, but she presumed it was only natural—after all, he had spent most of his life in France and Saint-Domingue.

'Do you think so?' she asked, nervously smoothing down her dress. 'My aunt always tells me so.' She could find no resemblance to herself in his features.

Hélène stood just inside the doorway beside her mother. She thought it a strange scene, this meeting between strangers who were going to play father and daughter.

Carroll smiled graciously at them. 'I wish to spend some time alone with my daughter,' he said.

Now that they were alone, Isabella felt a little awkward. 'You were not expecting to see me so soon,' she said. 'Unfortunately my uncle was against my leaving his house, and so I took the first opportunity of travelling, in what I fear were highly irregular circumstances.'

A frown crossed his face, and he looked at her keenly, as if he were about to inquire into those circumstances. Then he seemed to change his mind, and his face assumed a mask of gratification: 'So the lure of Paris was strong enough to entice you here, despite all the odds,' he said, showing that he still spoke English fluently, despite his French accent.

'I must admit it did hold a certain

attraction,' she replied. 'I thought Paris might have more to offer me than my life in Dublin.' She looked around at all the bookcases, built into the walls and painted the same off-white as the wood panelling. 'It is truly novel even to be received into a library such as this—there are so few books in my uncle's house, and I recently developed a longing to become acquainted with works of French philosophy.'

'You surprise me, though I remember all the volumes I used to read in my time as a captain—they whiled away many a long voyage. Is that how you distracted yourself?'

'Yes, I used to read all the newspapers my uncle brought home, and whatever books and pamphlets came my way. I heard about the French *philosophes* from a physician friend. He was so articulate on Irish politics compared to the others of my acquaintance, who interested themselves in such trivial and unimportant matters.'

'Then it is right that you should have come to me now, before your tastes have been too distinctly moulded,' he remarked, picking up a leather-bound volume and perusing it thoughtfully. 'I think it most beneficial that you read. It will certainly advance your French. But you will perhaps require some guidance in your choice of reading matter. Some light verse, a judiciously selected novel or two . . .'

'I understand,' said Isabella. 'What are your personal preferences?' she asked, hoping to gather some insight into his character.

He looked closely at her, as if considering what she should be told. 'I imagine I have something in common with your physician,' he said finally. 'I have always been fascinated by the theories of Newton and Locke, and the debate they sparked amongst our *philosophes* on the nature of matter and whether all psychological phenomena have in fact a physiological explanation.'

'I regret I am unfamiliar with their ideas,' said Isabella.

He smiled paternally. 'You speak as though they were beyond comprehension. You see, then, why guidance is necessary?'

Outside the door, Brighid was listening at the keyhole, and despairing of them ever getting to the point. Hélène was some distance along the passageway before she realised her mother was no longer with her, and she returned to find her.

'What are you doing?'

'Be quiet,' her mother whispered. 'I am trying to learn what exactly happened in Dublin.'

Hélène was a little disgusted. 'But surely the servants will see you and you'll be found out,' she said.

'It is a risk worth taking. The more one knows, the better,' Brighid answered. She looked scornfully at her daughter. 'Go and wait for me in my apartment, then.'

Hélène did as she was told. This apartment was distinctly shabbier than the others, though a faint aura of grandeur still clung to the faded tapestries. Her mother soon arrived with a triumphant glow.

'You will not believe what I have just heard. What a headstrong young woman! Running off to Paris in the company of a young doctor and an elderly abbé to escape a highly respectable marriage arranged by her uncle! She may be cleverer than I think she is, and perhaps plans to make a more spectacular match here. I imagine this is what her father believes, judging by his condoning of her conduct. But I think it more likely that she is foolish and romantic, preferring to indulge her whims rather than secure her future. What is your opinion of her?'

Hélène had been expecting some singularity of conduct, but she was highly startled by this. She was torn between envy of her cousin, and admiration for her daring.

'I like her,' she said finally.

'That is good, though it might be best not to allow sentiment to get the upper hand. You could perhaps strive to make yourself indispensable to her, but it is wise not to depend too heavily on the vagaries of a young woman's favour. It would be better to acquaint yourself with her weaknesses while gaining her confidence . . .'

Brighid looked at her daughter to see if she

was following her meaning, but Eibhlín did not seem to be listening. Did she not realise that this was not enough? Carroll's favour was not lost, but his attention was elsewhere now. She and her daughter had staked so much on his vague promises that any provision could only ever be an insufficient reward.

'I think this young physician may be of particular interest to us,' said Brighid in a slightly altered tone. 'Perhaps you could try to find out the precise nature of her feelings for him? I think it likely that he is not quite the prospective husband Carroll has in mind for his only daughter.'

Hélène did not reply. She was wondering why Isabella should wish to cast everything aside and venture into the unknown, when she had been given all that she could possibly desire. Perhaps her mother was right. Carroll could offer a larger fortune and better prospects.

'She is in her room now, eating from a tray and writing to her aunt,' Brighid continued. 'I think you should go to her, find out if the letter contains anything of interest.'

A silent Hélène went to do her bidding, though her own curiosity was equally eager to be indulged.

* * *

Isabella had just finished writing to Pamela

Murtogh. It was a difficult letter, because she was aware that it would probably be read by all the Murtoghs and scrutinised for a number of purposes. Not wanting to compromise her friend in any way, she spoke only in vague terms of having been well received by her father so that Pamela might not be unquiet on her behalf. But it was rather more difficult to write to her aunt. What should she say?

'Dear Aunt,' she began. 'I am sorry if I have been a cause of anxiety and disappointment to you . . .' She looked up as Hélène entered.

'Who are you writing to?' Hélène asked, approaching the writing desk.

'My aunt,' said Isabella. She unclasped the miniature she was wearing around her neck and handed it to Hélène.

'I see the likeness,' said Hélène, studying it carefully. The eyes were certainly similar, though the aunt's face lacked the defined structure of her niece's. 'I'm sure she'll be relieved to learn you arrived safely.'

Hélène's eye then fell on the single bag Isabella had arrived with. 'What have you done with the rest of your things?' she asked. 'I would have expected several trunks of gowns and possessions. Was your departure so hasty that there was no time to make the necessary arrangements?'

'I brought all that I required,' said Isabella, folding away her letter and choosing not to confide in her new cousin until they were better acquainted. 'Did *you* arrive in Paris all weighed down with trunks and trunks of silks?'

'Indeed no. I have very few belongings,' answered Hélène quietly.

Isabella looked at her curiously. Hélène was again dressed in that plain black dress. 'Forgive me for asking this, but are you in mourning?'

'No,' Hélène replied, taken aback. Then she saw that Isabella was examining her dress. 'This is what we wore in the convent,' she explained.

'You were in a convent?' Isabella asked curiously. 'What was it like?'

Hélène fiddled uneasily with the gold chain of the miniature she was still holding. 'Most of the girls seemed to like it well enough,' she replied. 'It was very kind of your father, to take such trouble with my education.'

'My father sent you there?' Isabella was startled by this.

'For three years, while my mother was with him in Saint-Domingue. And what about you? I suppose you had lessons at home in Dublin?'

Isabella smiled. 'I had a wonderful old governess, who had been to France. She gave me this . . .' Isabella rummaged in her bag and took out the story of the Wild Geese. Hélène turned the pages with interest as Isabella observed her intently, wondering as to the nature of her cousins' connection with her father. 'Was the convent in Paris?' Isabella asked.

'Yes, but I saw nothing of Paris, confined as I was within grey stone walls.'

'Was that difficult for you?' Isabella thought it must have been awful, to have been cloistered for all that time.

'I wasn't accustomed to being indoors, so I suppose it was,' Hélène replied, placing Isabella's notebook on the writing desk. 'You are curious, I know, but convent life is so uneventful, I really have nothing of interest to tell you about it.'

Isabella was disappointed. But it was quite obvious to her that Hélène had been unhappy there. 'So that is your convent dress,' said Isabella. 'Now I understand why you are to accompany me to the fashion houses and *couturières*. My father says we are both to have everything we think we might need. This confused me, because I thought you must be in mourning, and he had to leave before I could ask him. But I'm glad you're coming, because I dislike fittings, and I speak very little French.'

'Your father has offered to buy me clothes? Are you certain of this?' Hélène asked cautiously, not wanting to seem over-eager in case it were a mistake.

'Oh yes. It might even be fun, though I must admit I didn't come to Paris to tour the fashion districts. My father even wants to provide me with a lady's maid, though I must confess to an aversion to the thought. Our maidservant

Molly in Dublin . . . In any case, it is hardly practical when I do not speak French, so I am to have a French master immediately.'

What kind of girl actively discourages the attendance of a French lady's maid? wondered Hélène, surprised. 'I'll teach you French, if you like,' she suggested, motivated as much by a concern to protect her cousin from the pitfalls of her own experience as by an interest in securing some kind of influence over her.

But it was already becoming clear to Hélène that Isabella was not quite what she had expected her to be, and that her Dublin cousin would continue to surprise her.

CHAPTER FOUR

Carroll was on the whole satisfied with Isabella, although he had been more troubled than he cared to betray by the particulars she had related to him. He was impressed by what he chose to interpret as a touching display of filial loyalty in her determination to leave her uncle's house. He was a little alarmed, however, that she had been capable of escaping undetected and surviving such a perilous journey unscathed. She had also spoken of Mr M'Guire with a disquieting lack of awe or respect for his position as one of the most prominent Catholics in Ireland, though to be sure, this might simply be explained by her frustration with life in such a provincial backwater.

Peadar Carroll was now a very wealthy man. His years in Saint-Domingue had proved highly lucrative, but they had also exacted a harsh toll on a once robust constitution. Now in his late forties, he had intended to live out the remainder of his life in opulent retirement in Paris. However, he had always been a man of tireless energies, which had enabled him to achieve his worldly position, and once settled in Paris, he discovered that his drive was not blunted by age, ill-health, or dissipation. Instead it preyed on him, leading to ennui and melancholy. So in order to distract himself, he devised a new intrigue.

Other Irishmen who had had successful mercantile careers in France had been fortunate enough to receive letters-patent from the King. These *titres de noblesse* were a recognition by the King of noble status that had been lost in Ireland, and to secure them, one had to produce for the scrutiny of the King's Herald the relevant papers proving that one's family had once possessed such status. Carroll's family had not in fact belonged to the old Gaelic aristocracy, and this impediment, combined with the distance from Saint-Domingue to Paris, had prevented any attempt on his part to attain his own *titre*. But as it considerably boosted his consequence to do so, he often spoke of cousin Brighid's noble family as if he and they shared the same blood and lineage, and when Brighid applied to him for assistance, it had appealed to both his sense of showmanship and his imagination to take her into his household.

Brighid's pedigree was easily proven, and there was always the possibility of making it his own . . . Carroll had had this in mind three years ago when he had written to Brighid. But they had been a particularly trying and interminably long three years, during which his wife clung more tenaciously to life than life perhaps deserved. Whatever his intentions may have been towards Brighid and the daughter he had had educated so expensively, those final three years in Saint-Domingue had been such that, by the time he had arrived in Paris, his ambitions had changed somewhat. They settled now on his own daughter and a new intrigue to secure a title in his own right, without recourse to Brighid's pedigree.

Lack of pedigree was a problem, but not an insurmountable one. He cultivated an acquaintance with an elderly man of Irish family who had some influence at court and who also had the ear of a genealogist who could draw up a pedigree to match the exacting standards of the King's reputedly incorruptible Herald. Carroll bemoaned his predicament in words that intimated in clear but unspoken terms the reality of the situation.

His elderly acquaintance O'Shea responded by proposing a mutually agreeable solution to a dilemma of his own.

O'Shea had a nephew in the Irish Brigade, a captain who had distinguished himself in the American war. Unfortunately, military success alone did not in itself guarantee promotion, and it certainly did not prove financially rewarding. What the captain required was a wife, preferably a well-connected one, but a wealthy one would suffice. Carroll had a child, did he not? An only daughter? Surely he was as anxious to see her well settled as he himself was to see his nephew. It would be no small matter to persuade the genealogist to fill in all those puzzling blanks in a satisfactory manner, and if Carroll's hopes were set on those *lettres de reconnaissance*, well . . . a marriage alliance with the O'Sheas could only go in his favour.

Carroll had agreed tacitly to the match, but he was not one to rush in. If Isabella were to prove unpromising, then such a match could only surpass his expectations. However, if she had been blessed with some of her mother's beauty, and even a modicum of charm, then perhaps he could do better for them both than the young captain, whose veneer of *politesse* had been so roughly applied.

The initial interview with Isabella had left Carroll unsure. She was all that he had hoped for in appearance and manner, but her character could prove cause for concern. The situation he was in required some delicate manoeuvring, not to mention a pliable daughter. Perhaps she, like her cousin, should have been removed some years ago to the seclusion of a convent. But it was too late for that now. Instead, he thought it best to proceed slowly, avoid the topic of marriage, introduce the captain to her as an acquaintance of his, and see how well they liked each other. Meanwhile, her wardrobe had to be attended to as a matter of urgency. He wanted her to look every bit the young woman of fashion.

Accompanied by Brighid, Isabella and Hélène set off into a very wet, stormy afternoon. Rain softened the view from the carriage of the artfully shaped, bare winter trees and the gracefully proportioned *hôtels* on the wide streets. Isabella attempted unsuccessfully to see into the rooms they passed, wondering with curiosity about their occupants as she kept an ear to her cousins' conversation. From the letters of her former schoolfellows, Hélène had gleaned a surprisingly detailed knowledge of the Parisian fashion districts.

'Rose Bertin is by far the best and most famed *couturière*,' she told Isabella. 'But I do not think she would deign to accept such a client as you. She is a great favourite of the Queen, you know.'

'Let's avoid her then, shall we?' said Isabella

sharply. 'Nobody need deign anything, if we can help it.'

Hélène shrugged, but it was she who had instructed the *cocher* to take them to the busy Rue Saint-Honoré, where Rose Bertin had her extravagant premises, as did many other modistes, some of whom she hoped would be as elegant as Bertin. They would certainly be as costly, though Carroll had specifically told her mother they could have everything they might possibly require, and she intended to take full advantage of that. Their destination was on the Rive Droite, and so they had to cross the Seine. The sight of the tormented water pleased Isabella so much that she forgot her ill-humour at being obliged to spend her very first day in Paris being fitted for new clothes.

The Rue Saint-Honoré was full of mercers and fashion houses for those who could afford it. Isabella soon found herself standing in the gilded interior of the *couturière* of Hélène's choice. The Frenchwoman dismissed her Dublin clothes as poor examples of *le style anglais*, and pulled at her sleeves and skirt in a manner that suggested Isabella should consider herself privileged to be dressed by her. Having so little French, and anxious not to vex her father, she relied heavily on Hélène's judgement and knowledge of the minutiae of fashion as to trimmings and headdresses. It was Hélène who negotiated in animated

French for shot taffeta skirts with the skirt opening at just this particular angle, sleeves adorned with these particular lace ruffles. Because Carroll had instructed them to buy dress for every occasion, Hélène even insisted on one of the formal boned bodices required for court wear, even though she knew that court ladies avoided them if possible because they were so painful to wear.

'Surely this is a little excessive,' Isabella protested. 'We are hardly likely to be received at court.'

But Hélène insisted. 'It is wise to be prepared for every eventuality,' she said a little strangely, and her mother agreed.

Isabella gave in, attributing her cousin's lack of proportion to her convent experience—after years of restrictive confinement, Hélène must simply be overwhelmed by the world's temptations. She, on the other hand, simply wished for a new pelisse to replace the one that had badly survived the journey to Paris. While Hélène and Brighid were imparting their final, interminable instructions regarding those bodices, she decided to wait outside. The shop was over-embellished and under-heated, and she had tarried long enough. She was more than a little tired and hungry.

Despite the rain and the twilight, the Rue Saint-Honoré was as busy and congested as it had been earlier, with pedestrians threading their way between carriages, and pausing to look in the luxuriously appointed windows of the shops. Beside her, a young man in a black *surtout* was nailing a placard to a tree on the street corner. Intrigued, she waited until he had disappeared before going over to take a closer look. His words stared boldly back at her in French from the white page.

'Isabella!' said Hélène, horrified, coming at her from behind. 'We were looking for you everywhere. You mustn't disappear like that, anything could happen to you.'

'What does it mean?' she asked, indicating the placard.

'I believe it says something like "You Nobles, who squander your ill-gotten gains on finery to parade yourselves at the corrupt court of an Impotent King and Whore Queen, beware. Our day will come,"' Hélène translated. 'Why on earth would anyone write such a thing?'

Isabella laughed. 'Someone who wants to change things, perhaps,' she suggested, remembering all that Dr Connor had told her and wondering where he was now.

'Here is my mother,' said Hélène, looking hastily over her shoulder. 'Let us speak no more of this.'

'Where have you been, my dear?' Brighid smiled thinly.

'Why, you're absolutely soaked through. Just as well we were about to proceed to a *pelletier-fourreur*, to get that new pelisse we promised you. Come along now.'

Brighid ushered them out of the rain and into the nearby furrier's, where Hélène ordered two Russian beaver pelisses with matching muffs for herself and Isabella while her cousin reflected with secret satisfaction on the placard until she was called on to give her opinion on Hélène's choice of Canadian polecat and lamb trimmings.

Although she was in fact grateful for her cousin's assistance, Isabella felt there was something not quite open about Hélène. Her character and thoughts were completely indiscernible, and so Isabella had not been as free with her confidences as she might have been. The more she saw of her cousin, the more she thought she noticed a lack of freshness about her. Was this also something to be attributed to her years in the convent? Perhaps it was this that made her seem older than she really was. And yet Hélène resembled nothing more than an excited child when each and every item, from the daintiest slipper to the softest leather glove, had been safely secured and placed in the *commodes* of Carroll's *hôtel*, where they could not now be taken from her. Isabella had not thought she could be so animated, and was amused.

'Perhaps you would have been better suited to living with my aunt than I was,' she said with feeling. 'She would have loved a niece who valued her clothes as much as you do. I fear I was a disappointment to her. She would have liked me to marry Mr M'Guire just for the gowns.'

Seeing that her guard had softened, Hélène pressed her to continue. 'Is this Mr M'Guire the reason you left so hastily?' she asked, hoping to finally discover what had made her cousin act as she did.

'He was one of the reasons,' said Isabella reflectively, wondering how Dr Connor was faring with his Parisian friends and what he would have made of the placard. 'My aunt's tales had always inspired in me a wish to visit France, not to mention my governess's tales of the Wild Geese . . . Then I became acquainted with someone, a physician, whose French education seemed to have instilled in him an ability to articulate, in eloquent philosophical terms, all the reasons for my disenchantment with my Dublin life.'

Hélène's ears quickened. This then was the young doctor whom her mother had cited. Half-guiltily, she asked: 'Is this the Dr Connor who accompanied you to France?'

Isabella looked at her sharply.

'Forgive me. My mother mentioned someone of the kind, in confidence of course.'

Would her father have discussed the matter with his cousin? Isabella wondered with surprise.

'You must have been more than mere casual acquaintances, if you were able to prevail on him to take you to France,' Hélène continued. 'I suppose it might even be considered romantic, after a fashion. Is he wealthy?'

'You misunderstand me,' said Isabella hastily. 'We became friends within a brief period of time only because I understood something of his frustrations and he something of mine. It was so refreshing to be able to speak frankly with someone, to escape the pressures of Dublin life, if only for a few moments.'

'So you do find him more appealing than the other men of your acquaintance? I should like to meet him, to form an opinion of his future prospects.'

There were times when Hélène reminded Isabella of the O'Brien sisters in Dublin. Did everything have to be reduced to prospects and husbands? 'I do not think it possible,' she answered. 'He felt it better that we follow our separate paths, rather than complicate matters even further, and so he continued on alone, to join his friends in the University Quarter.'

Hélène reflected on this, though to Isabella's relief she said no more about it. But later that night, when her thoughts again turned to her cousin, Hélène was struck by the irony of the situation. She knew that she herself would go to any lengths to secure a wealthy husband and a handsome settlement. And she was equally convinced that Isabella had gone to some considerable lengths to escape just these things. It was a puzzle. Why was her mother so convinced that Isabella would prove a threat to their future? There was quite possibly no conflict of interest, even if Carroll did favour his own daughter.

CHAPTER FIVE

The next morning found Isabella in her father's library, her eye wandering from locked bookcase to locked bookcase, her hand leafing through a leather-bound volume of which she could understand but a few words. Outside the window, Paris rain continued to blur the view, falling silently, because there was no wind.

'I had hoped to see something of the city, now that we are finally finished with fittings and *couturières*,' said Isabella, peering at what she could discern of the distorted yellow limestone *hôtels* across the street. 'Would it really be folly to venture out in that?'

'Folly indeed,' replied her father. 'Particularly to run the risk of a cold, when I have taken a box for the Opéra tonight. We are to be accompanied by a young friend of mine—a Captain O'Shea, who distinguished himself during the American war. I suggest you conserve your strength for that, *ma fille*.'

'A captain from the Irish Brigade?' Isabella asked with interest.

Her father smiled. 'He is a most remarkable fellow, and will be honoured, I'm sure, to make your acquaintance.'

A captain from the Irish Brigade. It was something to look forward to. Isabella had never before met an officer, although some members of the brigade had been known to visit Dublin, and had been much talked about. One had even been pointed out to her in a drawing room once: an elderly man so frail of build and heavily powdered that she had found it difficult to credit the tales of his valour on the battlefield of Fontenoy. But this was a young Irishman, who had fought as recently as the American war. He would have interesting stories of his own to tell. Once she had verified that her cousins would also be accompanying them, she went in search of Hélène to tell her about this captain.

At the appointed hour, the two girls entered the salon in full evening dress. Hélène had virtually transformed herself with her own delicate, precise skill and with careful instructions to the new lady's maid. The silver embroidery and pale blue of her gown perfectly echoed the subtle dusting of powder in her hair. Isabella thought it created an enchanting impression, as if Hélène had been frosted with a shimmering ice, and she was offset perfectly by the pale pinks of the salon. Carroll's mind was too full of other considerations to pay Hélène more than an initial passing glance, but this glance crystallised into a favourably strong impression. He complimented her in French, resolving to give some thought to her future when other, more pressing, issues had been dealt with. And he was more than satisfied with Isabella's appearance, feeling that the deep blue of her gown emphasised the radiance of her complexion, and suggested a vibrancy and good health.

'Now I truly see your mother brought back to life,' he exclaimed. 'The French fashions become her well, do they not?' he said to his cousin Brighid, who smiled agreement.

Hélène's keen ears heard the sound of a servant approaching. Anticipating the announcement of a visitor, she decided to steal away to take a look at the captain as he waited in the *vestibule.* She was filled with curiosity about him, and knew that she would not be able to observe him intently in company without him noticing. In the dull glow of the *vestibule*, she saw a young man dressed in full uniform, even with a sword. She noted that his breeches were as fashionably tight as any Frenchman's, and that his hair was concealed under a wig. Indeed, only his pale, freckled skin and large build betrayed him as an Irishman. He started toward her, alerted to her presence by the sound of her new high-heeled slippers. Although a little embarrassed at being discovered, she stepped forward and greeted him with poise, confident of the power of her embroidered silk, which gently caught the candlelight.

He smiled in appreciation. 'I was told you were charming, but nothing had prepared me for how lovely you are,' he said in the French-accented English of a stranger to the tongue, a common trait among Irishmen who had long since made their home in France.

Hélène was pleasantly startled. Did he really think so? She tasted the idea for a moment, savoured it, allowed something to awaken inside her that suggested a vague promise to be fulfilled.

'Yes, your father is so pleased to be reunited with you at last,' he continued after a considered pause.

Of course, Hélène thought, slapped back into the reality of the situation. His compliments weren't intended for me at all. I wonder if they are even genuine expressions of appreciation, or just empty platitudes designed to flatter potential brides?

'Come this way,' she said, her smile no longer making her face glow. Why should I be the one to enlighten him? If a penniless girl cannot be praised solely on her own merits, then she can at least prolong the fleeting impression that she may, on occasion, be mistaken for someone more privileged.

In the cool brilliance of the salon, the captain advanced expectantly, greeting

Monsieur Carroll with a familiarity that struck Hélène as faintly disrespectful. But then, I must bear in mind that he is not a dependent of undefined status, she thought as she watched him being presented to her cousin.

'*Enchanté*,' he told Isabella, kissing her hand and lingering over it longer than necessary. Isabella pulled it back.

The captain saw that she was studying his appearance, and smiled. 'Does the uniform please you, Mademoiselle?'

'On the contrary, I was just thinking how similar it was to the English one,' she replied, more frankly than she had intended. 'You must forgive me, I am merely dismayed that an Irish Brigade should choose to dress its men in the red coat of an English soldier.'

'You astound me, Mademoiselle,' he laughed, greatly amused. 'Surely you are aware, at least in part, of the origins of our illustrious brigade?'

'Yes, you were followers of King James, but . . .'

'And King James was, after all, the rightful King of England?'

Of course, she thought. His men would have adopted the uniform of the English Army. She was nonetheless disappointed. 'Surely that must lead to some confusion, when the Irish Brigade faces the English Army on the battlefield?' she mused. 'How can you tell which men to fight?'

Carroll smiled benignly. 'Let our thoughts turn to more pleasing distractions: *Monsieur le Capitaine*, would you be so good as to escort my daughter to the carriage while I attend to my cousins?'

Hélène gave one last look at her reflection in the salon looking-glasses before following the others. When will they see me, really see me? she wondered. When will I command their attention as Isabella does?

It was a large carriage, but still the width of the girl's skirts made it difficult to accommodate them all comfortably. They were therefore thankful when they had crossed the river, and arrived at the Opéra on the Boulevard Saint-Martin.

'It is beautiful, is it not, Mademoiselle?' said the captain with satisfaction, 'Perfectly proportioned, *très élegant* . . .'

'Yes, surprising, really, that it was built in less than three months,' said Hélène, taking Isabella by the arm. 'The first two Opéras were destroyed by fire, you know. I believe a number of spectators were burned alive when the last *salle* went up in flames.'

'Burned alive, you say,' Isabella repeated apprehensively, dazzled by the heat and the swarms of brightly dressed, heavily made-up Parisians as they stepped inside.

'Why do you tell her such stories?' exclaimed the captain. 'You will only succeed in frightening her for the remainder of the evening.'

Exasperated by this, Isabella took the opportunity, afforded by the crowd to separate herself from the captain for a few brief moments while they were being guided to her father's box. She waved her fan to cool herself, looking out with curiosity on the Opéra in all its wooden splendour, absorbing what detail she could of an audience so large it was indistinct, until the curtain went up. Although she understood little of the proceedings, she found herself entranced and unsettled by the violence of the passions displayed on stage by the heavily painted players.

The captain, who seemed bored by the entertainment, glanced at her from time to time. 'It is refreshing to see how deeply affected a newcomer can be by such a spectacle,' he observed during the interval. 'But of course, Dublin does not boast a theatre of consequence, and must make do with the over-priced warbling of English touring companies.'

'You are mistaken,' replied Isabella shortly. 'We have two very fine theatres. And the audience is very discerning. Consequently, only the finest of Italian musicians, or the most fêted of English players, are invited for a season.' She turned to Hélène. 'How do you find the performance, Cousin?'

'Forgive me, I didn't hear the question,' said Hélène with a distracted air. 'I was admiring an old friend of mine from the convent. Elisabeth, or *Madame la Marquise*, as I should call her now. She appears to be leaving.'

All eyes turned towards the elegant Marquise, now a tiny distant figure, quitting her box.

'You are acquainted with the *Marquise*?' asked the captain, sounding surprised that Hélène should know someone of such consequence.

Hélène smiled. Who would have thought that her former tormentor would now inadvertently perform such a favour?

'It is a tolerable production,' her mother was saying to Carroll in French. 'But I must boast that my daughter's talents are infinitely superior. You know how carefully they were cultivated in the French style by her convent masters.'

'I defer to your judgement. But I detect a touch of ennui in the captain's demeanour. I believe your Irish airs would be more to his taste. The harp is his favourite instrument, and he has asked most particularly to hear you play.'

The performance then recommenced. Afterwards, the captain returned to the *Hótel de Carroll* with them, only for Carroll to find a letter calling him away again on business which could not wait. He made his apologies, urged the captain to remain, and prepared to leave. Brighid went to see him off.

'What could have happened?' Isabella wondered with dismay. Her father seemed to be as constantly occupied as her uncle had been.

Hélène shrugged her shoulders. 'Perhaps an urgent summons from his mistress. I understand she can be rather troublesome.'

'His mistress?' Isabella wondered if she had misheard.

'Yes. He keeps her in a little house outside Paris. That is why he is so often from home.'

Isabella was somewhat taken aback, as much by Hélène's plainness of speech in front of the captain as by the information.

'You seem a little perturbed,' remarked the captain. 'Perhaps you are shocked by the ways of Paris? *Bon courage*, Mademoiselle. One winter here, and all your awkward provincial manners will have been smoothed away.'

I am not shocked, I am merely surprised, and I hope I will never develop your affectations, thought Isabella angrily. 'Am I to thank you for your condescension?' she inquired.

Brighid returned and noted that the conversation was not proceeding smoothly. She guided the captain to a seat, saying, 'Monsieur Carroll said you wanted to hear me play?'

'Indeed, Madame,' he said eagerly. 'I have had a hankering to hear the native music of my poor land ever since Monsieur Carroll first boasted to me of your skill.'

There was a note of patronising ennui in his voice, as if this was some minor curiosity designed to tempt his jaded palate, like an oriental cabinet, or a classical statue. Hélène watched him through her fan as her mother played, and was gratified to see the effect it had on him. Isabella was grateful for the diversion, but she found herself unsettled by the music. She was enchanted by its evocation of a lost Gaelic world, but it had an impenetrable quality, as if she were somehow denied access to it, and by extension a whole tradition that was as unfamiliar to her as Paris, with its mistresses and its *moeurs*.

'Bravo,' cried the captain, when Brighid had smoothed away her final, dying strains. 'It is truly wonderful to hear one of our ancient and noble traditions come to life again, though the keenness of my joy is matched only by pain at what our poor country has suffered, how even now she lies in dejection, still waiting in vain for the Stuarts to release her from the tyranny of the Hanovers.'

'You amaze me,' said Isabella. 'Surely not even the Irish Brigades could think of a resurrection of the Stuart cause?'

'My dear Mademoiselle,' he smiled. 'What a pitiful thing it is to see a young Irishwoman so disheartened by the oppression of her poor country as to think deliverance impossible.'

'*Monsieur le Capitaine*, I am not quite so

pitiful as you think me. As a child, my governess told me stories of our country's history—she was particularly partial to King James and Bonnie Prince Charlie. But she said that after the Battle of Culloden, the Stuart Cause had died completely.'

'She passed her lack of hope on to you, then.'

'No, she was pragmatic, like my aunt and uncle. My aunt would always shake her head at those stories and tell me that there was more to be gained from professing loyalty to the present English King.'

'Who are we to question her aunt's authority?' remarked Brighid, primarily addressing Isabella. 'After all, she has always known what was best for her niece, has she not?'

Isabella felt uncomfortable under her gaze, as if her cousin could see deeper into her than she liked. Thank you, Cousin, for that gentle reminder of the poor terms on which I parted with Aunt, she thought. Though the less you know about it, the better.

'Despite my reluctance to tear myself away,' said the captain, 'I have a supper engagement I must keep. You will pardon me, on this occasion?'

'Of course,' said Isabella with deliberately exaggerated politeness.

Hélène took the opportunity to show him out. 'You must forgive my cousin,' she said.

'She is fresh from Dublin, and her thoughts are somewhat . . . preoccupied.'

'I understand,' said the captain, though he did not.

They were now standing exactly where they had been when they had first encountered each other. Hélène smiled slowly. You would have had a better reception from me, she thought. Not that I would have been overly eager to jump into matrimony with you, but we might have understood each other. I have your measure now: You are an ambitious young man craving money and position, and you have already attained a certain degree of success. You are sufficiently attractive a proposition to justify your presumption. This Mademoiselle Carroll from Dublin should be more than grateful for your attentions. Well, I imagine your person and manner are not displeasing by French standards, but as far as they are concerned, you lack the appearance, charm and wit necessary to tip the balance in your favour. Military prestige, and an uncle with a little influence at court count for something, certainly, but not everything, I suspect. That is why you will return here.

'*Au revoir, Monsieur le Capitaine*,' she said. 'I feel confident we shall meet again.'

CHAPTER SIX

Despite her disappointment in him, the captain did not prey on Isabella's thoughts as he did on her cousin's. The following morning saw the delivery of a letter from Aunt. She opened it with more than a little dread.

My Dear Niece,

I must confess my relief on being enlightened as to your whereabouts, and on being assured that you survived such a perilous escapade without mishap. It came as no surprise to me that you chose so rashly to throw in your lot with your father, for a while we did fear worse.

As you must have anticipated, Mr Gregory Murtogh took an exceedingly malicious pleasure in spreading the rumour that you had eloped with Dr Connor. I am sure you can appreciate the devastating effect this had on your uncle and me, not to mention Mr M'Guire. It was a most unfortunate business, though to be sure, I remain rather partial to the young doctor, and might not have objected to him.

I believe the time for recrimination has now passed, so I will not dwell on how deeply you have wounded your uncle, and how he has vowed never to see you again. If I appear softer than I should be, it is only because your uncle has decreed that all relations between us must henceforth cease, and I do not wish to part with you on bitter terms.

In short, Isabella, you have made your choice, and must now remain under your father's protection. I will therefore confine myself to a few pieces of good advice.

Firstly, your good name has not escaped unscathed from this affair. It would be one thing if Dr Connor had had intentions towards you: a hasty marriage and a discreet time lapse before returning to Dublin would have smoothed things over. But, it was quite another thing for you to settle on him as a travelling companion with only a priest to vouchsafe his good conduct. You are indeed fortunate that the abbé wrote to me so promptly to assuage my fears, informing me that he had entrusted you at the earliest opportunity into the care of a widow of impeccable character. His name is both known and respected here; this, coupled with a letter from your father assuring us that you were safely received into his household, have enabled me to make some progress in salvaging the remains of your reputation.

You have a tendency, my dear, to act without considering the consequences, and if people are talking, you have only your own rashness to blame. So, in future, try to moderate your conduct, and if you cannot do so, then try not to involve others in your scrapes. I will take this opportunity to inform you that Pamela's part in all this has emerged. You have placed her in the most awkward of positions. Nevertheless, Pamela is such a good, sweet-natured, generous girl, one can hardly blame her for it, but really, Isabella, what were you thinking of?

Lastly, do bear in mind that this father you seek refuge with is in effect a complete stranger, and one who has spent most of his life in distant lands. This is not necessarily a cause for concern, and I do feel you must stay with him now. He is your only hope for the future. But remember that you are a young woman in a strange country. You will have no friends to turn to should things go wrong. So be on your guard, my dear Isabella.

Despite everything, I remain,
Your loving Aunt

On the first reading, Isabella took a strong objection to her aunt's tone. On the second, she became less vexed and more resigned. My aunt writes as though I were an unscrupulous fool, on the level of Gregory Murtogh, she thought. Why is it that a young woman who disobeys her uncle by going to Paris is a naughty child, to be punished and partially forgiven, when Dr Connor can do as he pleases?

Isabella was fully aware, however, of the demands she had made on him, and how galling it must be for him to be dependent for his good name on the word of an abbé with whom he was so much at odds. She grew pensive and read the letter again. What, then, is a prudent young woman? she wondered. She smiled, remembering Pamela's wedding preparations: if I were a dutiful niece, I would be sitting in my uncle's house, planning my trousseau like a good child, waiting for lots of costly new playthings to arrive from London.

'Is it very harsh?' asked Hélène, who had knocked and entered the boudoir on being informed by her mother that a letter had arrived for Isabella from Dublin.

'In a way,' replied Isabella, folding it and placing it in the bureau. 'My aunt writes that she has washed her hands of me. At least for the while. But I think it may be for the best. She did take good care of me and provide the with a home when I needed one, a secure and happy childhood, and I have no wish to sour the memory with any prolonged bad feeling.'

'You appear so composed,' remarked

Hélène. 'Are you not in the slightest bit distressed?'

In fact, Isabella had been affected by the letter, but she did not want to discuss it any further with Hélène. She wished to create some distance between herself and her aunt's words, so that they would not continue to echo so loudly inside her. Looking out of the window, she saw that it had stopped raining, and the winter sun was glinting dully off the pale, damp buildings.

'When is my father expected to return?' she asked.

'Not till nightfall, I believe.'

Nightfall? Isabella glanced fleetingly around the boudoir before finding her eyes pulled back to the window. 'Then I shall go out. I am finally going to see something of the city I came here for. Will you accompany me? I must first call on the abbé, if he is at home—you may find that tedious, but it is surely preferable to remaining here all day?'

'By all means. I'll order the carriage.'

Isabella smiled as her cousin left, wondering what her aunt would make of the two of them setting off alone sightseeing for the day. She had decided to call on the abbé instead of simply writing, because she felt it incumbent on her to thank him for his kindness in writing to Dublin so promptly. But it was still early, and there would be plenty of time afterwards to do as they pleased.

Hélène did not relish the prospect of a winter's day traipsing around Paris in her cousin's shadow, but at that moment, she would have accepted any excuse to escape the confines of her surroundings. Her mother had been particularly difficult all morning, speculating about the captain and what he could possibly have made of Isabella's conduct. She did not realise how it hurt when she remarked what a pity it was that her own daughter was not in Isabella's shoes—her Eibhlín would have acted far more graciously. Now, her mother would be anxious to learn the contents of the letter, so Hélène avoided her as she went about the house getting ready, informing her of their plans only when both girls were dressed to go out.

'It is such a beautiful day,' Isabella remarked, now that it was possible to see out of the carriage windows. 'I almost wish we had decided to walk.'

Hélène shook her head. 'Once we have left the clean wide streets of the Faubourg Saint-Germain, you will see how impossible walking is in Paris—it is far too dirty and crowded, and some of these streets are so long, they seem almost endless on foot. The speed and comfort of a carriage somewhat shortens them.'

She speaks as though she prefers them shorter, thought Isabella, observing how her cousin's gloved hand emerged again and again from her muff to stroke its fur in mute appreciation.

Hélène became conscious of her cousin's gaze. 'Are we also to call on Dr Connor?' she asked. 'I should very much like to compare him with Captain O'Shea.'

'I don't think that would be appropriate,' Isabella answered, a little more acerbically than she had intended because her aunt's reprimands were so fresh in her mind. Much as she would like to see Dr Connor, she felt she should really stick to her resolution to stay away.

Contrary to what Dr Connor's rants about the Catholic Church might have led her to expect, the abbé lived in a relatively modest apartment in a house on a busy street in Saint-Germain des Prés, which was not as far from Carroll's *Hôtel* as Hélène had thought. The old priest received Isabella warmly.

'I had intended to write to you,' he said. 'But as you can see, I remain indisposed. But I did write to your aunt, and your father called . . .' Here he was interrupted by a fit of coughing.

Isabella fetched him a drink, while Hélène stood as far away from him as possible, fearing she might catch the old man's illness.

'My father came to see you?' she asked, once he had recovered.

'He came to thank me for my good offices on your behalf. We spoke at length, and assuaged each other's fears,' he spoke with difficulty through a dry throat.

'He did not mention it. I wonder if he also spoke with Dr Connor?'

The abbé frowned, and indicated his inability to speak.

'We mustn't tire you,' said Isabella, noting how weak he seemed. 'Perhaps I'll call again, once you've recovered. Is there anything we can do? My cousin and I are going to spend the afternoon driving around Paris, if you have any errands you would like us to do for you?'

'My nephew in the Collège des Irlandais,' he whispered. 'He was to visit today. Would you be so good as to take him a note, putting off the visit for another occasion? It will not delay you long.'

'By all means,' smiled Isabella, glad of an excuse to visit such a famed institution. Once he had finished his note, she dragged a reluctant Hélène back into the carriage and they set off again. The Quartier Latin held no appeal for Hélène, who sighed with resignation as the carriage fought its way through the Parisian hordes. She considered it unhealthily infested with seminaries and convents, and could attribute Isabella's interest only to the fact that her physician had attended university there, and was even now breathing this foul air in some unfashionable street, too narrow to admit sunlight.

These thoughts were, however, forgotten once she caught a glimpse of the Palais du

Luxembourg. 'Look,' said Hélène, drawing Isabella's attention to it. 'Isn't it beautiful? Marie de Médicis had it built in the exact style of Italian palaces sometime early in the last century.'

'Really?' asked Isabella, studying it. 'Was she homesick for the land of her birth?'

'She must have been,' Hélène replied. 'I sympathise with her, I know how she must have felt.'

'How?' Isabella was mystified. 'Even if you missed Ireland as much as she missed Italy, you could never know how she felt! She was a queen! And she ruled France cruelly, but according to her own will.'

'I miss Ireland sometimes,' said Hélène quietly. 'And I like palaces. Especially old ones.' They evoked images of that long-lost and never seen castle of her mother's family, a castle that had now become as much a figment of her imagination as her mother's.

'Look, Hélène,' cried Isabella in astonishment when the carriage turned away from the Luxembourg. 'What is that enormous building ahead of us?'

'A church,' she replied, reluctantly detaching herself from her reflections and seeing the great architect Soufflot's recreation of the classical splendour of Rome's Panthéon rise before her in the heart of its square. 'The King's grandfather ordered it to be built in honour of Sainte Geneviève. It is not finished yet. Unsurprising really, given its size.'

'Is it really a church?' asked Isabella, amazed.

'Oh, yes. Sainte Geneviève is the patron saint of Paris, you know, and this quartier is heavily associated with her. I believe the King sought her help when he fell ill, and this was how he chose to express his gratitude for his subsequent cure,' Hélène gazed appraisingly at the vast edifice, whose main purpose seemed to be to dwarf all the other buildings around it, to impose the memory of that one cure over all else this place had ever known. Meanwhile, Isabella was attempting to picture the Irish College. Her old governess's brother had studied there, and so it had featured prominently in Isabella's history lessons. Finally, she was going to see it for herself. What would it be like?

There were actually two Irish Colleges now, one for priest—students who had already been ordained, and one for those who hadn't. The abbé's nephew was in the latter, which they found in a small street behind Soufflot's Pantheon. Hélène communicated their business in Irish to the College Superior while Isabella admired what she could of the establishment, its walls still new enough to gleam with fresh, light smoothness. A boy of about fourteen was dispatched to fetch the abbé's nephew, Donnchadh, who apprehended them a few minutes later with an eager nervousness, addressing them in English only when given permission to do so by his Superior, because it was the House Rule that they speak Irish at all times.

'It was very good of you to bring this note to me,' he said, smiling hesitantly.

'It was our pleasure,' said Isabella. 'You are truly blessed, to have such beautiful surroundings to study in. It almost compensates for the denial of such opportunities in Ireland. An acquaintance of mine once told me something of university life in Paris, and, I've always longed to visit this *quartier* ever since I was a child, listening to my governess's stories.'

A few words in Irish between the student and his Superior, and the two cousins were treated to a brief turn around the tranquil courtyard, and a viewing of the college chapel. Then Donnchadh received permission to show them something of the surrounding area in return for their kindness. With some excitement, he and Isabella arranged for the carriage to meet them by the banks of the Seine, at the point where the rue des Bernardins met the *quais*, and the three of them set off to see the Sorbonne and the other Collège des Irlandais.

It was cold. Hélène would rather have retained the carriage and its warm rugs. If Isabella must walk, why not promenade in a fashionable spot, such as in front of the Jardin des Tuileries, where they would have the opportunity to see and be seen? Somewhere she, Helene, could also attract attention, if only for a transient, illusory moment. She understood the cafés of the nearby Boulevard Saint-Germain were full of officers.

But instead, they descended steep, narrow, medieval streets, so crowded that Hélène feared her new clothes would be sullied beyond redemption. Such considerations did not seem to affect her cousin, or the unkempt student in his threadbare *surtout*, who cheerfully answered Isabella's constant stream of questions about his studies and life in the college. Thankfully, they eventually came out at the river, where Hélène spied the carriage awaiting them.

Donnchadh led them down steps by the bank of the Seine, and they came out at the water's edge, where the river flowed thickly and forked away from them. There, at the point where the waters separated, Isabella saw what looked like a castle rising from the water, intricate in its towers and arches. Even Hélène was struck with the beauty of the scene. The sun seemed brighter here, reflected in the water, but as the light intensified, the building began to show its age, almost as if it could not sustain its weight, and might succumb to the insistent pressure of the river. This gave it a momentary, enchanted effect, one that Isabella tried to fix in her mind so she would always remember it. Hélène turned away, finding the light, reflected in the stone of the cathedral and the waves, was far too strong for her eyes.

'That is Notre Dame de Paris,' said the student proudly. 'Do you want to cross over to the Île and see it?'

'I would prefer to wait in the carriage,' said Hélène quickly. 'I find myself somewhat fatigued.'

'Are you unwell?' asked Isabella, who had been gazing in silent awe.

'I am perfectly well, but it has been a long day, and we still have to call on Dr Connor. He lives somewhere in the vicinity, does he not?'

'Why do you want to see Dr Connor? Are you in need of professional attendance?' asked Isabella ironically, sensing her cousin merely wished to gratify her curiosity.

'No, but we simply must go. You have to tell him about your aunt's letter . . .'

Despite Isabella's strong inclination to go see him, her consciousness of the circumstances in which they had parted, and her aunt's letter, made her almost angry that Hélène should broach the subject in the presence of this student. In any case, she didn't want Dr Connor to think she was pestering him, pursuing him all the way to Paris . . .

'We can visit the cathedral another time,' suggested Donnchadh. 'I can see you to the doctor's house instead, if you like.'

Isabella gave in, and as Donnchadh insisted

in seeing them there safely, all three of them set off in the carriage.

CHAPTER SEVEN

On arriving in Paris, Connor had been warmly received into his friends' small but comfortable apartment in the University Quarter, on the second floor of a house a mere two blocks from where Connor had lived as a student. They loved this *quartier.* Situated at the heart of the book trade, it was considered unfashionable by the wealthy and the nobility, which kept the rents down.

The Bernards now had a new son to occupy much of their attention, and Dr Bernard's duties were particularly demanding, but they were so concerned at Connor's wearied appearance that they devoted what energies they could to improving his spirits. His days soon fell into a pattern of reading in the morning, accompanying his friend on visits to patients in the afternoon, and talking late into the night.

Often before dinner, Connor would take a walk, down the rue des Bernardins to the point where the quai faced Notre Dame and the eastern tip of the Île de la Cité across the water. He would then follow the river, admiring the scene until he reached the turn for the Rue Saint Jacques. He would make his way up this street slowly, pausing to browse in its bookshops, always eager to peruse the latest arrivals—those sealed with the approval of the King's censor, as well as others more clandestinely presented. These were the ones that had to be published in Holland and smuggled back to France, where they were sold secretly to a hungry reading public. Connor liked to look through the most recent tales of debauched nobles before turning to less graphic political works.

Sometimes, he would go as far as the Sorbonne, or even the Luxembourg, where clandestine *colporteurs* would be selling the latest news. Connor would often purchase a *nouvelle á main* or a pamphlet from one of these street peddlers and bring it home to Julie and Bernard.

As he began to feel better, he decided to commit some of his ideas to paper, and under his friends' encouragement, he arranged into a coherent structure all the thoughts he had expressed to the abbé on the uses and abuses of religious practices and their many conflicting interpretations. This became an article, published in a radical journal that had been granted a verbal *simple tolérance* by the lieutenant of police, guaranteeing that the authorities would turn a blind eye to its publication.

Connor was very pleased with his published

article, but as he wandered the anonymous, busy streets, he occasionally found his thoughts turning to Isabella, wondering how she fared, and as he could not settle on how best to approach her, he was greatly pleased when one day she knocked on the Bernards' door, along with her cousin and a young clerical student.

'Miss Carroll,' he exclaimed. 'This is indeed a pleasant surprise.'

Isabella flushed, thinking their unexplained presence very awkward. 'I wanted to alert you to the contents of a letter I have just recently received from my aunt,' she said quickly. 'I apologise for the intrusion.'

After the introductions had been made, Julie Bernard guided Donnchadh and Hélène to a seat.

'*Je vous remercie de nous avoir accueillis, Madame*,' said Hélène.

'You speak French well,' Julie remarked curiously in French.

'I spent three years in a convent in Paris,' Hélène explained a little diffidently.

Julie grew excited when she learned which one: she had spent a year in a sister convent in Rouen, preparing for her First Communion!

Isabella stood at a loss, not understanding a word of the exchange. Connor beckoned to her to join him at the window where they might discuss the letter as privately as possible. She told him about Gregory Murtogh, and her aunt's efforts to salvage her reputation.

'It is as I thought,' he said. 'Though less serious than it might have been. Do you have any regrets?'

'No,' she said quietly. 'In some ways I miss my life in Dublin, but I feel as if I had been given it under false pretences, as if it had never been mine to begin with.'

'Strong words indeed,' he remarked. 'I hope you fare better with your father. Is he everything you had hoped?'

There was nothing to suggest that her father had also been to see Dr Connor. Isabella thought about mentioning his visit to the abbé, but decided against it. 'He has been most solicitous for my comfort, but he is often from home, and I know very little of his affairs. Last night I saw more than I wished to of a friend of his—a conceited young captain from the Irish Brigade.'

Connor rolled his eyes. 'Did you not swoon at the sight of his uniform?'

'Indeed I did not—I was too stunned by his belief that Ireland was still waiting for the Stuarts to return.'

'These *émigrés*—they get all misty-eyed when it suits them, as if nothing has changed in the past hundred years. But it is all affectation, really—they are far too busy advancing themselves in French society to give much thought to Ireland. So, he is not a potential suitor, then?'

'I should think not. I didn't come all the way to Paris to land myself a husband, I came here to escape all that!'

Hélène was watching them. Madame Bernard and Donnchadh were deep in conversation, comparing convent life to the Collège des Irlandais. They both had such soft-coloured, happy memories that Hélène felt all too keenly the sombre loneliness of her own, and turned away. She found much to interest her in the two figures at the window, although she was unable to hear their actual words.

An infant was heard to wail in another room, the sound arresting Madame Bernard mid-sentence. She hastily excused herself, and Donnchadh turned to Hélène.

'They must be very old friends,' he said, seeing that her eyes were fixed on Connor and Isabella.

'No, though there is an unusual sympathy between them.'

He heard the strain in her voice and became concerned. 'I hope you are not too fatigued,' he said. 'It struck me earlier that you were not enjoying the walking tour as much as Mademoiselle Carroll.'

'You are too kind,' she replied, taken with his consideration. 'I was perhaps a little out of spirits, but I am perfectly well now, thank you.'

Hélène looked at him with fresh interest, and soon found herself warming to his manner. The easy, natural pleasure he took in Paris and his studies reminded her a little of Isabella. But because he posed no threat to her future, Hélène relaxed with him in a way she could not relax with her cousin.

As the conversation developed, he dropped his slow, melodic French for the freer cadences of his native Gaelic. He was more comfortable with Gaelic, he explained, although so many students took so wholeheartedly to French that it was a rule of the Collège des Irlandais that they speak Gaelic there, lest they forget their mother tongue altogether. It was a long time since Hélène had heard anyone other than her mother speak it, and as her mother spoke it primarily so that the servants would not understand her, Hélène had come to associate the language mainly with Brighid's scheming. But as she listened to Donnchadh's tales of fellow-students and football matches in the college courtyard, his voice evoked memories of her childhood, mild summer days while her father was still alive.

Connor was now telling Isabella about the article he had had published. As always, she proved a sympathetic listener, so eager to read his article that she persuaded him to lend her the original version, which was written in English, even though he maintained it was a raw sketch.

Madame Bernard returned, apologising for her lengthy absence. Isabella came to herself with a start, realising how late it must be, and apologised for staying so long. All were sorry to see the visit at an end, Hélène especially, because she found it hard to believe its refreshing, dream-like quality could ever be repeated, even though Madame pressed an invitation on all three of them to call again, and Donnchadh said awkwardly that he would welcome any future opportunity to converse again with her in Gaelic. Connor then gave Isabella his densely written sheets, and she stored them respectfully in her Russian beaver muff.

After they left Donnchadh outside the gates of the Collège des Irlandais, Isabella found Hélène's silence so pronounced that she feared she had vexed her cousin by conversing so exclusively with Dr Connor all afternoon.

'I hope you have not been bored?' she asked. 'I'm sorry you and Donnchadh were thrown together like that, but he is a likeable fellow, is he not?'

'Very much so,' Hélène replied. 'I enjoyed his company immensely.' She drifted back into silence, attempting to prolong the flavour of the afternoon.

CHAPTER EIGHT

Night had already fallen by the time Isabella and Hélène reached home. In the library, Carroll was waiting for them with his cousin. Brighid brushed past Isabella without saying anything, taking Hélène with her.

'When I placed a carriage at your disposal, I meant you to use it, but we have been awaiting your return with some anxiety,' Isabella's father began.

'It is later than I thought, but if I had known you would be at home . . .'

'Yes, of course, the blame is entirely mine. Yesterday I was called away without warning, and today I await you with such impatience only because I must leave for Nantes, and I wanted to take my leave of you in person.'

'So soon?' she asked with dismay. 'On business?'

He sighed. 'I had a plan, you understand, of how I would settle in Paris, and everything would follow in proper course. But instead, events are happening out of sequence. First you arrive, sooner than expected, so I am from home more than I would wish, and cannot arrange things as I would like. Now I find I am to be away for some weeks.'

'It doesn't matter. You will not be away so very long. My cousins and I will simply make the best of it, and I feel sure you will find us just as you leave us,' said Isabella, resigned.

'That is the very promise I was hoping to extract, to carry away the reassurance that everything will remain just as it is during my absence,' he smiled. 'It will be a quiet time for you, knowing so few people in Paris, but you have your cousins, and the captain will call again.'

'We will make him welcome,' said Isabella politely. 'But you mustn't worry on my account. Hélène is teaching me French, and that should keep me occupied. And I have several friends here of my own.'

'Friends? Oh, yes, the abbé, though I find it difficult to believe he will always be able to devote as much time to you as he did today.'

'The abbé is unwell. We visited his nephew in the Collège des Irlandais, and then Dr Connor at his friends, the Bernards,' she said uneasily.

'Dr Connor,' he nodded. 'It will of course be difficult to guide your conduct from Nantes, but I know you realise the dangers of showing him too marked a sign of favour, and I will trust to your good sense.'

Isabella chose not to inquire any further into the nature of her good sense. He then took his leave of her without further discussion, though Isabella noticed that, before setting off on his journey, he exchanged some serious words with the coachman who had driven their carriage that afternoon.

*   *   *

Brighid seemed more bemused and anxious than Hélène had anticipated.

'Carroll is leaving. He has been called to Nantes on pressing business, and might be detained there for some weeks. I am to remain in charge of the household, and take full responsibility for Isabella until his return. It is more than likely that the captain will call again, and if so, he is to be made welcome and treated with the utmost hospitality.'

'The captain? It will be interesting to see how he chooses to play his cards,' mused Hélène, more to herself than to her mother.

'Indeed, though it is not the captain who is of most concern to me,' answered Brighid. 'Once again, Carroll does not take me into his confidence, as he might perhaps have done a year ago. I believe there is some problem or other regarding the cargo of one of his ships, though I do not see how that would justify such a hasty departure.'

'Is that what vexes you?' asked Hélène vaguely, her mind engaged on the captain: would Isabella rebuff him, and how would he respond?

'Not in itself Eibhlín, you are not listening to me, and your future depends on it. I think our cousin is playing some kind of game. From reading some of his papers, I have discovered that he is attempting to secure a *titre de noblesse*, a curious endeavour, since his ancestry is less than illustrious. Nevertheless, he is waiting to see how he succeeds.'

'Why not simply purchase a *secrétaire du roi*?' Hélène asked, remembering that the ambitious bourgeois families of girls in the convent had done so.

'Because, child, it does not carry the same prestige. Society is contemptuous of anyone whose pedigree is not six centuries old. For a *titre de noblesse,* he is marrying his daughter to the captain, though again, he is hoping to do better for her.'

'Is he indeed?' said Hélène.

'However, that can hardly progress any further until he returns, although we are to push his daughter at the captain at every opportunity. I fear he has tired of me, and we are being sidelined in favour of his daughter. I am no longer anything more than a glorified housekeeper, and he indulges you only at her request, as if you were her plaything. I sincerely hope *she* does not tire of you soon.'

Go raibh maith agat, a mháthair, thought Hélène. Your observations are as kind as ever. But as she was hungry, she decided to avoid provoking her mother and precipitating an argument that might keep her from her supper. 'What should I do then?' she asked.

'Oh, there is little either of us can do at the

moment, other than use his absence as best we can, and await his return.'

CHAPTER NINE

Several evenings later found all three cousins assembled in the salon. Brighid was listening to Hélène play some of the showiest pieces of her repertoire on the harpsichord, while Isabella's attention was devoted to Connor's article, which she had hidden inside one of her father's volumes, and was straining her eyes to read by firelight. She had read it many times before, but she was fascinated by the confidence with which he had distilled his thoughts on paper—it seemed to give them an import and an authority that an argument with an abbé in a half-forgotten inn could never have. She was therefore unwilling to be interrupted when their visitor was announced.

Monsieur le Capitaine, thought Hélène with a half-malicious amusement as he entered the salon. Self-interest brought you back very soon. Nevertheless, she fingered the polecat trim on her gown, relieved that she had dressed with care. Her mother was also glad she had prepared herself for this eventuality, and curled her lip in anticipation as she noticed how reluctantly Isabella closed her book—could the girl's indifference go unnoticed?

'What are you reading, Mademoiselle?' he asked, seating himself beside her on the sofa.

'A novel and informative piece of work,' she answered, pressing it tightly shut with both hands. 'I have of late been attempting to improve my woefully inadequate education.'

'That is commendable, in a young woman ignorant of so many matters,' he said, trying to conceal his puzzlement. Had her education been neglected? he wondered. Surely her family had been prosperous enough to ensure she had been taught reading, writing, and some accomplishments? He even thought he remembered her talking about some governess on his last visit.

'You, on the other hand, are brimming with tales of the battlefield and the world,' said Hélène, not wishing to be excluded from the sparring. 'I understand you distinguished yourself during the American war?'

He glowed with pride, confident now. 'That is true, in a manner of speaking, although Grenada was my finest moment, when the great Dillon led our regiment to victory against the English garrison.'

'I remember hearing glowing reports of him,' smiled Brighid. 'I arrived in Saint-Domingue not long after the war ended, not the most reassuring of times. But my courage was bolstered by the thought that the scion of one of our great Irish families had vanquished the British Army in those very lands. He then governed Saint Christopher until the peace, did he not?'

'How did the people of Grenada respond to these events?' asked Isabella, her mind picturing redcoated Irishmen fighting redcoated Englishmen in a land that must be far too hot for such exertion. 'Did they not object to other countries fighting out their grievances on their soil?'

'You misunderstand the situation,' answered the captain benignly. 'Grenada is an English colony, and as we were fighting on behalf of our American friends who had risen against English rule, it was a brilliant coup to capture such an island so early in the campaign. But then, our Brigade has such an illustrious history, and the Dillons are a noble family—our Colonel's deceased wife was a favourite lady-in-waiting of the Queen.'

'On the contrary, *Capitaine*, you misunderstand me,' said Isabella dryly. 'Ireland, for example, is also an English colony. If the French had decided to capture it during the war, and then fought the British Army on our soil, I imagine it would have been of huge significance, particularly in light of the role of the Irish Brigade in the French Army. What I am asking you is, what significance did this war have for the people of Grenada? Was it simply a nuisance?'

'There is no comparison between Grenada

and Ireland, if that is what you mean,' said the captain.

'I understand what you are trying to say,' Brighid told Isabella, taken aback by her reasoning. 'But life in that part of the world is very different, and fraught with perils you are thankfully ignorant of. She turned to the captain with interest. 'It must have been a very turbulent time. Was there unrest among the slaves?'

'Slaves?' Isabella asked, surprised.

The captain really did not know what to make of her. '*Les nègres*, Mademoiselle. They work the estates.'

'They are Africans, brought to the West Indies by ship, and sold to the estate owners,' Brighid added.

'People are bought to work the land?' Isabella said uneasily. She hesitated, then asked: 'Did my father own Africans?'

'Of course,' said Brighid, noting Isabella's discomfort and wondering where it might lead.

'Do not look so alarmed, Mademoiselle,' said Captain O'Shea, in an attempt at reassurance. 'After all, they are not people, like you or I.'

'*Monsieur le Capitaine*,' said Isabella, struggling to contain her anger, 'I am unaware of the nature of the connection between you and my father, but I can assure you that it does not permit you to presume a connection between us or an assumption that I might share any of your opinions.'

'Come now, Mademoiselle,' he said angrily, feeling he had suffered her long enough. 'You cannot fault me for treating you with the same courtesy that would be welcomed by most others of your sex.'

'It amuses them to have their thoughts and feelings so consistently insulted?' she inquired.

'My poor Isabella, you are looking flushed,' exclaimed Brighid, thinking it in everyone's interests to put an end to this particular interview. 'You really must excuse us,' she smiled meaningfully at the captain. 'But as she is unwell . . .'

'I understand,' he said, standing up to take his leave.

'My daughter will see you out,' she continued, touching her daughter's shoulder. Hélène, still seated at the harpsichord, was surprised and intrigued by the exchange that had just taken place. *'Eibhlín,'* her mother whispered gently. *'Tóg do chuid ama.'* Hélène understood: Do not hasten back, I have something to attend to here.

Once they had left, Brighid took her place at the harp and coaxed the strings. In the forefront of her mind, she held the knowledge of the circumstances in which Isabella had parted with her aunt and uncle.

'It surprises me that you were unaware of the nature of your father's business in Saint-Domingue,' she said. 'Your father did intend several of his favourites for this house, but they died on the crossing, and he decided not to send for any more, having acquired a taste for European servants.'

She produced soft waves of sound that seeped into Isabella's consciousness like tainted water. Brighid could see the girl becoming more troubled.

'Why distress yourself unduly?' Brighid asked. 'I admit the thought can be disconcerting at first. Indeed, more than a few of us are a little taken aback on arriving in the colonies when we see how things are done, but one soon grows accustomed to it.'

'What is it one grows accustomed to?' Isabella persisted. 'I know so little . . . What is life like on my father's estate?'

Brighid bent her head over her instrument, considering what to say. Could her words precipitate an estrangement between father and daughter? She hesitated, fearing Carroll's wrath. 'Your father is a *Grand Blanc*, widely respected among the *Colons.* He has a large *Habitation,* which, like all other estates, requires a large quantity of slaves for tending the sugar cane.'

'My father's wealth, then, is generated from the production and sale of sugar. That much, I believe I was aware of. What I failed to realise was, firstly, that he required a large number of workers, and secondly, that he bought Africans for that purpose. But why resort to such an ugly practice, why take such extreme measures? Africa is so very far away . . .'

'My dear, as I told you before, the exigencies of life are very different in Saint-Domingue. The heat enervates white people—at first I could not bear it, and found it a struggle to survive from day to day—The *nègres,* on the other hand, were born and bred in the eye of the blistering sun. They are far more capable of tending the cane than Europeans are, and could even be considered fortunate in a way. I believe most of them were slaves in their own countries, and the others either prisoners of war or criminals sentenced to death, before the intervention of the traders.'

'Are they then grateful to the *colons?*' Isabella asked incredulously. 'Is there no show of discontent, no resentment at being forced to do work anyone else would balk at, in a land they did not choose?'

'We are all of us victims of circumstance. In this world, choice is the luxury of few,' Brighid exclaimed resentfully. Composing herself, she added: 'My dear, nobody gives the *nègres* a second thought. If you wish to pursue the matter, I can show you some particulars that will answer your questions, but I cannot take responsibility for having done so. Your father left you in my charge, and I cannot have him accuse me of poisoning your fancies on his return.'

'You speak as though you think him guilty,' said Isabella. She had often felt that her cousin disliked her. Now, she felt this feeling confirmed. 'Do you then think the *nègres* less fortunate than you just said?'

'No, my dear. Rather, it is the fact that I am about to compromise my position here by granting you access to his private papers by means of duplicate keys he is unaware I possess.'

'I understand,' said Isabella with distaste. 'You want my word that my father will not learn of this. But I hesitate to rifle through the belongings of another.'

'As you wish,' Brighid shrugged. 'But rest assured, you will not find what you seek by other means, as your father will never respond to questions phrased in such a way. Nor did your uncle, I imagine, though I believe you were curious about those business affairs that took him away so often, and occupied so many hours at his desk?'

What did it matter? thought Isabella. These papers had already been exposed to her cousin's eyes. What difference did it really make if she were to see them too? 'Very well. Let us go now, then,' she said.

Brighid led Isabella to the library, where she unlocked the *cartonnier* beside the *secrétaire*. 'Baptism records,' she said, handing Isabella a sheaf of papers. 'All the slaves were baptised, though they persisted in their heathen practices, being incapable of grasping even the simplest catechism. But your father found these a useful way of keeping track of his numbers.'

She continued to rummage among the contents: 'Some notes regarding the *Code Noir*. Your father followed these guidelines quite closely, providing the specified food and clothing. He also referred to it for guidance on discipline matters, ordering the necessary whippings for those who stole from him, and punishing more serious offences as he saw fit . . .'

Isabella's newly acquired, elementary French enabled her to identify a few words: Food, Clothing, Slave, Property. All written in her father's hand: *Discipline. Article XXXVI. Batrus de verges, Margués d'une fleur de lis*.

All the time observing her closely, Brighid handed her a leather-bound ledger. 'This details the instances of runaway slaves.'

'Whatever are you doing?' asked Hélène, coming upon them in the library.

Isabella could not respond. She was tracing out the dates of recovered slaves, and the consequent date and method of death. Hélène gazed at her, perplexed. She had returned to the empty salon with a little seed of triumph. Captain O'Shea had lost some of his self-possession for just a moment when, with an amused sparkle, she had apologised for Isabella's behaviour. He had muttered something about despairing of the situation, and she had seized the opportunity to proffer whatever assistance she could give. He had hastily informed her of a particular café, where he could be found at a particular hour, should she ever have any information to impart. Even before he had finished, she could sense that he regretted taking her into his confidence, and that he was wondering what could have possessed him. Nevertheless, what was done was done, and Hélène felt she had somehow gained the upper hand. She was now surprised to discover that Isabella had developed an ashen pallor in her absence.

'What is the matter? Are you unwell?' she asked.

'Would that my father had remained a ship captain and never owned a single acre of sugar cane,' she said finally.

'He kept the ships' logs from his seafaring days,' said Brighid, selecting another key, and another old ledger. 'It was his success as captain of a *négrier* that enabled him to buy his own ships, you know. Let's see . . . details of how much silk, textiles, arms and munitions brought to Africa to barter with the traders, how many *nègres* secured . . . that seems quite a lot to be stored in the hold of one ship, I don't wonder so few of them survived the crossing to Saint-Domingue.'

'Are you made of stone?' Isabella exclaimed. 'You have witnessed at close hand human suffering of a kind I didn't even know existed, and yet you remain unmoved! I respected my father for succeeding in the world despite all the disadvantages of being an Irish Catholic from the poorest, most barren corner of the land. Now I see what price he has paid for that success.'

Hélène followed Isabella from the room. 'Do not attach too much significance to my mother's words. I feel sure it was her intention to provoke you,' she said.

'Did you know about the slaves on my father's *habitation?*'

'Just what my mother told me in her letters.'

'And did you not find it distressing to learn how cruelly they were treated?'

By now, they had reached Isabella's boudoir. Hélène drew a chair up to the fire and sat down. 'Life in Saint-Domingue never struck me as particularly pleasant,' she said cautiously. 'But I cannot say that I ever gave the *nègres* much thought. I felt so alone and miserable in the convent. I was quite preoccupied with my own sorrows.'

'I understand,' said Isabella, not pausing long enough to consider whether she did or not. 'But you are older now, reunited with your mother, and living in the opulent splendour of this *hôtel.* Are you not even a little uneasy that all this is maintained by the labour of *nègres,* stolen from their own countries and forced to tend the sugar cane under pain of punishment, mutilation, or death?'

'You think too much of these things,' said Hélène uncomfortably. 'My mother and I have no other friends, we have no choice but to rely on the kindness of Cousin Carroll. He rescued us when we lost my father's farm and were starving in a cabin exposed to the full weight of the Atlantic wind. He is the only thing between us and the streets.'

'Then I too am in the same boat. But I can't possibly remain here any longer.'

'You mustn't be foolish,' Hélène exclaimed. 'Where could you go? You have no money, no friends, and you do not even speak French.'

'That much is true. I find myself utterly alone. I left my uncle's house knowing that a place awaited me in my father's, but I have nowhere to turn now. I have well and truly burned my bridges, but it cannot be helped.'

Hélène pulled back the heavy curtains, opening the window and shutters to the wind and rain that had been laying siege to the house all night long. 'That, my dear Isabella, is the Parisian winter. You want to go out into it? Catch your death of cold wandering the streets in the company of beggars? Your father struggled his entire life to shield himself and his from that. Why inquire too closely into the means?'

Isabella came to stand by Hélène at the window. 'Can you ignore suffering simply by closing your window, when everything in this *hôtel*, from the polecat trim on your gown to your dinner of champagne and oysters, has been paid for in blood?'

'What a sensitive conscience you have,' remarked Hélène uneasily, shutting the window. 'But it is easy for you to find fault with everything, because you have never experienced hardship. Compose yourself, and reflect that your father's fortune is no different from that of many others.'

'You remind me a little of my aunt,' said Isabella quietly.

'You will achieve nothing by leaving here,' said Hélène, lighting the room. 'Cast those thoughts aside, at least until morning. You will see things more clearly when you are rested.'

Isabella seemed so dispirited that Hélène could only leave her as she was until morning. She went in search of her mother, and found her in her apartment, drinking carefully measured liquid from heavily leaded crystal. 'What a scene,' she said. 'It leaves me in need of a searing shot of Saint-Domingue rum.'

'It was badly done,' said Hélène, noting with disquiet how quickly her mother emptied her glass. 'The day you came to fetch me from the convent, you told me that Carroll's entire fortune would not recompense you for your years in Saint-Domingue, but I cannot understand why you use Isabella so. Perhaps you seek to drive her from under his roof?'

'Come now, Eibhlín. Our merchant

princess's tantrums are entirely of her own making.'

'Her sensibilities are singular, and highly susceptible,' Hélène admitted. 'But you played them skilfully: I witnessed the final part of your scene, and saw how close you brought her to tears.'

Her mother rose with some difficulty. 'Help me to bed, Eibhlín. My health is not what it once was, and the momentary relief of that pernicious drink will have exacted its own toll by morning. You have seen how Isabella is with the captain. She cannot leave things alone. She craves knowledge so badly, why should I have held back?'

'Because she has led a sheltered life,' said Hélène. 'She has been carefully and delicately woven, like the finest silk, and she is just as easily torn.'

'Oh, I am inclined to think her more robust. She has already shown an ability to fend for herself.'

'With the help of her friends, yes,' said Hélène doubtfully. 'There is one in particular, who holds considerable sway over her imagination. If only you had left the matter in my hands, I might have seen to it that she disappointed her father without jeopardising all her chances of future happiness.'

'You mean marriage to the physician, I suppose,' said her mother scornfully. 'Struggling to make ends meet on a limited income, left penniless should he die first . . . though I understand Dear, Misguided Aunt has a special liking for him? Would that they had both remained in Dublin and resolved the matter there.'

'There has been no declaration, no acknowledgement of feeling, even. For reasons of their own, they were both drawn to Paris first, and it is here it must be settled,' said Hélène thoughtfully. 'But there is so little time now.'

Brighid closed her eyes. 'Spare me your tender tale, and pour me another drink before you go, if only to ward off my dreams a little longer.'

CHAPTER TEN

Isabella locked the door after Hélène's departure, knowing that in seeking shelter in this newly furnished apartment, she was essentially wrapping herself in the treacherous folds of her father's wealth. And I know so little, she thought. How did I come to be so ill-equipped to live in the world?

She looked out of the window, far into the rain-strewn Parisian night, remembering all the hopes she had woven around this city. France, where so many Wild Geese had found shelter. A Catholic country with a benign king, where the quest for worldly success, to compensate for wrongs committed at home, would surely not harden the soul to the point where one became like her uncle, caring nothing for the suffering of others as long as one's own family had silk gowns.

My father, the *Grand Blanc*, she thought. Look how wrong I was. She remained there for some time, lost in contemplation of the papers she had taken with her from the library.

*   *   *

The following morning, Hélène brought up a breakfast tray of coffee and *petits pains*, and spoke coaxingly to Isabella from behind the locked door. 'You should try to eat a little—you mustn't make yourself ill.'

The door opened. 'Thank you Hélène, I'm not a child.'

Nevertheless, she drank the coffee, angry that such a small thing as breakfast could bespeak complicity with this household. She then got ready to go out.

'Where are you going?' Hélène asked, uneasily watching her.

'Do not distress yourself,' said Isabella ironically. 'As you have already made clear, it is not yet in my power to leave this household.'

Hélène pondered this for a moment, and then hurried off to see to her own toilette, intending to accompany Isabella wherever she went.

'Isabella!' she exclaimed, stopping her in the hall. 'I am looking forward to our walk after yesterday's rain.' She then led her silent cousin through the *vestibule* and out into the street.

'Why the show?' Isabella fumed when they were some distance from the house.

'Because you could not have left alone. It was bad enough that you did not order the carriage. The fewer tales the servants have to tell your father, the better.' She lowered her voice: 'I understand his wrath is to be feared and avoided at all costs.'

What a strange girl, Isabella thought. So pitiless last night, and now, almost frightened on my behalf. 'Thank you for your concern,' she said more calmly. 'I see that the *moeurs* of fashionable society are to be adhered to at all times. I wish to visit Dr Connor, and as I am unfamiliar with these streets, I would be grateful if you could direct me there. But I wish to visit him alone.'

It is as I had hoped, thought Hélène. Perhaps everything will turn out as planned. There is the danger that he might be put off by her constant dramas, but as I believe most of her opinions were shaped by him, there is no reason why he shouldn't be somewhat charmed by her turning to him.

'Very well,' she said. 'I will accompany you there, and return for you later.'

*   *   *

Connor was not alone. His visitor was a woman in her late twenties, who stood in the Bernards' drawing-room with proprietorial ease and assurance. She was very fashionably dressed. Everything, from her elaborate coiffure to her pointed, jewelled shoes, looked as if it had been artfully assembled: there were numerous ornaments twisted into the coils of her hair—flowers, birds, gazebos, shepherdesses, to name but a few. Her eyes swiftly ran over Isabella with a mocking scrutiny before she laughed and said something to Connor in such rapid French that Isabella could not follow. Isabella became conscious that she had not taken any particular pains with her own toilette. She was wearing her Dublin dress, and though it was certainly not old, its simplicity made it seem rather rough and unpolished next to this strange lady. But what should I care, thought Isabella angrily. I did not come here to compete with the epitome of Parisian elegance.

Connor made a hasty response to the lady, before turning to speak to Isabella in English, and introducing the Frenchwoman as Madame Fourier. She raised her eyebrows at the description of Isabella as an *Irlandaise*, and again her eyes examined her, as though she would be mildly amused to learn the reason for the *Irlandaise*'s visit. Then she departed, accompanied by Madame Bernard.

'Is her husband a friend of the Bernards?' Isabella asked, wondering who she was.

'Madame Fourier is a widow,' he answered, tidying a few books and pamphlets that lay scattered on a table. 'Her late husband was a very learned man, as was her father, I believe. He gave her the benefit of an enlightened education. She is well-read in several languages, and acquainted with some of the best works of modern philosophy, which is truly rare indeed. She was also sufficiently impressed with my article to invite me to her salon.'

'Indeed?' asked Isabella, wondering that her toilette left so much time for reading.

'Yes, and she also brought me a copy of the latest *Gazette de Leyde*. It's published abroad, and reveals what actually happens behind the closed doors of government institutions and *parlements*.'

'How fascinating,' said Isabella, looking with interest at the newspaper he showed her. 'I too have read your article. But that is not the reason for my calling. There is something I must show you. It concerns my father's Saint-Domingue estate.'

She handed him the first sheaf of papers, detailing punishments on the plantation. His countenance proved difficult to read, but it had perceptibly darkened by the time he looked up.

'Where did you get these?' he asked.

'My father's cousin Brighid showed them to me, not trusting I should find them so distressing.'

'Did she indeed,' he said, his attention returning to the papers. 'What motive could she have had, then? Is she Mademoiselle Ní Fhlathartaigh's mother?'

'Yes.'

He drew his own conclusions and continued studying the material. 'Then the *colons* are every bit as barbaric as I suspected,' he said finally.

'Doctor Connor, did you know that my father owned slaves?'

'I didn't know he was the proprietor of a Saint-Domingue estate.'

'I didn't understand the significance of the fact until last night. I would scarcely have credited my cousin Brighid's words, had she not shown me those papers. I might have thought that my father could not commit such atrocities, and that things were perhaps not as they seemed. But the words speak clearly: my father has inflicted unimaginable cruelties. I had been told he made the estate far more profitable than it had been under its previous owners, and now I see how.'

'According to these notes on the *Code Noir*, he consulted regularly with his fellow *colons*. One was as barbaric as the next.'

'But to think an Irishman who had suffered

from the Penal Code all his life could in all good conscience inflict the *Code Noir*.'

'What is conscience when there is a profit to be made?' was the physician's ironic reply.

She fingered the closed ship logs, which she had delicately placed on a table, sensible of what they contained. 'My cousin told me that his first success was as captain of a *négrier*, which provided him with the capital to buy his own ships. I wonder that my aunt never told me. She would have known, would she not? She was with my mother in Nantes when I was born.'

'Nantes is one of France's main slave ports, so it is scarcely surprising that your father would have had some involvement in it, and it is likely that your mother and aunt knew about it. But they would have taken it as part of his business. Think of your uncle: a merchant owns a number of ships, which he uses to export and import a variety of goods. Your father would have exported silk and textiles to Africa, and imported sugar and coffee from Saint-Domingue. The slaves that were carried in the intermediary passage, referred to here as *bois d'ébène*, would have been considered as another form of good.'

'But they were not dealing in ebony wood,' said Isabella. 'Did that never trouble them?'

'I have only ever stopped in Nantes briefly, but slavery and the slave trade are so much a part of life there that people simply take it for granted without giving it much thought. The plantations of Saint-Domingue are a very long way from here.'

'I see. And Cousin Brighid said the Church had given the *colons* its blessing, because the slaves were rescued by baptism,' said Isabella, recalling Brighid's words.

'Of course. Just as the plantations of Ireland were justified on the basis that the Catholics were superstitious pagans.'

'She also said most of the *nègres* were criminals, sentenced to death in their own country, but rescued from this fate by slavery. Another barbaric justification.'

'It is,' he agreed. 'But it is a very old rationalisation. There is a long and ancient history of legal bondage and servitude. Many of the *philosophes* write rapturously about the Greek and Roman civilisations, but they too were founded on the labour of slaves, many of whom were captured during war, and enslaved instead of killed. But I believe that in some instances, they could actually earn their freedom back.'

'But there are no longer any slaves in Europe, are there?' she asked.

'We no longer have captives forced to work the land, if that is what you mean, but the serfs of Russia, for instance, exist in a form of legal bondage. They are the property of the landlord, and must work for him so many days a week in return for their miserable plot of land. Indeed, the Irish peasants exist in such a state of misery that their lot too could be considered similar to that of the serfs.'

'But they are not slaves? They are free to go where they please?'

'For the little good it does them. Though there was a time when Cromwell had thousands of them sent to the colonies as indentured servants—a human traffic as abominable as your father's.'

'Then it is a practice deeply ingrained into the commerce of the world,' said Isabella slowly. 'The *Code Noir* was composed at the behest of the same monarchy that offered sanctuary to the Stuarts and their Irish followers. So the French kings are every bit as bad as you told me they were.'

'Kings, noblemen, and merchants are all alike in wishing to safeguard their own interests. Saint-Domingue is one of Louis's most prized possessions, the jewel of the Antilles, because of all the wealth generated from the cane-fields.'

'He could not then be persuaded to abolish slavery?'

'In a court as corrupt as his?' Connor scoffed. 'Do you really think the voice of compassion and humanity could be heard above the clamourings of the *colons* who keep him rich in taxes? Or the cries of the Nantes merchants that the livelihood of their city would be ruined, their shipyards laid to waste

. . . ? It would be rejected as detrimental to France's economy. I imagine the only way to convince *them* that abolition is in their best interests would be if it were more profitable to employ free men.'

'But what about the Enlightenment?' she asked. 'Surely the *philosophes* have condemned slavery?'

'On the contrary, of all the books and pamphlets I have read, very few have addressed the subject of slavery in the French colonies. They quite simply haven't concerned themselves with it,' he replied.

'What then are their concerns?'

Connor shrugged his shoulders. 'You are acquainted with many of them—a move towards reason, and a re-evaluation of religion, a debate on the merits of different models of political economy . . .'

'I understand, and this concept of materialism my father talks about,' said Isabella, disappointed. 'Is that it, then?'

'The concept of slavery tends to be explored only in a symbolic context,' said Connor thoughtfully. 'Rousseau wrote that Man is born free, but is everywhere in chains, because civilised society fetters man to the extent that the best one can ever hope for is to exchange one form of slavery for another. He is dead now, but he was one of the best thinkers of the age, though many of his ideas are so diametrically opposed to the prevailing schools of thought that he did not consider himself to be a *philosophe* at all.'

'What else did he write?' she asked.

'Oh, many things,' said Connor, his mind running. 'He wrote that people such as the native Caribs of the Antilles existed in a pure state of nature, unfettered by worldly vices and pursuits.'

'Was he unaware that the Antilles were divided into *habitations* such as my father's?'

'Rousseau had never been to the Antilles—he simply used the image of the Savage, with his simple diet and vigorous, well-exercised limbs, as a vehicle to analyse the ills of civilised society, where fine clothes hide our weak, diseased bodies, and intrigue corrupts our minds.'

Isabella absorbed this in silence.

'Then, in *The Social Contract*, he talked about the ancient civilisations of Greece and Rome, and stated that society is so corrupt that slavery is the best we can do,' Connor continued.

'He condones slavery, then?'

'On the contrary, he condemned society for being too corrupt to function in a better manner. He saw everyone, from the richest to the poorest, as a slave. The rich man is a slave to his own desire for money, luxury and position, and so he enslaves the poor man to provide those luxuries with the fruit of his toil.'

'What is the solution, then? How does one

return to an uncorrupt existence?'

'One flees the city, I suppose, to lead a simpler life in the country,' Connor smiled faintly.

'I can identify with the need for flight,' said Isabella. 'But having already fled Dublin for Paris, I find myself with nowhere to go now. I cannot remain in my father's house, but what can I do? I seem to have achieved nothing by leaving my uncle's house.'

'Well, I don't recommend the country,' said Connor. 'I grew up there, on an estate managed by my father, who was every bit as corrupt as yours.'

'Was he? When I think of the country, I think of my friend Pamela Murtogh. Country society does not seem so very different from the city's. But at least you were able to leave. What use is my conscience if I have to stay in my father's house anyway?'

'It is an intolerable situation,' he said, troubled. At least his education and profession had given him the freedom to seek his own way in the world, whereas this young woman could choose only between the protection of her father and that of her uncle.

Isabella sighed, and turned her thoughts away from her own predicament. 'Has there been anything at all written specifically about the *nègres* of Saint-Domingue?' she asked.

'Some men have written accounts of their voyages. The Abbé Raynal's *Histoire*

Philosophique et Politique des Indes would be the most interesting to you. Several years ago, I took an interest in reading descriptions of the colonies. I was curious to learn what similarities exist between the English and French treatment of their respective colonies. The abbé calls for an abolition of slavery, albeit a gradual one, because he claims the *nègres* have been so brutalised by their experience that an immediate emancipation would be too abrupt—instead, he recommends a period of transition and acclimatisation.'

'It is singular, is it not, the thought that they would need time to grow accustomed to freedom,' she said, turning the concept over in her mind.

'It is almost akin to the belief that the Catholics of Ireland would be ill-equipped to manage their own affairs if the remaining Penal Laws were lifted,' he agreed.

'Very few French writers have concerned themselves with slavery then?'

'As I have said, the Antilles are a long way away. There is so much poverty to be seen here on the streets of Paris. That has a greater impact on society's sensibilities. One attempts to alleviate one's conscience through charity and benevolence, distributing food and clothing among the poor during winter, preferably in full view of one's most influential acquaintances. The deplorable state of France quite naturally preoccupies a lot of writers, and when there are so many restraints on what one is even permitted by law to publish . . .'

Isabella brightened at this: 'I know that the power of the printed word holds a particular fascination for you, and I thought about this when I was reading your article—you might be a Catholic physician, who can never hope for political office in his own country, but you can at least record your ideas on paper, where they might one day leave an indelible impression on a reader's mind.'

'That is true,' he smiled.

'Then why not write an article or a pamphlet, addressing the incongruity of the Irish involvement in the slave trade, tracing the path these men have followed to become *Grands Blancs*? It would show the lengths some people will go to secure worldly position, and you could plead for the abolition of this dreadful system far more eloquently than I ever could.'

'Perhaps,' he said reluctantly, looking as if many obstacles were coming to mind. 'But I have no experience of the colonies.'

'Use the documentation I have given you. Much of what you need to know is there.'

'You would wish me to denounce your father, then?' he asked in a voice full of reservations. 'Have you given any thought to your position? It is one thing for me to write about the role of Irishmen as plantation owners. It is quite another thing for your father and your family name to be implicated in the matter, and it is something else again to use material that you have taken from his personal papers.'

'I understand,' she said. 'I would not wish to create difficulties for you. It was foolish of me, but I came to Paris hoping to find a more sympathetic world, and instead I found a house infinitely more corrupt than the one I had left behind. I suppose I thought that if I could persuade you to write a political work, then that would at least be something, but . . .'

'What cunning traps society sets,' he exclaimed. 'It is easy for me to sit here condemning the world, yet were it not for consideration of your place in that world, I would gladly offer you my own protection. The Bernards would not object to your staying here, and I could get lodgings elsewhere and write whatever I chose. But the world would misinterpret that protection, and should you ever return to Dublin, your name would be gravely compromised. I cannot write such a piece, much as I would like to.'

'I am confused,' said Isabella. 'Though I must insist that I did not come here to impose on your kindness.'

'Do you have any idea of the steps your father might take if he learned of your involvement in such a project?' he asked.

Connor walked to the window and looked out, attempting to gather his thoughts. The sky was dull, but the street was full of activity. Suddenly, a young man burst through the crowd and rushed up the steps of the house. Connor heard a commotion at the door.

'If you'll excuse me for just one moment,' he said hastily, leaving the room.

Isabella went to the window, wondering what he had seen there, if anything. She heard a clock chime, and realised it was a great deal later than she had thought. Had she really been there so long?

Connor returned with a note in hand. 'It would appear that your cousin Mademoiselle Ní Fhlathartaigh has been busy in your absence,' he said hurriedly, skimming the contents again. 'She requests me to bring you immediately to this address. She requires me to attend a friend of hers.' He paused, perplexed. 'What the devil has she been doing?' he asked. 'And how does she know you're here?'

'She insisted on accompanying me here, but I've no idea what she's been doing. Perhaps we should go—it is late, and she had arranged to collect me here at about this time.'

Whatever their respective doubts, they therefore set off together.

CHAPTER ELEVEN

That morning, Hélène had initially been annoyed on being left alone by Isabella. It is all very well for her, she thought. Mademoiselle Carroll may create as many scenes as she likes about her father, his ships, and his *habitation*, but she refuses to appreciate that it gives her the power to do as she pleases. She runs to her physician for solace without once taking into consideration that I must find something to do until it is time to fetch her. But then Hélène recollected that Captain O'Shea might well be at his café at this hour, and her spirits lifted. After all, she thought, Isabella did not want me to accompany her. It was I who insisted, having her best interests at heart.

As she made her way on foot towards the Boulevard Saint-Germain, she was struck by a sense of freedom. She too could do as she pleased, if only for a few hours. Her courage almost deserted her when she entered the café and saw the captain engaged in rowdy conversation with a number of other officers, some dressed in the red of the Irish Brigade, some in the blue of the French Army. Having come this far, she made herself advance, a little hesitantly. He was the first of his party to see her, and looked startled, but this quickly gave way to a sense of triumph at being sought out by such a fashionably dressed young woman, alone and unchaperoned.

'Mademoiselle Ní Fhlathartaigh! To what do I owe this pleasure?' he asked, addressing her in French.

The others turned their drink-clouded eyes and flushed faces towards her, and made a few ribald noises of appreciation. From their indistinct speech and stale appearances, it was clear to her that they had been up all last night, engaged in some debauchery or other, but there was nevertheless something contemptuous and humiliating in their glances.

'I have a rather disappointing message for you,' she said coldly. 'From that charming heiress who responded so badly to your recent attentions.'

The officers laughed and whistled at this, amused at the captain's quickly suppressed flash of anger.

'I will wait for you outside,' added Hélène, having seen her shot hit its target. He should never have suggested she come here. Did he think so little of her, that he could so easily expose her to the ridicule of his fellow-officers?

He soon joined her, with a smooth self-possession. 'So,' he said. 'What news of *la belle Isabelle*?'

'Mademoiselle Carroll,' said Hélène with an icy politeness, 'has made it perfectly clear that you can never win her affections. Indeed, as you seem capable only of incurring her most vehement dislike . . .' She indicated that the situation was hopeless, feigning a deliberately affected gesture of compassion.

The captain was unsurprised. He gave her a sly smile. 'Mademoiselle Carroll made her feelings perfectly clear last night. Was this the sole purpose of your visit?'

She flushed. 'It had been my intention to offer you some insight into my cousin's tastes and fancies, so as to improve your chances,' she said uncomfortably. 'But on reflection, I fear that any such attempt would be futile, and as you are in more urgent need of sleep, and dare I suggest it, a change of clothes, I think it best to bid you good day.'

The captain sighed, adjusting his wig and viewing his burgundy-stained coat with distaste to the cold morning light. 'You must forgive my bad temper,' he said. 'I have had a long night. Allow me to take you home. You were ill-advised to come here alone—I should never have suggested it.'

Was she dismissed? she wondered. Because she had nothing of note to impart, she could no longer command his attention.

'That is very kind of you,' she said distantly. 'But I have other plans. I had intended to call on a young acquaintance of mine, a student at the Irish College.'

This seemed at last to make an impression on him. 'A clerical student?' he asked with interest.

'Yes,' she answered. 'We met quite recently and struck up a most remarkable friendship.'

'What kind of friendship could you possibly have with a soon to be ordained priesteen?'

She lowered her eyes, deliberately refrained from answering for a moment, then added: 'I was hoping you would be of some assistance to me, as I cannot very well call there alone, and ask to see him . . .'

'Was that the real purpose of your visit, to implicate me in your intrigue?' he asked, wounded pride mingling with amusement. 'Could Mademoiselle Carroll not have accompanied you?'

'There are some matters I think it best to conceal from her,' said Hélène, smiling as sweetly as she could.

The captain deliberated, and evidently decided this was a diverting way of starting his new day, for he offered her his arm and they set off at a brisk pace. Hélène struggled to keep up with him, marvelling that he could hold up so well after a long night of dissipation.

'I am glad the demands of debauchery have not yet taken their toll of your constitution,' she remarked.

'And I that society has not yet taught you to curb your tongue,' he responded. But he hailed a *fiacre* to take them the remainder of the short journey to the Irish College. He seemed fresher now after the exertion in the cold air. 'I am indeed blessed with a formidable constitution,' he said. 'It can sustain the rigours of any climate, and I can function for days with little or no sleep, which is a marked advantage on the battlefield. But it is here in Paris, when I am reduced to fighting the tedium of all-night card games, that I find myself tested to the limit.'

'I understand,' smiled Hélène. 'I imagine the constantly flowing liquor is yet another hindrance.'

'Do not judge me by my stains,' he said wryly. 'My means are so limited that I only drink what I must—for obvious reasons, I find this both prudent and rewarding. Though it is hardly pleasant to be constantly surrounded by drunken officers, who cannot function effectively in a battle situation, but think their military skills superior to your own, merely because their position in society guarantees them automatic promotion.'

'But surely wars are won on the basis of military strategy, and only the most brilliant officers triumph?' she asked curiously.

'I'm afraid the truth is not so simple,' he said warming to the subject now that he had the sympathetic ear of a beautiful girl. 'Certainly merit can advance your cause, particularly in a time of war, but social rank will always play its part against you—the French aristocracy looks after its own, and ensures they are given the least dangerous postings, while officers like me risk our lives on a daily basis. Do not be fooled by the reputation of the Irish Brigades. The lives of our men will always be dispensed with first, and we will always be placed in the most foolhardy of situations.'

'Our countrymen's exploits on the battlefields of the world are famed throughout Ireland! I had no idea they were treated so badly, though Sarsfield's death at the Battle of Landen is the most famous of all, when he looked at his blood and said: "Would that this were shed for Ireland." But what about Fontenoy, when we avenged the Treaty of Limerick?'

'Our men were used most shamefully at Fontenoy,' exclaimed the captain. 'That charge against the British Array was brave and courageous, I could never deny them that, but for all those men to be thrown so casually to their deaths . . . and many of them at the hands of fellow countrymen fighting on the English side . . . So few Irishmen now venture their lives as foot-soldiers in the Brigades, that we are reduced to recruiting among foreign mercenaries and petty thieves!'

'So the Irish Brigades are Irish in name only!' Hélène was struck by this, and pondered it a moment. 'The odds are against you, Captain. I wonder that you do not resign your commission altogether.'

He shook his head emphatically: 'Make no mistake, I have a taste for the military life, and my uncle has some influence at court. This, coupled with my reputation, is what sustains me in Paris.'

Of course, thought Hélène. Those card games form part of a carefully planned strategy to ingratiate yourself with the power brokers of French society. Such dedication will surely pay off. 'But career advancement does not in itself promise financial reward,' she said.

'No,' he answered, amused. 'That too must be worked towards.'

'Indeed,' she said acerbically. 'Though your attentions to Mademoiselle Carroll are likely to be in vain. Perhaps it is time to look elsewhere.'

He was silent, and Hélène wondered if she had gone too far. 'It is now for you to forgive me,' she said.

He smiled stiffly. 'What is your exact relation to Mademoiselle Carroll?' he asked.

'We are cousins of sorts—my mother is a cousin of Monsieur Carroll.'

'Of course,' he said as he helped her from the coach. They paused outside the large gates of the Collège des Irlandais. 'Would you like me to make the arrangements for you to take your young man out for the day?'

Hélène's eyes flashed appreciation as he knocked on the entrance and deployed what charm he possessed on the college superiors.

'Mademoiselle Ní Fhlathartaigh!' exclaimed Donnchadh with surprise, making it clear this was no pre-arranged meeting. 'To what do I owe this honour?'

'I was simply longing to renew our Gaelic conversation,' Hélène said, pausing to think up a more substantial excuse.

The captain noticed her discomfort and laughed, but decided to come to her rescue. 'And I had heard such wonderful reports that I too was longing to meet you,' he said.

Donnchadh seemed a little baffled by this, but his attention had now been seized by the captain's uniform. 'A captain in the Irish Brigade? I have often dreamed of taking my place on the battlefield!'

The captain looked at the young student and shook his head. 'Such battles are better fought in dreams,' he said. 'Though several of my fellow officcrs did see fit to abandon their studies here in favour of a commission.'

'Did they indeed?' asked Hélène, looking at Donnchadh in a new light, trying to picture him in an officer's red coat.

He coloured a little under her gaze, and the captain cleared his throat. 'The *fiacre* awaits us, if you're quite ready to leave,' he said.

All three arranged themselves in the *fiacre*. The captain seemed a little put out by her attention to Donnchadh, and Hélène was secretly pleased. Leaning slightly towards the student, she said: 'I so enjoyed the last afternoon we spent together, Donnchadh. What do you recommend we do today?'

'If you don't object,' remarked the captain, 'I'd like to return home first to change my coat.'

Hélène silently welcomed this opportunity to see his uncle's house. She knew from her mother's words not to anticipate too much, but the *fiacre* brought them to a street not far from Carroll's, and a house that was attractive from the outside, though the inside was very sparsely furnished. The Captain left them in a small salon, muttering vague assurances about returning shortly.

Now alone together, Hélène smiled tentatively at Donnchadh. 'I'm sorry you weren't expecting me today,' she said. 'But I did want to see you again. It is not often I get to speak Gaelic, so when I found myself with the opportunity . . .'

'The pleasure is all mine, Mademoiselle,' he replied in Irish, sounding a little embarrassed. He avoided her eyes, fidgeted in the threadbare bergère he was sitting in, then got up to examine a pair of swords. 'I wonder if these are the captain's?' he said, taking one in his hand and affecting a pose. 'I am Captain O'Shea, of Dillon's. Face me at your peril.'

Several moments later, the Captain himself returned, still in his stained uniform, to see Donnchadh waving a perfectly good sword about in the most foolhardy manner, and Mademoiselle Ní Fhlathartaigh lapping it up as if she'd never seen a man wield a weapon before.

'Be careful with that' he exclaimed. 'You could hit Mademoiselle.'

'No, he won't,' said Hélène, laughing. 'He has defeated many an imaginary foe in your absence.'

'Well, as he has not the experience to do so, it is best he lays that sword aside.'

Hélène raised her eyebrows at this, and turned to Donnchadh.

'Perhaps I flatter myself unduly,' countered the student, his hackles raised by the captain's snub. 'But in Ireland, I learned something of the use of a pistol and a sword. I should dearly welcome an opportunity to test my skills against yours.'

'What say you, Captain?' asked Hélène challengingly. 'I have yet to see that famed military prowess of yours in action.'

Did she doubt his reputation? he wondered angrily, glowering back at them. This Mademoiselle Ní Fhlathartaigh and her clerical student might find they had bitten off more than they could chew. 'Why not?' he said, taking down the other sword. He'd show them a thing or two. 'Let's go outside, then.'

Out they went, into an empty winter garden. The captain and the student arranged themselves in an open space at some distance from Hélène, and their swords clashed with a wary, antagonistic playfulness. She sat on a bench to watch them, but the cold stone became unbearable, and she stood up again.

'Hélène, look at this,' called Donnchadh, as he waved his sword wildly.

'Bravo, Donachadh, I am impressed,' she said, pulling her Russian beaver pelisse tightly around her for warmth, and burying her gloved hands deep inside her muff. She then began to walk back and forth, taking care not to come too close to the others. She laughed to see the captain trip over some winterdead bush and fall to the ground, only to jump up again and run at his opponent with a pretended renewal of vigour. But Donnchadh seemed impatient.

'I wish you wouldn't hold back, just because you are an officer and I a mere student,' he complained, his face bright from the exercise and the bright air. 'I'm told I can wield a sword more skilfully than most, and I should enjoy a real challenge,' he said with a sidelong glance at Hélène.

The captain looked doubtful, but as he was clearly enjoying himself too much to desist, he sprang at Donnchadh, his sword moving so fast that it blurred into a shining mirage. 'What say you now, Mademoiselle Ní Fhlathartaigh?' he asked gloatingly.

Hélène's eyes widened with awe and concern, but when she saw that Donnchadh could keep pace with him, she forgot her fears. He must have been telling the truth about his military exploits, she thought. 'You have all my admiration, Captain,' she called back. 'I imagine you reign supreme on the battlefield.'

And who would have expected a postulant priest to hold his own so well? she thought, wondering how an onlooker would view this scene. Would they think a duel was being fought over her? The idea thrilled her: Hélène, whose charms were such that men risked their lives to win her hand. She gazed at the scene with a heightened interest. 'Come on, Donnchadh!' she exhorted. 'Show the captain what you're made of!'

But then suddenly Donnchadh fell. When he failed to rise, the Captain went and bent over him anxiously. 'Do not distress yourself, it is not a deep wound,' he assured the prone figure.

Hélène ran over, and gasped at the gushing blood. 'You must send for a doctor at once,' she told the captain.

He hesitated, his face white. 'But who can we send for? This is my uncle's house, you understand. Who can we trust not to misrepresent this to my fellow officers?'

Hélène stared at him scornfully. A wounded opponent lay before him on the winter ground, and this was his first concern? 'We will send for Doctor Connor, then,' she said coldly. 'You are unacquainted with him, but I can vouch for his discretion. Oh, and we will ask Mademoiselle Carroll to accompany him! do not think it wise for us to remain apart any longer today.'

She saw from his face that he understood her cousin was the reason for the doctor's discretion. But he hastened to the house to do her bidding while she assured Donnchadh that Dr Connor was the very best doctor in Paris.

CHAPTER TWELVE

In her frantic note to Dr Connor, Hélène had omitted to explain that the specified address was that of the captain. Isabella was therefore startled when he rushed forward anxiously to greet them at the door.

'Captain O'Shea!' she said. 'What brings you here?'

'This is my uncle's house,' he said hastily. 'Doctor Connor, I believe? I am exceedingly grateful for your promptness.'

'Doctor Connor, this is Captain O'Shea, whom I believe you may have heard me speak of?' said Isabella.

She saw a glimmer of recognition in the physician's eyes as he looked at the captain afresh. So this was the Jacobite officer her father favoured, he thought, taking in everything from the sturdy build to the much-stained coat and the grey-shadowed eyes. The captain glowered slightly, conscious that he was being seen in the worst possible light by his rival.

'If you'll follow me, I have a friend in urgent need of your attention,' he said.

The captain led them to the room where Hélène was sitting by the bedside of the pale and wounded student. The doctor looked from Donnchadh's wound to the captain's blood-splattered uniform, and drew his own conclusions.

'To what does he owe this honour?' Connor inquired of the captain as he examined the wound more closely.

'It was merely in jest,' said the Captain, flustered. 'I had not intended even to scratch him—but I should never have agreed to pit my skills against his, even in play.'

'You did this?' exclaimed Isabella. 'And you excuse it as a jest! I only dread to think what damage you wreak on the battlefield.'

'You are indeed fortunate that you cannot imagine the reality of a battlefield,' he responded indignantly. 'You are thankfully blind to the true cost of defending your liberty!'

Much as he might agree with Isabella in sentiment, Dr Connor felt it his duty to intervene—Domnchadh was struggling to get a word in, and any exertion on his part was inadvisable. 'Miss Carroll, I should be grateful if you and your cousin could wait in another room—there are far too many people here. Captain O'Shea, I would ask you to remain, as I need to know exactly what took place.'

Hélène led Isabella into the adjoining room, which again was small and sparsely furnished.

'So, Cousin,' said Isabella, walking around the room. 'I find you on rather friendlier terms with both the captain and Donnchadh than I had realised. Might I ask what led to such a bloody altercation?'

'It was a mock duel of sorts,' said Hélène. 'Donnchadh was enchanted by the notion of fighting a real soldier, and the captain was only too happy to oblige.'

She thought of Donnchadh's face as he fell, and the deepest sense of guilt arose within her. If only I had not brought the captain to see him. Such foolishness. Though I did wish to see them, both of them. If only it had not ended so badly.

Isabella looked out of the window, down at the bare garden. 'And is this where he fell to shed real blood?' she asked, seeing the signs below. Leaving her cousin, she found her way outside, drawn to the scene of battle.

Hélène remained where she was, brooding and worrying as the daylight faded. Then Dr Connor came in, looking as though he too had a lot on his mind.

'Your friend's wound should heal easily,' he said. 'It was not especially deep.'

'You are too kind,' she said, uncomfortable. 'I am exceedingly grateful to you.'

Walking to the window, he stood there, troubled. Wondering what detained him there, Hélène joined him, and saw her cousin still pacing the garden. Her eyes met those of the physician. What did he seek in Paris, she wondered, that he thought to find in the Bernards' cramped apartment?

'There is nothing else for it, she must return home with you,' he said at last. 'I trust you will be so kind as to ensure your mother does not unduly torment her?'

Hélène raised her eyebrows at this. 'Is that how you account for Mademoiselle's distress?'

The doctor winced, but what could he say? For all his philosophising about the corruption of society, there was very little practical help he could offer Isabella. The cruel irony of the situation was that any steps he might take to remove her from that household or to further her cause could only serve to compromise her fixture, particularly should she ever wish to return to Dublin. But what kind of future awaited her inside the walls of her father's *hôtel*? And why did he attribute so much importance to the scandal-mongers of her aunt's circle and his former Dublin patients? This was Paris, was it not? Why should he afflict her with his own crippling confusions?

'I believe Mademoiselle Carroll has already elaborated on her distress, for the benefit of your mother's ear as well as your own,' he said shortly. 'As her anxiety has doubtless been compounded by our errand here, I suggest you fetch her and set her mind at rest while I take leave of our patient.'

For Donnchadh's benefit, he composed himself as best he could, promising to return the next day. But the anger rose in him again when, on leaving the sick room, the captain indicated that he should follow him into the salon.

'I am deeply indebted to you,' said the Captain with genuine feeling, though now that the danger was past, some of his smooth pomp was creeping back into his manner.

'I am delighted to have been of service,' replied Connor ironically. He noticed the gold of the captain's stained uniform gleaming in the flickering candlelight. Turning away, his eye fell on a well-thumbed paper lying on an old console table. The *Gazette de France*, that fawning courtier of the King, slavishly printing every last, absolutist detail of his appointment calendar for the edification of his supposedly adulatory subjects, thought Connor. This captain clearly took his social aspirations very seriously. 'How old were you when you came to France?' he asked.

'Twelve,' ventured the captain cautiously, as if the information might somehow compromise him.

'Yes,' said the doctor, considering the

information. 'By now, I imagine you have become so French in your ways that your Irish birth is no longer anything more than a minor impediment. You must forgive my frankness—my rudeness, even, but Mademoiselle Carroll has told me quite a lot about you, and the circumstances are such . . .'

'That you quite disapprove of me,' finished the captain. 'I apologise wholeheartedly for creating such a crisis, though as a physician, you must have encountered similar situations before.'

'It being your profession to destroy others, and mine to clean up the mess?'

'What mess could you be here to clean up?' The abbé's voice made Connor jump. The old man had come silently into the room and now looked baffled at finding Dr Connor there, until he saw Isabella entering the salon, followed by Hélène. 'Mademoiselle Carroll,' he exclaimed. 'I am most disappointed in you,' his tone implying: 'I thought you had severed all connections with that disreputable young man?'

'Now what is the meaning of the note I was sent? Has something happened to my nephew?' the abbé asked, becoming agitated.

'Allow me to present myself,' said the captain hastily. 'I am Captain O'Shea, of Dillon's Regiment. It is I who summoned you here to my uncle's house. You are acquainted with him, I know.'

'Yes, and I am honoured to make your acquaintance, Captain,' the abbé replied, his voice urging the captain to get to the point.

'I fear it is a rather dubious honour he has done you today, Abbé,' remarked Isabella.

The captain coloured a little. 'Yes, well, it was most unfortunate, really. Your nephew most earnestly requested me to do him the favour of clashing swords, so to speak, and as I felt I really could not refuse . . . Of course I had not intended to wound him, but . . .'

'Fortunately his condition is far from grave, and I have sutured the wound,' Connor interjected. 'But he is sleeping now, and I would be inclined to let him rest.'

'The doctor rendered us a most satisfactory service, though indeed I barely grazed your nephew.'

'It was but a playful skirmish, then?' asked the abbé gravely, but looking much relieved.

'Upon my word as an officer, I assure you he is no worse than a child who fell and cut his knee in play. It was merely as a precautionary measure that I summoned Dr Connor here and alerted you to the incident as Donnchadh's nearest and most esteemed relation . . .' Here the captain bowed to the abbé as Isabella looked on in disbelief.

'In that case, take me to him immediately, and we'll say no more of it.' The abbé then turned to Connor. 'I believe I should thank you for your services,' he said coldly. 'They will no longer be required. My nephew will in future be attended by a physician of higher calibre in every respect.'

Hastily, the captain led him out of the room while the remaining three absorbed the snub. Hélène mused on the significance of the respect the abbé had shown for the captain's rank and name, Isabella was indignant on Connor's behalf, and Connor found himself forming a resolution. If the captain could wound as he pleased and get away with it, then why should he, Connor, hesitate to write the pamphlet he wanted to write?

'Mademoiselle Carroll, you and I have some unfinished business,' he said finally.

'You wish to pursue that matter, then,' she said intently.

Hélène's eyes narrowed with speculation, having caught something pass silently between them. 'Mademoiselle Carroll and I will call here tomorrow morning to visit Donnchadh. I suggest she call on you afterwards.' This way, she, Hélène, would have a way of seeing both Donnchadh and the captain the next day.

Isabella flushed. 'The doctor and I can make our own arrangements, Cousin,' she said sharply. 'Meanwhile, I suggest we remove ourselves from this odious house before the abbé returns.'

CHAPTER THIRTEEN

The next day was cold, colder than ever. Hélène had been anxiously anticipating her mother's questions, but instead she complained of a chill and a headache.

'Put some more coal on the fire, Eibhlín. This winter is interminable,' she said, drinking the hot Saint-Domingue coffee and examining the skyline sourly, as if it were something that had been put there uniquely to spite her.

'Perhaps it will snow,' said Hélène hopefully, remembering how winter had sometimes buried the convent in a clean, achingly beautiful shroud. 'Wouldn't it be lovely, to see Paris transformed?'

'The snow would be reduced to brown slush in a matter of minutes,' said her mother shivering. Then she softened. 'Do you remember the winter when you were six?' she asked. 'It snowed for three days and three nights, and then it stopped. Do you remember how brilliant the sky was afterwards? The light against the mountains was magical, the air so silent. Of course it brought much hardship with it—several of our neighbours died, not to mention your father's best cow. But I've often thought of that winter . . . now *that*, my dear, was snow.'

Isabella opened the door and paused

uncomfortably on the threshold. She was wearing a *caraco* over her gown and pulled it tightly around her to shut out the chill of the room. 'Good morning, Cousin,' she said, addressing Hélène. 'We have some errands this morning, I think?'

Hélène looked uneasily at her mother, but the remembrance of the snow had shadowed the older woman's countenance with a weariness that made her turn away, dismissing the two girls. They exchanged few words between them as they fetched their fur pelisses and muffs and set off to call on Donnchadh.

Now that her initial panic over his wound had died down, Hélène's imagination had returned to the thrill of the moment before Donnchadh fell, when they had both been showing off for her benefit, as if they were fighting for her favour. It was a pleasing fancy, one that had quickened her pulse as she made ready to go out. Deep down, she knew it was probably foolishness, but it made the prospect of the day far more exciting: herself and the captain, together at Donnchadh's bedside! After all, Isabella had her physician. Why should she not have something too?

But they reached the captain's house only to be told that Donnchadh had been removed by the abbé to his own home, where he could be cared for by his uncle until he was fit to return to the Collège des Irlandais. Hélène was hugely disappointed, but told herself that the captain would be sure to visit Donnchadh, no matter where he was. Accordingly, they made their way to the abbé's. He received them warmly, assuring them that his nephew was sufficiently himself to receive visitors.

'He is healing remarkably well. I immediately sent for my own physician and a surgeon to verify that the wound had been sutured correctly, but fortunately the injury was not as bad as it might have been.'

'Or perhaps Doctor Connor's skill is greater than you give him credit for,' remarked Isabella, again provoked at the slur on her friend.

The abbé frowned at her. 'Am I to surmise that you have resumed your connection with him, despite all I have said on the matter?'

Isabella remained silent. A volume of images and memories rushed through her head—Connor's exchange with the abbé that night in the inn, her father visiting the abbé to verify her story . . . It all conspired to create a sense of frustration and a fear that her own thoughts and wishes would ultimately prove irrelevant, because she could not take her fate into her own hands.

'I came here only to inquire after Donnchadh,' she said. 'So if you will excuse me, I have another engagement.'

Hélène winced at the awkwardness of this hasty departure. 'I believe she had to see a *couturière*,' she told the abbé with a conciliating smile.

He appeared unconvinced, but let the matter drop, and brought her in to see his nephew.

Donnchadh's spirits had improved immensely. 'Mademoiselle Ní Fhlathartaigh!' he exclaimed. 'Have you come to rescue me from the tedium of my sickbed?'

'I doubt I am fit for such a task,' she said apologetically, though she was savouring the warmth of her welcome. 'My conduct yesterday was completely and utterly foolish. I don't know what I was thinking of, dragging the captain to visit you, and then allowing things to get so out of hand.'

Donnchadh grimaced at the reference, and touched his wound. 'Nevertheless, you had the presence of mind to summon a doctor quickly,' he said with a quick look of defiant embarrassment at his uncle.

'Has the captain been to visit today?' she asked, feigning nonchalance, sitting herself down at an old spinet which stood near the bed.

'Not yet, but he has promised to.'

She hadn't trussed him, then. If she could only prolong her call, she just might receive the reward of being the crucial third party to the interview that would then take place between wounder and wounded. But would the abbé think her presence proper, now that she was alone? To give herself time to reflect, she turned to the spinet and began to play. It was slightly out of tune, but as it had clearly been made with superior craftsmanship a long time ago, the sound was not as awful as it might have been. Its age lent it a melancholy tone, but with an almost warm timbre.

'Mademoiselle, I did not know you played so beautifully,' said the abbé with delight.

'Nor I,' agreed his nephew. 'It's a rare treat, to hear such music on a dreary winter's day.'

'And it is rare for me to hear such praise,' answered Hélène, genuinely touched. With the exception of Beaufils, the praise accorded her by her tutors and her mother had usually been tempered with criticism, faulting her for this, urging her to that. Brighid had always demanded that Eibhlín capture the precise style of her ancestors without being able to pinpoint exactly where her daughter failed in it. Even from Saint-Domingue, she had sent her instructions. And in the convent, the nuns' greatest praise was bestowed only on the girls with the most generous purses. But these two listeners had no underlying motives. Their words were truly meant, for her own musicianship, exactly as it was.

Helene touched the keys again. A shadow seemed to fall over the window, and she looked up to see it had begun to snow. Delicate, clean flakes, darkening the sky. Where were Connor and Isabella? she wondered.

*   *   *

Despite the cold, Connor and Isabella had gone to the Palais Royal.

'It is the Paris mansion of the Duc D'Orléans,' Connor explained, impatiently drumming his fingers against the window as the hackney coach began to negotiate its way through the treacherously narrow streets. 'The King has exiled him by *lettre de cachet* to the Château de Villers-Cotteret, and the Bernards and I are anxious to learn the latest news. Exiled, simply for observing that the King could not legally order the parlement to register Brienne's new loan edict!'

'But in that case, surely we cannot simply knock on the door and demand information?' asked Isabella, confused.

'Oh, no. Forgive me, I should have spoken more clearly. The Duc opened his gardens and galleries to the public some years ago—it is full of charming *allés* and curiosities, but it is the coffee-houses and bookshops that are of most interest to me. It has always been possible to hear the latest developments there, because the police are not allowed inside the grounds, and the Duc encourages the exchange of opinion and the circulation of ideas.'

They had now crossed the Seine by the Pont Neuf. Isabella shivered with cold as they entered the gardens of the Palais Royal. Two men and a woman were huddled on a bench, studying a piece of paper with animated interest. As they moved away, one of the men left the paper lying on the ground, and Connor hastily went to see what they had been reading. He scanned it quickly before handing it to Isabella—a hastily scrawled handbill, it simply recounted yesterday's gossip from Versailles. But then he espied a *colporteur*, and after exchanging a brief word with Isabella, went to inspect his wares. She watched, fascinated by the furtive transaction. The *colporteur* hurried off to another *allée*, only to be accosted while still in sight by another man. Isabella wondered if these people would ever seek out Connor's pamphlet with the same interest. If, of course he writes it, she added to herself.

Then the snow came, and despite its initial beauty, and the way it adorned the bare branches and soil like winter flowers, it soaked through the hems of her skirts and petticoats, weighing down her fur pelisse and his surtout. Like so many others, they decided it was time to seek shelter in a nearby café.

Inside, the atmosphere was heated and lively. Angry voices loudly debated the sorry state of the kingdom, whether or not the *Etats-Généraux* would ever be convoked, and even if they were, what powers could they possibly have against the despotic tyranny of a weak King and his incompetent ministers. Connor listened eagerly until they had been served their hot chocolate, whereupon he turned his attention back to their own affairs.

'Yesterday evening, at Madame Fourier's salon, I met an American journalist. He was on the final night of an extended sojourn in Paris,' he told Isabella. 'An interesting fellow. We discussed the subject of slavery in the Americas in some depth. Some states have actually abolished the institution.'

'Indeed? Some states, but not all?' she asked with a keen interest.

'No, but some did feel in all conscience that they could not condone it. The Quakers felt it went against the teachings of the bible, and were sufficiently powerful to ensure that abolition was passed by state legislature in Pennsylvania. Laws have also been passed in Vermont, Rhode Island, Connecticut, and even Massachusetts, I think. The other states choose to disagree, though I find it ironic that they should also uphold the American Constitution, which states so clearly that all men are born equal. Nevertheless, we should not be too surprised: it is not as economically lucrative for them to abolish slavery as it was to rebel against colonial rule.'

His words were as hard-edged as ever. Isabella shook her head. 'You speak as though everyone were cut from the same cloth, as though mercantile enterprise could only be pursued at the expense of others. I know there is some truth in that, but I cannot believe everyone insensible to the true cost of their endeavours. For all the Cousins Hélène and Brighid in the world, who choose to ignore it because their situation blinds them to all else, there may be just as many ignorant nieces and daughters like myself, who are simply unaware of the reality of their guardians' business affairs.'

'Of course. The Society of Friends has become increasingly uneasy about the plight of the Africans, and a small group is being set up in England to see what might possibly be done. Already, there are some individuals, like Granville Sharp, who have successfully exploited the ambiguity of England's slavery laws to secure the freedom of several slaves, though the slave trade and the institution of slavery itself in the colonies remain as intact as ever.'

'But there is at least something to hope for,' said Isabella.

'Something,' he echoed, before hesitating. 'The pamphlet you suggested is one that should be written, and one that I should like to write. But if I do so, it would be wiser for us not to meet again. I shudder to think what your father would do if he ever learned of your involvement. He would almost certainly shut you up in a convent for the rest of your life. Either that, or marry you off at once.'

'You think I could be disposed of so easily?'

she said, knowing as she spoke that it was true. 'Then don't think of it. I can at least take responsibility for myself.'

He looked doubtful, but was reluctant to press the issue. 'Of course, a pamphlet by an unknown author is unlikely to have any significant repercussions,' he said, attempting to reassure himself. 'Although it would be considered highly seditious, and of course would not be passed by the King's censors. So we'll have to print it privately and distribute it as we can through the people we know—the Bernards and their friends, such people. It would then be unlikely to come to your father's attention.'

'But not distributing it openly would defeat the purpose of the exercise! It should be circulated and debated in places such as this.'

He looked from the *journal* that lay on the edge of the table to all those others that had gathered in the coffee-house, and his countenance took on a distant, preoccupied expression that Isabella could not read. He is worried, and does not wish to confide in me, she thought. But as the snow continued to fall, they both placed their respective doubts aside and resumed a less personal discussion.

CHAPTER FOURTEEN

The captain did not call during Hélène's rather long visit to Donnchadh, and so she went home disappointed. But fortunately her mother had retired to her room, and so she was not called on to account for the day. Instead, she was free to dream of duelling officers and to practise her harpsichord for the remainder of the night.

The following morning, Brighid again remained in bed, and again Hélène found herself in a position of relative freedom. Knowing this could not last, she did not dwell on whether Isabella was meeting the doctor again, as she herself hastened to the abbé's apartment. Today, she was rewarded with a glimpse of the captain arriving just ahead of her, the red of his coat glaring against the snow-framed house.

'*Capitaine*,' said Hélène with a tinge of anticipation.

'Mademoiselle,' he said uncomfortably. 'May I have a moment with you, in private?'

'Certainly,' she replied, moving away from the door.

'Donnchadh is much improved, is he not?' he said as Hélène led him to the side of the house.

'I believe so, with no small thanks to Doctor

Connor.'

'I am relieved to hear it—I sought your opinion, as I understand you had a longer opportunity to observe him yesterday than I did. In that case, do you think he would look unfavourably on me if I told him I had to absent myself from Paris for a period of time?'

'Your regiment is being stationed elsewhere?' she asked in dismay. But the officers normally spent the winter in Paris, did they not? she thought to herself.

'No, it's not that.' He looked at her consideringly, hesitated, then decided to add: 'I have been invited to visit the home of a superior officer near Versailles.'

'Indeed? And is it to be a long visit?' she continued, her mind busy with speculation.

'That will depend—on a number of factors.' Something in his voice confirmed her suspicions.

'Your superior has a daughter, then.' She tried not to make it sound like an accusation, but her voice was bitter.

He looked at her sharply. 'You sound surprised,' he said.

'Not at all,' she replied. 'Mademoiselle Carroll remains impervious to your charms. Perhaps you will have better luck with a young *Française*, fresh from the convent and ready to marry as her father pleases. It does please him, I take it?'

'Do not mock me, Mademoiselle,' he said

wearily. 'I have explained my situation to you. Surely you of all people can understand the need to secure a future.'

'Of course. I only lament that my own opportunities to do so are considerably less plentiful than yours.' She then turned away from him, not wanting to sour their last moments together.

'I fear I have some sad news to impart,' she said, sweeping into the room where Donnchadh lay, eagerly anticipating their visit. 'Captain O'Shea is leaving us.'

'I am sorry to hear that,' said Donnchadh, though he didn't sound very disappointed. Instead, he studied them both closely.

The captain had followed her, and now sat uneasily in a chair by Donnchadh. 'It is I who should apologise,' he muttered thinly, furious with Hélène for having ruined the opportunity to break the news with more tact and subtlety. 'My presence is required at the home of a superior. Unfortunately his home is some distance away. I am most reluctant to go, being keenly aware of my duties towards you.'

'Captain O'Shea, I am as much responsible for my condition as you are. More so, in fact. It was I who suggested the escapade. You need not apologise for your absence.'

'That's settled, then,' said the captain with relief. 'I will write, of course, and if there's anything you require . . .'

'Thank you for your kindness, and I'll let

you know.'

'Quite. Well, if you'll excuse me . . .'

'You have preparations to make,' Hélène finished for him. The captain left. Hélène listened to the street door close behind him. 'I'm afraid you must make do with my company now,' she said finally. 'I shall try to amuse you as best I can.'

'It all seems rather sudden,' mused Donnchadh. 'He mentioned nothing of this yesterday. I wonder what called him away?'

'He is gone to get himself a wife.' She blurted it out without reflection and paused, amazed.

'I'm sorry,' said Donnchadh, examining her face with a new alertness. 'I didn't know there was an understanding between you.'

'There was nothing of the sort,' exclaimed Hélène. 'Anyway, he is prudent, and has a glittering career all mapped out for himself.'

'But he has disappointed you, and for that I'm sorry.'

'It's of little consequence, really. If I am a little attached to him, it is only because I recognise myself in him. I admire his ambition, and share his desire for position and advancement. He would make a formidable husband, but not for a penniless Irish girl, who could only hinder him. No, I believe I will follow his example, and find myself a husband who can provide me with all the comforts and security I crave, though I realise my prospects are somewhat less than glorious.'

'Mademoiselle!' he said, astonished. 'Is your outlook really so bleak? Have you so little faith in humanity?'

I imagine he has never given a single thought to material considerations, she thought, a little enviously. 'Pay no attention to me,' she said. 'You will soon be a priest, and you look to the future knowing that society will provide for you on account of your cloth. You will make a good living from sanctity and Christian charity, whereas I have nothing to look forward to, which makes me spiteful, and fearful that one day I will become my mother.'

'Life is hard for everyone, Mademoiselle,' Donnchadh exclaimed. 'Have you been in France so long that you have forgotten what it is to be a Catholic in Ireland?'

'On the contrary, I speak like this because I remember it all too keenly,' she said, touching the keys of the spinet.

'Then place your fears aside, and distract us both with some music. My uncle and I were delighted by your playing yesterday. It was quite beautiful.'

Such praise I hear only from him, Hélène thought, warming to his voice. And he is confined here, at least for a while longer. How many afternoons does that give me, to be myself? How many more opportunities will I have to steal away here? Almost as if they were already gone, flown into the past, Hélène looked around her, memorising each detail of the room. Daylight shining faintly on the worn keys, the red of her hem darkening against the faded carpet, and the gentle admiration of a slightly wounded clerical student.

The images stayed with her as she returned home with Isabella, who kept her now customary silence. But the moment they entered the *vestibule*, a servant came forward to tell them that Brighid had taken a turn for the worse during their absence, and that Monsieur Carroll's physician had been called. In alarm, Hélène went to her mother immediately.

'What did the doctor say?' she asked, guiltily noting the variety of new bottles assembled on the cabinet.

Her mother eased herself up in bed. 'Is it now you ask me, after being off gallivanting all day, while your sick mother was lying here in agony, with no one to care for her?'

Hélène said nothing, knowing that the best response was to let her mother's temper take its course.

'Well, don't just stand there. Go and see what those useless servants have done with my supper—and make sure it's still warm when it arrives.'

Hélène turned hastily to leave.

'Eibhlín?'

Hélène stopped again, noting the concerted effort at civility in her mother's voice.

'I spoke without reflection. In fact, I think it best that you stay away from me for a while. I would not like you to fall ill too. One of us must remain fit to keep an eye on Mademoiselle Isabella.'

'As you wish,' said Hélène, feeling a sense of relief.

'Eibhlín?'

Hélène smiled inquiringly, hoping her mother was not now going to ask awkward questions about how they had spent the day.

'You will do your best for me, won't you? I know you think me somewhat callous in that regard, but it's just that I worry so. What is to become of us?' Brighid broke off here in a fit of coughing.

Hé1ène hesitated, concerned. 'Are you sure you wouldn't prefer me at least to sleep in the next room, where I will hear you if . . .'

'Go,' her mother ordered as forcefully as she could. 'Do as you are told. And take my keys—you may have need of them.'

Even in sickness, my mother clings tenaciously to her intrigues, Hélène thought with some resentment. But she did as she was told. After seeing to her mother's supper, she went to Isabella's room. Her cousin was sitting at her bureau, and seemed to have hastily concealed some pages in a leather-bound volume. The pages remained visible, despite the fact that Isabella's hand rested over the book.

'You will be pleased to learn that you are to be temporarily free of my mother's presence,' said Hélène, noting the tension in Isabella's hands and wondering what the pages held.

'Your mother is unwell, then?' asked Isabella.

'Does that persuade you to join me for supper rather than eating here alone?' Hélène continued.

Isabella thought about it, then shrugged her shoulders, saying that she would be down presently. Hélène left, but the keys her mother had entrusted her with lay heavily on her skirt. Was it not time to acquaint herself with the substance of her cousin's frequent *rendez-vous* with the physician?

Isabella left, closing the door without locking it. Hélène waited a few moments, then returned to the empty room. Once inside, however, she discovered that the bureau had been locked, and the volume placed inside it. This made her hesitate. In the weeks before Isabella's arrival, she had been accustomed to wander from room to room out of sheer boredom, testing beds and opening wardrobes. But even so, she found she could not unlock a bureau that had been clearly designated another's private property without some unease. She knew she was crossing the line between idle curiosity and snooping.

But, then again, was she? she countered. She was acting, not only in her own interest, but in Isabella's. If these concealed sheets were important, then it was for the best that she read them so she could make an informed decision on how to act. Hélène turned the key and pulled out the volume. The first sheets consisted of scrappy notes, scrawled, scribbled out, and re-phrased. She skimmed them hastily, finding little of interest. Then she came to a clearly laid-out plan for an anti-slavery pamphlet, with a specific emphasis and denunciation of the Irish traders and upholders of the institution, to be written in English and translated into French. This she read carefully, despite her consciousness that Isabella could return at any moment.

Hélène knew nothing of political pamphlets, but was sufficiently cognizant of Paris and French society to be aware of what was considered unacceptable, and a written, published denunciation of one's father would certainly qualify as a transgression. She remembered one of her mother's letters, in which she mentioned that the *colons* had had the Jesuits expelled from Saint-Domingue for becoming too friendly with the slaves. What then would Carroll do with Isabella and her physician? She thought of the papers and ledgers her mother had shown Isabella, and she shuddered.

Outside, the snow lightened the night. Hélène thought longingly of Donnchadh's room and the tranquillity and admiration she had found there. What a foolish, foolish girl Isabella was. Not content at having thrown her uncle's fortune away, she had now settled on courting retribution from her father. To have snubbed the captain, sent him away to a country house where a more compliant creature awaited him with all those convent-acquired layers of modesty and greed. Hélène could almost have howled with frustration.

Isabella was lost, that much was clear. There was little Hélène could do, other than await the storm that would erupt sooner or later after Carroll's return. But his return was not imminent, and her mother was ill, too ill to pursue her own intrigues. That left an interval, which Hélène could fill as she pleased. Why trouble herself unduly about Isabella's fate, when Donnchadh awaited her so eagerly? Donnchadh's wound would heal just as surely as her mother would recover and Carroll would return. Why should she be the one to hasten the storm?

Hélène carefully folded the sheets, and replaced them where she had found them. She then composed herself and went to join Isabella for supper.

III

CHAPTER ONE

For several weeks, Paris lay buried under several feet of snow. The country roads became icy and treacherous, and so the post became infrequent and unreliable. The cold sank deeply into Brighid's bones, and she remained confined to her sickbed, with no word from Carroll, no sign that he had received the letter informing him of her illness. But both girls flourished in the frozen city which had given them a liberty of sorts.

Hélène continued to play the spinet for Donnchadh, each afternoon growing a stronger sense of herself. She felt as if she had finally been seen, truly seen, by someone else. Not only that, but it was as if he had held up a mirror to her, and she had seen herself reflected back for the first time. Her anxieties lessened as she learned there were others who doubted themselves, whose means were erratic. He was fortunate to be blessed with such an uncle, he told her—there were other students at the College who were often left wondering if and when their fees would arrive from home, but they trusted to God and the College that they would somehow be provided for.

Most of the time, the atmosphere was light, as Hélène recounted in Irish all the best stories she could remember from her childhood. But her consciousness that each day was a fleeting gift led to a growing melancholy as the snowflakes began to dissolve into rain: how much longer can this last? How much time do I have? She did not know that Isabella asked the same questions of herself with increasing sadness as each afternoon with Connor in the noisy, cheerful Bernard apartment drew to an end.

At first, Isabella had feared she was imposing herself—the Bernards could barely accommodate Connor, let alone a caller who came every afternoon to read from his books and debate the contents of a pamphlet that he continued to insist could not be distributed outside their network of friends. As it was so very cold, and the drawing-room fire the largest and the warmest, Julie Bernard could not very well take herself and her infant elsewhere, but she soon succeeded in reassuring Isabella that her presence was a pleasure, a distraction when the weather kept all other callers at home. And as the cold weather swelled the ranks of Bernard's patients, keeping him away from his family for most of the day, she convinced Isabella that she was glad of her company. Sometimes, Julie added her voice to those of Isabella and Connor, speaking softly so as not to disturb the sleeping child. All three did their best to soothe and amuse the little boy when he did awake.

Because of the constraints of the situation, Connor allowed himself to put his misgivings aside temporarily, and concentrate solely on the task at hand. He devoted so much time to it, and to Isabella, that Julie could not fail to notice it. She said nothing on the subject for the present, though she encouraged Isabella to talk of herself, and found much to interest her in the Irish girl's character. But as the snow began to melt, Connor's completion of the pamphlet drew near, and Isabella knew she could not postpone the decision about her future any longer.

She had written to her friend Pamela, confiding something of her troubles. One morning, as the carriages were beginning to move more freely and rapidly through the streets, she received the letter which she had half hoped for, and half dreaded, from Pamela. It began:

My poor Isabella,

What a dark and troubling turn your fate has taken since the day you left your uncle's house. You write that your conscience demands you sever all connections with your father, and indeed, I shudder to think what that odious widow will do should you remain there a moment longer. You must leave Paris immediately. I know I cannot prevail on you to ask your uncle's forgiveness and return to his protection, but I have spoken to my husband, and he agrees that you must come and live with us. I know your objections, but let me assure you, they are groundless. This place is so godforsaken that you need not fear a friend coming to visit, let alone your family knocking down the door, clamouring to remove you! Mr M'Guire remains a close friend of the family, but I believe he is to be married soon, and there is no danger from that quarter.

Won't you come? I am so very lonely here, with nothing to relieve my solitude. Most of the peasants are very poor, but the O'Beirnes are considered good landlords, and we are at least Catholic. In any case, you will not be able to understand a word the tenants say, for they speak for the most part in Gaelic, and the rest is unintelligible.

Do come, Isabella. It'll be just like old times, and the countryside in winter does have a brutal beauty of sorts.

I remain,
your loving friend,
Pamela O'Beirne

It is very kind of her, thought Isabella. But I do not wish to go. We have both changed so much since we last met, and I fear we should soon come into conflict, and make each other miserable. She read the letter again. Poor Pamela, marriage seems to have done little for her spirits. My presence—anyone's presence for that matter—would cheer her immensely. I should go. Indeed I must go, for I cannot remain here much longer, and I have nowhere else to turn.

The resolution was nonetheless made with a sinking heart. Once I go there, I will become the worst possible form of dependent, preying on Pamela's happier memories of Dublin for every scrap of kindness she shows me. Why can I not think of an escape? Am I so useless that I must spend my entire life going from one household to the next, always unable to provide for myself?

She told herself that perhaps the O'Beirnes were not so very bad; perhaps she could perform some services for Pamela to repay her generosity. She would have to tell Connor about the letter and ask his advice. She placed the letter in her muff and fastened her pelisse securely.

* * *

In the Bernards' apartment, Connor had just told Julie that he had prevailed on the printer to have copies of the pamphlet ready that afternoon.

'So soon?' she asked with surprise.

'I told him it was of the utmost importance. Isabella will be pleased.'

'All this to please *Isabelle*?' She shook her head in amazement. 'My dear Connor, I do believe your interest in her extends beyond the bounds of political philosophy.'

Connor responded with an awkward laugh. 'You forget her present circumstances are so troubling . . .'

'What troubles you, then?' she asked teasingly. But on seeing his face, her voice took a more serious turn. 'Why do you hesitate so, when she has clearly captured your affections, and you hers?'

He was slow to reply. 'My circumstances are hardly ideal. I have little to offer . . . anyone.'

'A skilled physician? Jean-Claude always told me you were one of the finest students at the University, and I believed him.' Now it was Julie who hesitated. 'Jean-Claude also said he had never known a man so afflicted with self-doubt,' she said gently. 'I remember how awkward and timid you were when he first brought you to my father's house, this newly arrived Irish boy who had learnt his impeccable French from an elderly priest. But I also remember how much you had gained in confidence and spirits by the time you left us. What became of that confidence and spirits?'

Connor smiled briefly at the memory. 'I fear they were too new and tender to withstand the journey home,' he said, before taking himself to the window to end the conversation. Julie feared she had said too much, and occupied herself with the baby. She was surprised when Connor spoke again after a few moments.

'Isabella came to Paris because she did not wish to be married.'

'But of course,' said Julie, adopting a lighter tone. 'How could she contemplate the infinitely corrupt Mr M'Guire once she had set eyes on the handsome young doctor?'

'I believe the truth is a little grimmer than that. Her mother died within a year of marriage, from an illness contracted during her birth, and her aunt's health has been ruined by a lifetime of miscarriages and stillbirths—not one of Mrs Reily's own children survived infancy.'

Julie's eyes lost their twinkle as she looked down at her baby's head. 'It is a common fear,' she murmured. 'But at least she would be marrying a physician.' She lapsed into silence, before recovering something of a sly smile. 'The advantages of marrying a physician are manifold—perhaps you could endeavour to postpone the birth of your first child?'

'Julie, stop, I beg of you,' he urged. 'She is due here at any moment, and she mustn't hear you talk like that.' He looked out of the window again, and sure enough, saw Isabella approaching their door.

Julie deposited the baby in its cradle and rushed to greet her. '*Isabelle*,' she exclaimed, kissing her on both cheeks. 'Connor and I were just talking about you. Do you realise how much time and energy he has devoted to this pamphlet? It really has become very dear to him.'

'Yes, it has all been very worthwhile,' he added, frowning at Julie, who chose to ignore his embarrassment.

'*Les deux Irlandais*, adrift in all the contradictions of Paris, they come together in their search for meaning. *Vous me dîtes que ce ne signifie rien*?' smiled Julie.

'You must excuse her—I believe she has been reading too much poetry of late,' said Connor hastily. 'Isabella, I have a surprise for you—even as we speak, our pamphlet is fresh off the printing press and awaiting our collection.'

'So soon?' she asked with dismay. Was it over, then, the one piece of her life in which she had not been at odds with herself? 'But that's wonderful,' she added, remembering herself.

'Yes, Michel promised to print it last night, and I've arranged to meet him in a nearby tavern. Shall we walk? It's much less cold today.'

'By all means,' she smiled, taking her leave of Julie and the baby.

Once they were outside, an awkwardness rose between them. The conversation with Julie was still fresh in Connor's mind, and

Isabella could feel Pamela's letter in her muff.

'Have you had news from your father?' he asked finally.

'You must want to know what my plans are,' she began. But she was loth to continue. 'Let's not talk about it, at least until later.'

The manner in which she spoke implied a bleak decision of some kind, one that he would not wish her to have to make. If only he himself weren't so riddled with confusions, so unsure of what step to take. Did she really know her own heart? he wondered. Perhaps she did have those feelings for him that Julie had spoken of, but how could she identify their true nature, when they were so bound up in gratitude for his assistance?

'I do hope everything went to plan,' he said, turning his thoughts back to the moment. 'Michel works by day as a master's journeyman in an authorised shop, but he has a small printing press hidden in a closet, and at night, he prints works like mine. He has already been raided by the police once this year, so whenever he fears a repeat visit, he has his press concealed somewhere else.'

'He must be very brave,' remarked Isabella. 'Does his master know?'

'Oh yes. He pretends not to, of course, but he allows Michel to take type home, and is perfectly aware of what it is for.'

They turned the corner into a street thronged with people. Connor took Isabella's arm to guide her through. A one-horse cabriolet came crashing through, forcing everyone to jump back in alarm lest they be trampled on as its driver tore through without the least consideration for those he splattered with slush and filth. Connor and Isabella attempted unsuccessfully to shake their garments clean as the air around them filled with angry grumblings. Fortunately, they did not have much further to go.

Across the crowded tavern, Connor saw the printer sitting alone at a table, drink in hand, staring fixedly ahead of him with no indication that he had seen them.

'Connor,' he exclaimed, relieved, as they sat opposite him. 'It's good that you came now.' Leaning across the table, he whispered in French quickly: 'I was worried you'd be late—on my way here, I spoke to a *colporteur*, who has just had some pamphlets seized by the police, including one I printed only last week!' Under the table, he handed Connor an octavo pamphlet of thirty-two pages. 'The others are in a parcel, as you requested—you'll leave by the back way, where they are waiting for you.'

Isabella caught a glimpse of it before Connor concealed it hastily under his *surtout*. Now that it was no longer in his possession, the printer seemed a little more relaxed, and looked speculatively at his empty glass.

'But I really must tell you, *ce pamphlet est vraiment extraordinaire*,' he said respectfully.

‘The *colons* like to assure the world that they treat the *nègres* like children in need of a strong guiding hand, but I should not like to be the child of this unnamed *Grand Blanc*, whose documents you quote. Such atrocities, so dispassionately recorded by their perpetrator. Where did you find them?’

‘What is important is that I believe him to be typical of his kind,’ said Connor evasively.

‘Yes, though he is rather distinctively drawn. An Irishman, you write. I was very interested in all you had to say about the political situation of that troubled country. I brought it into the shop this morning, so that I could have another look at it before the day’s work started, and I was so engrossed in it that I did not hear the Chevalier de Sébastien come in. He of course wanted to know what I was reading, and prevailed on me to give him a copy.’

‘The Chevalier de Sébastien?’ asked Connor, horrified. ‘But I told you how important it was not to show it to anyone!’

‘*Mais oui*, but the Chevalier is such an important person. He moves in such exalted circles. I thought you’d be pleased.’

Isabella’s French had improved sufficiently to allow her to understand the substance of what had been said. ‘We want only friends to read it,’ she said in hesitant French.

The printer looked at Isabella, and the truth of the matter dawned on him. Shaking his head regretfully, he finished his drink and stood up to take his leave. *'Je suis vraiment désolé,'* he said. 'I didn't know.'

'Well,' said Connor. 'There is little we can do about it now, other than collect that parcel.'

Slowly, they made their way in the direction indicated. A serving girl caught their eye, and motioned that they should follow her into a storage room where she quickly loaded Connor with a very heavy parcel, before leading them in a flash into a narrow alleyway and leaving them there. Sagging under the weight, Connor quickly found his bearings, and judged it best to walk the few streets to the Bernards', despite the crowds, and possible police. The printer's tale of the *colporteur* had given him some cause for anxiety, but he had never yet been accosted by the police, and it would be more troublesome to engage a *fiacre* to carry them such a short distance.

'Who is this Chevalier?' asked Isabella, once they had set off.

'A minor noble with a taste for philosophy, but I do not think we need worry too much. He hardly moves in the same circles as your father.'

'It's good that he's read it. You have nothing to fear on my account. My friend Pamela has invited me to live with her in the O'Beirnes' country house in Ireland, and I think I shall accept. I have little choice, really,' she added sadly.

'But your friend is newly married, is she not, and you know little of her new connections.' He hesitated. 'Perhaps you should reconsider. I know the Bernards would gladly have you to stay if, if . . .'

'I have imposed enough on their kindness already, and besides, they live so close to my father's house. Once he has returned, and I have spoken to him, I think it will be best for everyone if I leave Paris immediately.'

'You are going to speak to him?' asked Connor apprehensively.

Isabella fidgeted uncomfortably with the letter in her muff. 'He is my father. His documents showed me what he truly is, and these last weeks have taught me how he became that person, but I am still filled with unanswered questions, which can only be addressed to him.'

'Isabella, don't do this,' said Connor, appalled. 'I understand what you're feeling, but the answers you seek can never be found. You will simply torment yourself, and unwittingly deliver yourself into his hands, to be broken as he chooses.'

They had now reached the Bernards' door. 'Julie will be waiting,' said Isabella. 'Don't let's talk about it now—at least not until Julie has seen these.'

But once inside, they found Hélène waiting for them, her skirts spread perfectly wide to avoid unnecessary creases. Julie had been speaking to her as politely as she could, though Isabella's story had done nothing to recommend this cousin to her, and it was hard to warm to someone who so plainly viewed her baby as something to be kept away from new clothes at all costs.

'I think we should leave now,' said Hélène, carefully rising to her feet.

'Now?' protested Isabella. 'But it is earlier than we had arranged.'

'Please,' said Hélène. 'My mother is much improved today. I'm afraid she'll ask awkward questions if we stay out any longer.'

'Then we will see you tomorrow, *Isabelle*,' said Julie, intervening. 'Do try to come. We shall be expecting you.'

Isabella reluctantly followed her cousin outside.

'What on earth was that large parcel the doctor was carrying?' Hélène asked.

'Oh, nothing of consequence.'

'It did not seem of no consequence to me.'

'It does not concern you,' said Isabella, her mind too full to dissimulate.

Hélène's face tightened. The two continued in silence.

CHAPTER TWO

Early that morning, Brighid had felt sufficiently recovered to resume her duties. The same post that had brought Pamela's letter to Isabella had also brought Brighid a letter from Carroll. He informed his cousin that he would soon be returning to Paris. All the arrangements had been made, and he would be home by the end of the week. Brighid folded the letter and sat by the fire. Outside, snow no longer fell. Footsteps had long since muddied the white-coated streets, reducing them to brown sludge. The sky was dark with clouds. But despite all this, she knew that, somewhere in the house, her daughter and Isabella were preparing to go out. In a few moments, there would be a knock on the door, and Eibhlín would attempt to bid her a hasty goodbye, as if she were still an invalid. Both girls would then rush headlong into the Parisian streetscape towards some mysterious attraction yet to be revealed.

As anticipated, the knock came.

'Look at you, hiding behind all that fur, like a sheep dressed up in a wolf's coat. What drives you out of doors on such a miserable day?' asked Brighid, observing her daughter closely. There was a freshness to the girl's complexion that she had not seen before, a light sparkle in her eyes that seemed to dull at the sight of her mother.

She has recovered full possession of her faculties, thought Hélène, surprised. The illness had dragged on so long and been so debilitating that she was unprepared to find her mother up and dressed. 'Are you sure you're well? Perhaps you should rest a while longer—you know how severely this climate affects you.'

'But not you?' Brighid asked.

'Oh, Isabella likes the cold—she finds it quite invigorating. I am happy to go with her—she is impatient for our daily walk near the Tuileries.'

Do you think me a fool, Brighid wondered as her smile narrowed. But she was so struck by the delicate sheen on the girl's countenance that she found herself letting Eibhlín go without any further ado.

Instantly, she regretted it. What had she been thinking of? Carroll was due home so soon, it was imperative that she find out what both girls had been up to during his absence and her illness. She balked at the limited avenues of possibility open to her. But there was no time to pursue this by gentler means: the girls would have to be followed. She shivered at the thought of those heavy clouds. Perhaps she could send a servant, under the pretext that Mademoiselle Carroll might require assistance should it rain during her *promenade?* She laughed at the ridiculousness of the premise, reluctantly acknowledging that it was better to go herself

It was bitterly cold outside. Brighid gritted her teeth and pulled her pelisse tightly around her. She went at speed and soon caught up with them, though she remained a good distance behind. From what she could see, they seemed in good spirits, though they said little. They were clearly as fond of exercise as Eibhlín had claimed: she found herself struggling to keep up with them, to keep them in view as they headed east towards Saint Germain des Prés, instead of across the river to their supposed destination, the Tuileries. But then, some time later, they separated. Brighid was bemused—had Eibhlín perhaps been dispatched to undertake some small commission before returning to join Isabella? Which girl should she follow? She could feel the remaining traces of her illness flaring up in the cold, and cursed the errand that had brought her out. What was she, that she should feel reduced to following a pair of girls halfway across Paris? She decided to pursue her own daughter, the evasiveness of their recent interview still fresh in her mind.

Hélène found Donnchadh waiting for her, leaning against the tree outside the house where the abbé lived. 'What are you doing?' she asked in dismay. 'You're not well enough to be outside.'

'Oh, there's nothing like a thaw and a fresh wind to blow away the cobwebs of a sickroom, and my return to the *Collège* is long overdue.'

'Not *long* overdue, surely.'

There was a silence, and he turned away from the disappointment in her eyes. 'Look at this place,' he exclaimed, running his hand along the bark of the tree. 'All forlorn and muddy. You would not believe how easily a touch of spring transforms it with some green here, a flower there . . .'

Hélène smiled faintly, thinking that she would not now see the tree in spring.

From a safe distance, Brighid watched her daughter in disbelief. A secret *rendez-vous* with a young man? Brighid took in the shabbiness of his appearance, the pitiful state of his *surtout.* Obviously a student of very scanty means. Silly, silly, girl. Did I not teach her better?

A woman of indeterminate age emerged from the house and made her way towards where Brighid was standing.

'*Je vous demande pardon*,' said Brighid, adroitly manoeuvring herself into the other woman's path. 'I am not usually so clumsy, but I was admiring your house. Is that fine young man perhaps your son?'

The Frenchwoman looked at her suspiciously before laughing scornfully at the idea of him being her son. '*Mais non, Madame*, that is the Abbe O'Donnell's nephew, a callow

Irish youth who got himself wounded in a duel with an officer. The girl prides herself on her sickbed charm, and comes to play music to him every afternoon, though I do not see why she bothers. He too is studying for the priesthood.'

'*Merci, Madame*,' she replied, horror-struck. Is this what Eibhlín has been doing all this time? I shudder to think what our dear Isabella has been up to. And her father due to arrive by the end of the week.

Her eyes returned to the young couple, who were now making their way inside. Forget Isabella, she told herself. What does she matter, when my daughter chooses to blossom in the company of a threadbare clerical student?

She was suddenly confronted by an array of emotions, and retreated to a nearby café to prepare herself for her next step. It was a dark, dirty place, its proprietors clearly unable or reluctant to relieve the winter dullness with more than the smallest expenditure of candles, soap and water. Those, at least, were economies Carroll never made.

Brighid knew what had to be done, but found herself too weary even to muster up the necessary disapproval. She sat there for several hours, allowing her thoughts to turn to her own childhood in Ireland. Eibhlín had shone with a certain dash of life that had reminded Brighid of her brothers, Tadhg and Ciarán. High-spirited lads, who would often make her laugh and laugh until her stomach hurt. The sensation of that laughter washed faintly over her again, and she bit her lip, hoping to quell it. But again, she found herself remembering summer nights, when her brothers would steal outside and race down to the seashore where a small group of people would be secretly awaiting a smuggler's ship from France. One night she had followed them outside, and when they had failed to threaten her back indoors, Ciarán had taken her up on his horse with him. She could still feel the exhilaration of flying through the night, her cheek cool, her heart beating fast. She watched the water by moonlight, hoping that the ship would never arrive, because then it would all be over, and she would have to go back home to bed. How times had changed. What she wouldn't give now to go back to that home and her family, all dead and gone.

She realised she was in danger of losing her self-command. Brighid forced herself to return to her surroundings, and judged it time to leave. I'm too old for this, she thought ruefully as she stepped back out on to the cold busy street and around the corner to the home of this student's uncle. But within a few minutes, she had been admitted into the apartment by the abbés housekeeper, and found herself alone with the young man. Eibhlín must have left, she thought as she looked around, taking in the old furniture and the faded curtains of the abbé's small reception room.

'Monsieur O'Donnell?' she asked him in French. He looked at her, baffled, wondering if he was supposed to know who she was. 'I am Madame Ní Fhlathartaigh. I believe you are acquainted with my daughter?'

'*Je suis vraiment honoré*,' stammered the student, unnerved by the nuance she had given the word 'acquainted'. 'I have often hoped to meet you, and for you to come visit me . . .'

His French was clumsy, but it was softly accented, even appealing in its rawness. Brighid realised how it must appeal to her daughter, accustomed for so long to the smooth cunning phrases of *les religieuses* and the prattling of silly convent girls.

'My daughter has left, then?' she asked.

'Yes.'

'Is your uncle at home?'

'Not at present—his duties often keep him from home.'

'Indeed?' So Eibhlín was often alone with her young man? Brighid absorbed this rather unsettling piece of information.

He hesitated, finding her manner cold. 'May I offer you some refreshment?' he asked.

'Please,' she replied, taking the opportunity to examine him more closely.

He handed her a glass of wine, his manner such a disarming mixture of nervousness and politeness that she found herself rushing to the point in a desire to terminate the interview.

'I feel I should almost apologise for putting you to so much trouble,' she said. 'You must think I have quite a lot to say to you, when really it is so very little that I might have spared us both the time and told you immediately. You must forgive me—I wanted to indulge my curiosity and sample your company for myself.'

'You speak as though there were something distasteful in it,' he responded, taken aback.

'Come now, Monsieur O'Donnell. Do you really expect me to believe your impending vows a sufficient guard against the considerable musical charms of my daughter? Particularly when she chooses to deploy them, without my consent, whiling away the long dreary hours of your confinement here?'

'Your implication is clear.' He reddened. 'But you are mistaken. There was nothing clandestine about it. If she came here against your wishes, then I am sorry. But there was nothing to conceal. I feel . . .'

'It matters little to me what you feel. If others were to learn of her meetings with you, they might interpret them as they wished, and her future would be jeopardised.' She smiled with what she hoped resembled sympathy tinged with regret, but there was such a sour taste in her mouth that she found it difficult.

'You disapprove of me so much?'

Brighid sighed, and spoke more frankly than she had intended. 'My circumstances are such that I cannot afford the luxury of approving or disapproving anything. I simply do the best I can for Eibhlín, and it is not in her interest to maintain a connection with a penniless young clerical student who has nothing to offer her.'

'I am sorry you choose to view our friendship in that light.'

It was evident he did feel something for her daughter, but what purpose could it possibly serve? Unless he were to pursue a profession, join the array, even, make a fortune for himself . . . But he did not strike her as the type to abandon his chosen path. He was so young, and so unsure of himself, it was best she nip this in the bud while she still could.

She stood up. 'Thank you for seeing me,' she said. 'I feel sure you'll make a fine priest some day.'

CHAPTER THREE

Her mother's words were as cold and sharp as the crystal chandelier in the unheated salon. Hélène turned away, unable to withstand the blow she had known would come, sooner or later.

'I am sorry,' said Brighid. 'Clearly these last years have been more difficult for you than I had realised. I only wish our lives had been very different.'

'He is studying to be a priest,' said Hélène, struggling not to be overcome. 'Do you think me such a fool?'

'Look at you,' said her mother gently. 'Shedding tears over some ragged little student. Believe me, I wouldn't have done what I did if I hadn't felt there was much more in store for you. But you must safeguard that future now, while you are still young enough to do so.'

'Oh, spare me your intrigues, at least for one night.'

'Intrigue? Is that how you see it?' I suppose it is as good a word as any, thought Brighid sadly. 'I am sorry, but I couldn't let the matter lie. This morning, I received a letter from Carroll: we are to expect him by the end of the week.'

'So everything else must be cast aside in a last effort to win that elusive favour of his? I curse the day you ever set your sights on this household.'

'Say what you will, but you'll soon find yourself cursing the loss of this roof over your head should Carroll find his daughter has been engaged in mischief during his absence. You must tell me, Eibhlín. What has Isabella been doing?'

Isabella, thought Hélène, dreading what was to come on Carroll's return. 'She is sleeping,' she said. 'Leave her be, at least until morning.'

Hélène attempted to think more clearly

once she had left her mother. It somehow seemed of vital importance to use these few hours before morning to put some perspective on the situation, but she was overwhelmed by a sense of grief. She always knew those afternoons could never be anything more than an interlude, a transient sense of space created by the flux of circumstance. A friendship like that could never have lasted, fortune would always dictate otherwise. But the manner in which it had been uprooted, thrown away, and the soil smoothed over with barren words of worldliness and regret . . . She felt as if something had been torn from her, not only Donnchadh and the soft dull sparkle of an old spinet in the winter sun, but something fundamental, which she could neither understand nor express.

Hélène had not intended to sleep, but the oblivion of the pillow offered such a tempting escape that she eventually succumbed to it, even though she remained so troubled that the slightest sound awoke her—a gust of wind, her mother's step in the corridor . . . Consequently, she was one of the few members of the household who heard Carroll arrive home in the early hours of the morning. Awakened by the muffled commotion, she hastily prepared herself and slipped quietly downstairs as he dispatched a servant for supper and retreated into his library.

Home rather earlier than expected, she

thought to herself. My own dear mother will be thrown off course. She almost smiled, and all the anger surged up inside her. Her mother had already done her worst. It little mattered what she chose to do next. This made Hélène reckless, and the next thing she knew, she was knocking on the library door and walking in without being able to account for her motives, other than a desire that this Cousin Carroll should somehow see her, really see her, for once in her life.

'Are your business affairs so pressing they cannot wait until morning?' she wondered aloud when she saw him perusing correspondence by candlelight.

At first he barely acknowledged her presence, other than to glance up quickly, but when he looked up again to find her studying him intently, he put his papers down and spoke. 'Well, Hélène, what keeps you up at this hour of the night?'

I have your attention now, she thought. But how long can I command it? One minute, maybe two? Whole years of our lives must depend on the vagaries of your favour.

'I am glad to have this opportunity to speak with you alone,' she continued. 'You always seem so preoccupied, rushing here and there, being called away so suddenly on business, that I sometimes wonder if you are even aware of my presence in your household?'

'I wonder you ask such a question,

considering the cost of your education,' he answered sharply, examining her more closely than she ever remembered him doing before. His gaze made her uncomfortable, but she stood her ground.

'Yes, I have often found it strange,' she said, 'that you should remove me from the only country and family I had known and place me in a French convent, when you failed to ensure that your own daughter could even speak a word of the language. What exactly did you intend doing with me?'

'Hélène, it is late, and I have had a long journey,' he said, looking tired and as if this were yet another strain he could not deal with at present. 'I will give some thought to your future, and we will talk again at a more opportune time.'

You will give some thought to my future at a more opportune time, Hélène repeated to herself with resentment and more than a little horror.

'It is not always prudent to push matters aside until such time as it pleases you to pick them up again,' she said defiantly. 'Look what became of Isabella.'

'What of Isabella?' he asked wearily, casting his papers aside.

Hélène saw with frustration how quickly he had forgotten his affairs at the mere mention of Isabella's name. Isabella, who had thrown all this away for the sake of a few pages of heartfelt rhetoric.

'You see fit to accuse me of ingratitude, and yet perhaps you will be surprised to learn that your daughter, this stranger, should treat you with even more contempt than she did her uncle.'

His eyes flashed, and she wondered if she had said too much.

'Why the hesitation, Cousin?' he asked. 'You are clearly burning to enlighten me on the latest little misdemeanour. Has she been cold to the captain?'

The captain. She thought of him then, being received by the daughter of that country house surrounded by snow-covered grounds.

'Perhaps you underestimate her. Isabella has been busy with her physician in your absence.'

'Doctor Connor? The young man she travelled with to Paris?'

'Yes. They have been working together on a seditious pamphlet. I believe it seeks to denounce the institution of slavery.'

'Sedition and slavery? Good Lord! What on earth have they been writing?'

'A condemnation of the Irishmen who sought to escape the constraints of a troubled Ireland by taking to the seas under a French flag and inflicting unimaginable cruelty on another race by enslaving them. In short, Cousin, I believe it is intended as an attack on you.'

Hélène saw his colour change and became frightened. He would have found out sooner or later, courtesy of her mother's machinations, or Isabella herself. What difference could it possibly make who told him? Oh, why had she been provoked so, today of all days, that she should have felt impelled to do this? Guiltily, she pondered the tone and delivery of her last words.

'Who planted such a notion in her head?' he demanded after a moment's reflection. 'I find it hard to believe she could act in this way without some provocation or encouragement.'

'It is perhaps not as surprising as all that,' she countered in a more conciliatory voice. 'Both my mother and your friend Captain O'Shea have spent time in the West Indies, making it an obvious topic of conversation. It was only natural that they should mention in passing certain particulars pertaining to life in those countries. But because this physician had taught Isabella to do so, she took an objection to your . . . business affairs, and concocted this scheme to assuage her conscience.'

'Did she make you her confidante, then?' he asked mockingly.

'Her confidante?' asked Hélène, retaliating in a like tone. 'Why Cousin, Isabella sees herself as the Day to my Night and believes that somehow sets her outside my sphere. She fails to realise it simply makes us opposing cards belonging to the same stack.'

Hélène met his eyes directly. He was surprised to see something new in hers, something of his own temperament in this young woman who shared so little of his blood. Was this recently acquired, or had he simply failed to notice it before?

'I understand,' he said. 'You snooped and pried with your own ends in mind. Well, you may go now. Your betrayal is complete.'

'But do you understand?' she asked disconsolately. 'This game was not of my making. You instigated it the day you wrote to my mother, offering sustenance in return for her presence in Saint-Domingue. You left us at such a disadvantage, in such uncertainty, it is hardly surprising we learned to play as we did. But it was never my choice, Cousin.'

'Choice? What a curious turn this has taken,' he remarked, adding coolly: 'If you wish to remain in this house, you will furnish me with the physician's address. Then you can retire for what remains of the night.'

Hélène suppressed her initial impulse to run. What had started as a simple need to impress her existence on her powerful cousin had somehow backfired. This was a mess of her own making. But what could she do? She wrote the address in her bold, clear hand, and hesitantly gave it to him, studying his face in an effort to guess his intentions.

'You have a fine hand,' he observed. 'Did the nuns teach you that?'

'No, Cousin, my mother did,' she almost laughed. 'The nuns could not even teach the girls to spell properly.'

'I didn't pay them to sharpen your tongue either,' he replied, though she could see she was now being dismissed from his thoughts.

Feeling lost and uncertain, she made her way back to her room. She opened her window, which faced onto the wall of the next house, all damp and dirty from the last remnants of the snow. Elsewhere, her cousin Isabella was sleeping, dreaming of her physician, oblivious to all that had been said. Hélène continued to sit there, chilled by the cold, desolate air.

CHAPTER FOUR

The following morning, it was not Hélène who awaited Isabella at the breakfast table, but her mother, still pale, and clearly agitated. Isabella was unprepared for this, and hesitated, unsure of what she should do.

'Eibhlín is indisposed. I am your sole breakfast companion,' Brighid announced. 'But your father has returned from Nantes,' she added, attempting to conceal her anxiety—he had been so brusque, so contemptuous . . . 'He asked most particularly to see you. He has gone out on business, but wants to see you on his return.'

'Of course,' said Isabella. 'I too would like to see him.' There was some defiance in her tone, but now that he was back, the thought of facing him was more daunting than she had imagined. Brighid's keen senses instantly detected the girl's confusion.

'You seem a little . . . troubled?' she probed. 'My dear Isabella, I know you do not think of me as a confidante, but I have the advantage of having lived in the world many more years than you. Perhaps I could advise you?'

Isabella was surprised. Were her thoughts so easily read? 'It is of little importance,' she replied, rising from the table.

'Little, indeed,' remarked Brighid coldly. 'It is so unimportant, it merely requires your presence at some secret *rendez-vous* every afternoon. Eibhlín has already confessed her own transgressions to me. Would it not be prudent of you to do the same, so that I can offer you some guidance on how best to approach your father?'

All at once, Isabella understood the full extent of the woman's dislike for her. It was a strange animosity, as if she wished to punish Isabella for something that had been done to her, as if it were all Isabella's fault.

'Thank you for your kindness. If your guidance is behind Hélène's indisposition, then I'll forego the honour.'

'Quitting the breakfast table so soon? Why,

you haven't touched a thing, and the coffee is particularly good this morning. Made from Saint-Domingue's finest coffee beans, you know.'

Fresh from the fields of my father's *habitation*, you mean. 'I have a prior engagement,' said Isabella hastily. 'There's something I must do this morning.'

'Why don't you sit back down, my dear,' smiled Brighid. 'Your father's instructions were clear: you are to remain here until his return. But I don't imagine he'll keep you waiting too long.'

* * *

As soon as she could, Isabella knocked on Hélène's door, but it was locked, and whatever the true state of her health, Hélène was clearly not willing to talk. Had the 'confession' been so distressing, Isabella wondered? But then, why should Hélène be anxious to talk to her when they had spoken so little of late? She turned away—her father would be home soon, what would she say to him? In her own chamber, she traced Connor's words over and over again, words she almost knew by heart, printed on paper which was already worn from too much handling.

It was dark when Brighid came, to say her father had returned and was waiting in the library. She found him engrossed in his reading.

'I've been reading a singular piece of work,' he said. 'A little florid in style, but both libellous and seditious in content. I believe you are familiar with it?'

He held it out to her, and she saw that it was Connor's pamphlet. Her hands went to her skirts, where she had hidden her copy. How then, had her father come by it?

'I am more than familiar with it. I conceived it as the only avenue of protest open to me, and inveigled someone to write it, against his better judgement,' she said, attempting to keep her voice steady.

'Indeed,' he said, her words seeming to intensify his already barely controlled anger. 'Well, I need not ask what precisely you thought to protest about—I have much to choose from here, do I not?' He took the pages back and affected to study them again, pacing back and forth by the fire.

'How did you come by it?' Isabella ventured, her throat dry. Connor's name was printed so clearly, it was impossible to hope he could somehow be kept out of this.

Ignoring her, he crumpled up the pages. 'Very poor form, even for a young man trying to cause a stir. I rather think I could do better myself, though I would tell my own story somewhat differently. *Alors*, let me see then,' he said, sitting down and picking up a quill as if he were really about to compose this work. 'I believe I would begin on the day my family were evicted from our smallholding, and suffered hard times the likes of which you have never known, before going on to describe how I was sent to try my fortune at one of the Irish merchant houses of Nantes. Your physician takes an inordinate interest in the Nantes *négriers*, dwelling on the suffering of the *bois d'ébène*, this human cargo, so many of whom died from what you presume to be appalling conditions. Can you conceive of what conditions were like for the captain and his crew, you who can conceive of this?' He held up Connor's crumpled pages, and then threw them into the fire from where he was sitting.

'All those months of sitting in sweltering discomfort off the coast of Africa, negotiating the purchase of those barbaric savages—criminals most of them—your physician cannot presume to speak of from experience, let alone authority. Have you ever suffered intense thirst for a period of months at a time? Strange tropical fevers unlike anything you have ever heard of, let alone know cures for? Can you imagine eighteen months in a stinking ship, from France to Africa, Africa to Saint-Domingue, and then back to France again? Nothing but a few books, some dry biscuits and salted meat to compensate for the rigours of the journey?'

'If it were truly so awful, why would you have undertaken these voyages?' Isabella challenged, finding her voice as she watched the fire blaze with a fresh burst of life from the consumption of Connor's words.

'Because, my dear, I was saving to buy my own ship, and that is how it is done: one prays for a handsome commission on the sale of the cargo to bring one closer to the day when one can stay in Nantes, establish a mercantile career, and marry a woman like your mother.'

My mother? Was she the reward, then, glistening in the distance like an ever-nearing harbour, in full view of all the other captains, agents, and merchants? The thought unsettled Isabella. 'So you did not care, then, for the suffering of those you stowed in the hold of your ship, and sold so far away? You simply thought of your commission, and the pretty daughters of other merchants, and remained unmoved. But what of my mother?'

'Your mother was a sweet-tempered thing, who would have wept tears at your insolence had she lived long enough to see it.'

Then perhaps it is a blessing that she did not, thought Isabella sadly.

'But back to my pamphlet. What would I write next? *Alors*, after your mother's death, I suffered some heavy losses in trade. This, coupled with the disappointment of a *négrier* that had just arrived back from its triangular passage with a paltry return on its few saleable *nègres,* not to mention a very poor quality sugar, persuaded me try my hand as agent in

Saint-Domingue to several families I had contracted a connection with. Consequently, I made the regrettable decision to leave you in your aunt's clearly negligent hands, and set sail for Saint-Domingue, where I married the heiress of the *habitation* that fills your young man with such horror, though I succeeded in turning it into one of the most profitable on the island. That makes for a more cheering tale, *non?*'

'That young man cautioned me against the dangers of looking too closely into the darkness,' said Isabella finally. 'I believe he was right.'

'He was fully cognizant of his own danger, then. Well, the law is clear in its treatment of such offenders. But if he wishes to play at being a *philosophe,* then I am only too happy to oblige and make the necessary arrangements. The *homme de plume* has been served with a *lettre de cachet*, his writings duly confiscated, and he himself thrown in the Bastille for his pains. But what does one do with this rather novel concept of the "conceiver", particularly when it possesses the dubious distinction of being one's only daughter?'

'You would have done better to throw *me* in the Bastille. If you are capable only of brutality, then you can at least attribute all the blame to me and act accordingly.'

'You cannot presume to pass judgement!

Your aunt and uncle shielded you from the suffering of most of your fellow countrymen, fed you, clothed you, introduced you to the best society they could. Here, you live in a magnificent *hôtel,* your dazzling future guaranteed. If your sensibilities have become too acute, then I imagine we only have ourselves to blame for our over-indulgence.'

'Who precisely are the "we" you talk of?' Isabella responded angrily. 'I was but an infant when my aunt brought me to Dublin, and we received nothing from you but a handful of letters all these years. If by over-indulgence you mean all these tightly-laced gowns you foisted on me, then you may give them to Hélène, for it was she who chose them. Fine clothes purchased with the blood of others are not to my taste.'

'Would you rather I had taken you to Saint-Domingue and filled your time with so many household cares that you had to plead for the assistance of a few Negro servants? And when your complexion and constitution had been ruined by the climate, what then? Make no mistake about it, this delicate distaste of yours is the product of too many sheltered years. But your sensibilities mean nothing to me. Your sole value is as my daughter, and you will conduct yourself accordingly.'

'What am I, then? Your prisoner?'

'No, my dear, you are free to do as you please. But I would not advise you to go out alone, or to attempt to contact this young man. The consequences could be disastrous for him. Now if you will excuse me, I have a supper engagement, but I expect to see you at my breakfast table tomorrow morning, where you will conduct yourself in a fitting manner.'

A manner fitting whom, Isabella asked herself as he left the library. Even to think of Connor's predicament was to become distraught beyond belief. How could she go through the motions of breakfasts and engagements, knowing all she did? But she must, if she did not wish any further harm to come to Connor. Could she even trust that there would be no further harm? Who would know? Who would dare tell her, within this new prison of hers? Hélène only, perhaps, but Hélène, always so disapproving: 'Do you wish to go out *again*, Isabella? We must pretend you have to see a *couturière*, that you require exercise, but who will believe you require exercise in the snow? Must be prudent, exercise caution, move slowly . . .' She must speak with Hélène.

'Hélène, I must speak with you,' said Isabella, urgently, knocking on the other girl's door.

From her cousin's voice, Hélène knew that what she had been dreading all day had finally happened. She considered sending her away, but what purpose would that serve? Sooner or later, they would have to speak, and so she opened the door. Isabella made an effort to gather her thoughts.

'My father has had Doctor Connor thrown into the Bastille, and there is no knowing what is to become of him.'

'The Bastille? But that's, that's . . .' Hélène was truly shocked.

'Prison. And in the depths of winter. The conditions must be appalling. And all because he wrote a small work condemning slavery. How could my father have known of it? How could it have come to his attention, let alone that of the authorities? Why, it was only printed yesterday!'

'Your father must have leaned on some friend of his to bribe the relevant officials,' said Hélène uncomfortably, thankful that Isabella was too distracted and her thoughts moving too fast to notice her cousin's guilty manner.

'Of course he did—he told me he had made the necessary arrangements, I can only guess at the particulars. But who told him about it? The only one who read it, other than the Bernards and the printer, was a nobleman, the Chevalier something or other. But how could *he* have identified my father?'

'Anything's possible,' said Hélène cautiously. 'I've been told the *colons* guard their position jealously, sensitive to even the slightest threat. But throwing him in prison? I imagine it was to punish you, though I had no idea the stakes were so high.'

The word was so unexpected that Isabella became instantly alert. 'What do you mean by stakes?' she asked.

'You and Doctor Connor must have known what you risked, courting the wrath of such a man as your father with your pamphlets and philosophy,' replied Hélène defensively.

'But you knew before I told you,' said Isabella softly, her eyes not wavering from the other girl's face.

'I read the few notes you brought home once,' Hélène admitted.

Isabella said nothing, but Hélène knew she had realised who was responsible.

'I am sorry,' said Hélène. 'I had no intention of telling him, but I was so vexed with my mother, and with you to a certain degree, and then he provoked me . . . I regretted it as soon as I'd spoken, but I couldn't have known his vengeance would be so swift.'

'You were *vexed*?' exclaimed Isabella with disbelief. 'Good God, Hélène. I never showed you anything but friendship, and goodwill, and you say you were *provoked*?'

'You know something of provocation, you who flits from one household to the next after the slightest altercation.'

'Is that how you see me?' asked Isabella slowly, wondering that she had never sensed her cousin's hostility before. 'Well, you may be sure I will be confined here for the duration of

Doctor Connor's . . .' She broke off here, unable to contemplate the situation. 'If only I had let him be,' she said sadly, more to herself than to Hélène. 'He came to Paris hoping to escape the constraints of Dublin society, to revisit his student days. Why did I burden him with all my troubles?'

'You could not have known this would happen,' Hélène offered with guilty sympathy. 'I am so sorry, Isabella, but circumstances had taken such a turn that someone was going to use this pamphlet against you . . . Me or my mother, what difference did it make?'

'Speak plainly, I don't understand you,' said Isabella, strengthening her guard.

'Very well. When you were born, you were given so many advantages, so many cards, if you like. But you became so critical of those cards that you never learned to play them. I, on the other hand, was never given any cards, but I was taught to play, and it was impressed upon me that I must endeavour to acquire some cards at all costs.'

'Am I to suppose that your knowledge of Doctor Connor's pamphlet became a card to play in some pretty little intrigue to elevate you in my father's favour?' asked Isabella scornfully.

'No, of course not. I'm simply saying that I couldn't help viewing it in that light.'

'Like mother, like daughter; she taught you well.'

'I do not expect you to understand.'

'Doctor Connor is in prison, I understand that, and while I am responsible for entangling him in this mess, you too have something to answer for.'

Isabella's eyes were drawn to the window. Behind the faded velvet curtains, she could hear the splattering of hailstones against glass. What conditions did Connor have to contend with? Were they really to remain trapped, devoid of hope, at the mercy of . . . Icy, icy composure, she thought. That is what I must call upon to see me through. If I am to be forced to play the well-conducted house prisoner, then I can at least conceal everything.

CHAPTER FIVE

Across the river, the Bastille prison dominated the workshops and courtyards of the furniture-making Faubourg SaintAntoine. The Bernards had tried repeatedly to see Connor. They had even succeeded in getting as far as the governor, only to be told he was allowed no visitors, no letters, and no walks on the terrace. Each abortive attempt ended with a walk around the fortress, trying to guess where he was being held—in one of the towers, or in the dungeons? Remembering all the dramatic accounts they had read of the suffering of the inmates, they looked up fearfully at the soldiers on the battlements.

The governor had informed the Bernards that Connor had been imprisoned under a *lettre de cachet*, because of the seditious content of his writings. So much had already been made clear to them the night Connor was seized along with every copy of his freshly printed pamphlet. He had insisted to the police that their *lettre de cachet* was an abuse of power, manufactured by Monsieur Carroll for his own ends, but they had not listened. After tearing the Bernard's apartment apart looking for incriminating material, they had dragged Connor protesting from the house and to the Bastille as ordered. The Bernards had been powerless to stop them, just as at the Bastille they found themselves powerless against the moat and the walls that separated them from their friend.

Angry and frightened, they had returned home, attempting to assuage their servant's fears, calm the baby, and put their home back in order. Despite the violence of the raid, they found it was mainly books and little else that had been damaged. Then, after as much deliberation as the predicament allowed, the Bernards decided that Julie would try to see Isabella. Early the next morning, a *fiacre* took her from their apartment in the University Quarter to the clean, airy streets of the

Faubourg Saint-Germain where the imposing Hôtel de Carroll stood, separated from its neighbours by its bare garden, windows shuttered against the cold morning. But Isabella too was allowed no visitors. When Julie persisted in her request, Carroll's servant simply slammed the door in her face. Incensed, she turned away. From the gate, she scrutinised the coolly elegant building, wondering if Isabella could see her, but the long, wide windows remained shuttered, guarding its inmates as jealously as the Bastille did her own. Later that day, Jean-Claude Bernard made an attempt to see Carroll, only to be told he was not at home.

In vain, they called on everyone they knew, asking for assistance. All were horrified at the thought of incarceration in the Bastille. The Bernards told them all about Carroll, the monstrous *colon*, and how Connor had feared he would exploit the censorship laws as revenge for his denunciation of slavery.

'I understand this Carroll has connections at court,' concluded Julie to her particular friend Madame Fourier, the elegant hostess whose salon Connor had attended. 'Which of course leaves us powerless against him. Is there really nothing we can do? Our dear friend is imprisoned for daring to speak out against evil, like so many writers before him!'

'I regret there is nothing I can do,' said Madame Fourier. 'But the pamphlet must really be extraordinary to exact such retribution. I should very much like to read it, if there is a copy to be found in the city. My poor Connor. This will do his literary reputation no harm at all! He was at any rate fortunate not to have been thrown in Bicêtre like a common criminal.'

These sentiments were echoed by the Chevalier de Sébastien, the nobleman who had taken that first copy from the printer, and who now appeared to be the sole possessor of the ill-fated work.

'I regret I cannot intercede on his behalf,' he told Bernard. 'I have my own troubles with the authorities, you understand. But the *Bastille? Alors*, I must have that pamphlet copied and give it to a few men of taste, so that we may judge its merits more clearly.'

'Its merits are irrelevant,' said Bernard. 'Our friend was imprisoned by the unscrupulous *colon* he writes so eloquently about. If you have read it with any care, then you will understand why we fear for his fate.'

'What a singular form of retribution,' mused the Chevalier. 'To have this unknown Irishman treated in the same way as the great Voltaire and others whose work actually posed a threat to the King.'

'You speak as though a spell in the Bastille was a badge of honour,' fumed Bernard. 'Do you not recall the effect it has had on so many inmates, those who suffered a lifetime of melancholy and nervous disorders after their release, and I speak only of those fortunate enough to have been released? But we have reason to believe that the infamous *colon* acted solely to break Connor's connection with his daughter and to threaten her into submission.'

'There is a daughter involved? This Connor is really something, *non?* I of course understand your concern, but why worry unduly? If this *colon* wished to resort to barbarity, well, dare I say there are infinitely less troublesome ways of disposing of an unsuitable young man?'

'Indeed. Such is the present state of France, that it takes little trouble to arrange an incarceration by *lettre de cachet*, while those who claim to oppose the absolutism of a foolish, incompetent King can only sit by and watch, helpless against the suffering of their friend.'

The infinitely infuriated Jean-Claude Bernard had to concede defeat, and returned home, dejected, to Julie and the baby. Again, they left the infant in their servant's hands, crossed the river Seine, and found themselves outside the Bastille, daunted by its impenetrability. They spoke to the guards and the passersby, gathering what fragments of gossip and information they could. They learned that the looming, melancholy state prison was almost empty, that the madman who shouted from his tower window was the notorious Marquis de Sade, and that the Bastille housed only two madmen in total, the other being an elderly Irishman, a Comte de Whyte Malville, formerly of the Irish Brigades. There were several other prisoners—dissolute, debauched, guilty of petty crimes that bore no similarity to Connor's, although one of them had attempted to assassinate the King. The Bernards failed, therefore, to gauge Connor's situation by comparing it to that of his fellow-inmates.

When they had appealed to everyone they could think of, but could not bear to slacken their efforts, Julie paid a visit to the Collège des Irlandais. The College Superior received her kindly and sympathetically, though he was unacquainted with either Monsieur Carroll or the young doctor, and granted her request to speak with the newly returned Donnchadh.

'I know Mademoiselle Hélène has a particular regard for you,' said Julie once she had recounted her sorry tale. 'I thought perhaps you might have seen her, that you night have learned something other than the little we have been able to ascertain?'

But no, Donnchadh had not seen her since his recovery and return to the College. He stumbled over his words, attempting to reconcile his brief memory of the calm physician, who had so carefully sutured his wound, with his uncle's scathing descriptions of the young man's morals, and now this new unsettling element of Monsieur Carroll and the *lettre de cachet.* 'Is Mademoiselle Ní Fhlathartaigh safe?' he asked in a worried tone. 'And what of Mademoiselle Carroll?'

'They are in Monsieur Carroll's house, though that hardly qualifies as safe. I know of no reason to be unquiet on Mademoiselle Hélène's behalf, though I worry for *Isabelle* . . . For all their sakes, it is imperative that Doctor Connor be released. Is there really nothing you can do?'

Donnchadh floundered, feeling at sea and unable to articulate his own distress. 'I know that one of the chaplains at the Bastille is an Irish priest,' he volunteered at last. 'The Abbé Thomas MacMahon from Galway. We could ask him to keep an eye out for Doctor Connor—it isn't much, I know, but it is the best I can suggest.'

The ministrations of a fellow countryman, thought Julie, disheartened. Is that the best we can do for him, the sole consolation we can offer? 'Thank you for your kindness,' she said sadly, and left to return home to her baby. She tried to picture Connor with this Abbé MacMahon, because it seemed on the surface to be the least foreboding image she could find, but she soon abandoned the effort. An Irish chaplain, and an Irish gaoler, she thought, that does not reassure me at all.

*   *   *

Inside the Bastille, Connor was listening to the Abbé say Mass. You have the air and manner of my old teacher, Father Ó'Murchú, and something of his voice, he thought. I can almost hear him, though he is five years in his grave, and long may he lie in it, for he would not rest easy if he had seen what was to become of me.

It was raining the night the guards took me outside. On the opposite side of the street, I recognised the carriage from Isabella's first visit, and caught a glimpse of the man I assume to be Monsieur Carroll, *Grand Blanc*, peering out from behind his window. He has come to watch, I thought, witness the manifestation of his power, see them drag me to the Bastille as a spectacle for his amusement. But then he called to the driver in a bored, peremptory tone to drive on, not to linger in such a drab, narrow street, as if he had been passing reluctantly through and I were nothing to him. I was never under any illusions. I knew he would move swiftly if he learned about Isabella—I can only blame myself for hesitating so long, for failing to anticipate this.

I have invested the shadows with the stories of all those who were ever incarcerated here. *Philosophes*, most of them wiser than me, some of them not, all of whom dared more than I did. It is ironic, is it not, that Carroll should have me sent here? Is he mocking my insignificance, or elevating my few pages? If I have the opportunity to do it again, I will make sure that it is for a real reason. I will not again become the puppet of an intriguing Irish *colon*, I will have that pamphlet read by as many people as possible, just as Isabella desired. I would fight back against the corruption of the world, I would fight hard.

How long must I stay here? Two years, like Linguet? A lifetime, like those who crossed the path of the so-called *Louis le Bien-Aimé*, until I'm old and white-haired, health destroyed and eyes blinded by the darkness?

Julie was rocking the baby in a cradle by the fire, trying to lull him to sleep. She worried that he might have caught cold. Beside her on a table lay a reprinted copy of Connor's pamphlet. The Chevalier had been true to his word. He had circulated the promised copies, and Connor was being talked of by those few discerning friends. Much good may it do him, thought Julie, before she was interrupted by a caller.

Donnchadh advanced slowly into the room. 'I went to see my uncle yesterday,' he said. 'He is ill-disposed towards your friend, but I pleaded with him to make inquiries, in the name of Christian compassion, if nothing else, and today I received this.' He held out a brief, hastily-scrawled note. 'Doctor Connor is well-treated, though low in spirits. He occupies a cell in one of the towers, and has a bed, a table and chair, and a fire. He is also allowed clean linen, and pencil and paper.'

'That much is something,' said Julie. 'Thank you for your kindness.'

The sound of his mother's voice unsettled the baby again. Donnchadh stood in the middle of the room awkwardly, wanting to express a torrent of sentiments, but not knowing what to do. Despite the demands of the child, she saw his hesitancy and confusion.

'Read this,' she said, indicating the reprinted pamphlet. 'Acquaint yourself with his sins while I tend to the child.'

This pamphlet had been troubling Donnchadh ever since he learned of its existence. What precisely had the physician written about Monsieur Carroll, and was it true? What was he to make of his own uncle's denunciation of Dr Connor's character and philosophies? Who was right, the uncle who had fostered his vocation in him, or this physician? All the implications and possible conclusions made his head spin, as did one additional recurrent anxiety: what was to become of Hélène in all this? Brushing the thought of her away, he began to read. But the pamphlet filled him only with greater conflict and doubt. He looked up to find Julie's eyes on him now that the baby was sleeping.

'What is to become of him?' she said quietly.

I don't know,' said Donnchadh, at a loss. 'But I pray for him, and now that I have read his writing, I pray for the poor souls of Monsieur Carroll's *habitation*.'

CHAPTER SIX

After informing Isabella of Connor's imprisonment, Carroll's first step had been to extend some rather lavish hospitality to the other *colons* who had settled in Paris to live on the remittances of their Saint-Domingue estates. These were large supper parties and entertainments, designed to distract attention from the coolly composed and barely concealed revulsion of this Irish daughter. There were always so many people invited that Isabella found she could escape each cluster of them after receiving their compliments on her appearance and the vaguest protestations of friendship and interest. Anything more, and she pretended not to understand, though she was terrified of angering her father.

Only two weeks had passed since Connor had been imprisoned, and already significant changes had been made inside the *hôtel*. Carroll never spoke of Connor, or of the pamphlet, but neither Isabella, nor Hélène, nor her mother, were fooled when he hired several new servants, ostensibly to cope with the additional strain on the household of this sudden bout of entertainment. Isabella was placed entirely in the hands of a new lady's maid whose duties disguised her true purpose, which was to guard and frame the Irlandaise's every movement. All three Irishwomen hated Angélique—Hélène and Brighid were as much at the mercy of her constant prying as Isabella.

Hélène avoided Isabella as much as she could. Those enchanted, snow-trimmed days now seemed so very far away; she had lost both the captain and Donnchadh, and now she had lost Isabella her physician as well. She had received no word from Donnchadh, and although she knew she could not really have expected it, she was nonetheless disappointed. He has returned to the *Collège* by now, she thought, and neither Isabella nor myself has anything to look forward to other than blackness and despair.

There is not an ounce of fight left in her, thought Brighid, watching her daughter. '*Ná bí buartha, Eibhlín*,' she said. 'It will all come right in the end.'

'*Brigitte*,' said the self-important Angélique, strutting into Brighid's room with Isabella in tow. 'Monsieur has hired musicians to play for his guests tonight, and he wishes you to oversee their choice of music and ensure they have everything they require.'

'Of course,' smiled Brighid thinly. Not only were she and her daughter excluded from the night's proceedings, but they were not even to be called upon to play. How things had changed.

Hélène watched Isabella being led off to have her hair dressed.

'You see to these musicians, Eibhlín,' said her mother. 'You are better fitted for the task than I am.'

Hélène found them in the kitchen, eating all that was put in front of them. Not wanting to interrupt them, she went to the window, wondering what was happening outside. Within moments, her eye caught a familiar shadow hastily hiding itself beside the back entrance. Her blood quickened, and she felt a surge of life flow through her. Could she steal this one opportunity? Capture this one moment before she thought better of it? She slipped unnoticed from the room.

'Donnchadh,' she whispered once outside, pulling him out of view. 'I thought I'd never see you again,' she said with some excitement.

He flushed, and stepped back from her. 'I wasn't going to speak to you, I just wanted to know you were safe,' he said.

'None of us is safe, Donnchadh,' she said in Gaelic, wondering why he was shrinking away from her. Did he know about Connor? 'The physician is imprisoned, and we are all at my cousin's mercy. I don't know what is to become of us.'

'I know, and I've been praying for you, night

and day.'

'Donnchadh,' she said, putting her hand on his arm. 'What earthly good are prayers?'

He gave her a startled, agitated glance, flung her hand away as if it were a leper's, and ran off into the night. Hélène returned indoors to the musicians, confused. How could he spurn her so, after going to such lengths to see her? Had she done something wrong, said something wrong? Showing the musicians into the empty salon, she wondered what to make of his behaviour, and thought of all their afternoons together when he was recovering from his wound. She sat at the harpsichord to show how Carroll liked one of his favourite pieces played, but the music served only to remind her of the abbé's old spinet, and she shook her head sadly, excusing herself from the salon on the pretext of needing to fetch another piece of music.

'Bravo, Mademoiselle,' said a drunken young *colon*, falling over her the moment she stepped outside the salon, and grabbing the sheets of music from her hand. 'I heard your playing from the *vestibule.* Carroll promised us some fine musicians tonight, but he did not tell us it would be such a pretty piece.'

'Well it's not,' said Hélène, pulling her sheets back. 'And if you wish to appreciate the music, then I suggest you refrain from drinking any more of that rum.'

'Ooh,' he said mockingly. 'You're a fiery

little wench, aren't you? In which gutter did he find *you*?'

'You dare speak to my ward with such disrespect?' asked Carroll, coming upon them at that moment.

'Your *ward*?' The young man was taken aback. 'Forgive me, I misunderstood, and her playing was so beautiful, I . . .'

'She yields an intriguing result, does she not?' observed Carroll dryly. 'But still a little raw for Parisian society.'

Am I his ward, then, wondered Hélène? For as long as he continues to treat me as a servant of undefined rôle, I will remain easy prey to all these drunken *colons* he has thrown his house open to. She could hear the sound of guests arriving. Angrily, she decided she could now abandon the musicians to their own devices, and went to her chamber, where she could brood in peace.

About an hour later, Angélique flounced in. 'Monsieur says you are to dress immediately—the musicians he hired are disappointing, and he wishes *you* to entertain his guests.'

Does he indeed? thought Hélène. Well, in that case, I am going to make myself so much the fashionable *Parisienne*, that not a single person in that *salon* will dare insult me.

Some time later, she made her entrance, her elegant dress and coiffure fortifying her against the strangers' glances. How dare any of you set yourselves above me, she thought.

Seating herself at the harpsichord, she began to play just as she had been taught.

A considerable interval passed before Carroll told her she might stop. Standing up, she met Isabella's eyes across the room. Her cousin's gaze seemed reproachful, as if she were asking how Hélène could play while Connor languished in prison. Hélène observed how stiff and guarded Isabella's movements were, and held herself responsible. I'm so sorry, she thought, I did not mean to make you so unhappy. Without realising she had done so, she found she had made her way to her cousin's side.

'Your music surprised me,' Isabella said. 'I had not suspected you of sensibility.' She then turned abruptly and left the salon.

In her boudoir, Isabella grabbed some paper and began to write the only letter she could think of:

> Dear Aunt,
>
> I find myself in such difficulties that I must appeal to you for your forgiveness and immediate succour. It has taken me this long to realise that I am every bit as rash and foolish as you once warned. Hoping that you still harbour some remembrance of the happy years we spent together, I can only pray that you find it in your heart, and within your power, to offer me the assistance I so

desperately seek

I often recall the words you spoke, when you told me that money was the only way to shield oneself against disaster in a world like this. But how can one do so at the expense of so many others? On learning the true nature of my father's 'business affairs', all those forcibly carried in the hold of his ship to Saint-Domingue, and the conditions on his *habitation*, I turned to Dr Connor. He is a thinker of unusual abilities, and I persuaded him to write a pamphlet denouncing my father and those of his kind. Little did I know my father would then have a *lettre de cachet* served on him. Dr Connor has been imprisoned in the Bastille, while I am confined to the house. What am I to do, Aunt?

Forgive me if I make little sense, for I am so dreadfully confused, and do not know my own mind. Won't you speak to my uncle? You both know the world better than I. Perhaps you could find a way to have Dr Connor freed? Though you are so very far away . . .

She heard Angélique outside, talking with another servant. Hastily, she threw the unfinished letter on the fire, knowing that Angélique would find it otherwise.

'Mademoiselle,' said Angélique, her eyes

darting suspiciously around the room. 'You left so suddenly, your father was concerned.'

'It is nothing,' said Isabella. 'My head aches a little from all the voices.'

'Do you wish to retire, then?' Angélique asked, tearing at Isabella's hair as she set about dismantling the evening's coiffure.

Isabella winced, and tried to distract herself from Angélique's rough hands so that her discomfort wouldn't show. She returned to the schemes she constantly dreamed up for securing Connor's release. Perhaps the prison authorities would realise it had all been a terrible mistake, though that was highly unlikely. Or perhaps, a large sum of money would somehow fall into her hands. She could then march out of the *hôtel* and down to the Bastille, where she would bargain for his release. But once there, who would she approach? Her mind faltered over this detail. Hélène would excel at this kind of thing, she who played her cards to such deadly effect. But Isabella?

In any case, where could such a large sum of money come from? Could its origins be anything but corrupt? Though indeed, her attempting to buy Connor's liberty was in itself a form of corruption, was it not? What was she to do? she wondered, observing the witch Angélique through the *miroir de toilette.* What was Connor to do?

CHAPTER SEVEN

Hélène had not yet lost her habit of listening out for callers, hurrying down to the *vestibule* whenever she heard the front door open. The next morning, however, she was unnerved to find herself face to face with Captain O'Shea. All the things she had thought to say should she ever see him again had left her, and she found herself lost for words.

'*Capitaine*,' she said finally. 'Am I to congratulate you? Was your mission successful?'

'Such pleasantries are a little premature,' he replied in some embarrassment. 'Monsieur Carroll, I came as soon as I could.'

Her cousin had appeared so silently behind her that she almost jumped. 'I am grateful for your condescension,' he said, indicating that the captain should join him.

Hélène glanced sharply at the captain as he followed her cousin into the library, and immediately formed the only conclusion she could: marriage to Isabella, she thought, staring at the closed door. Moments later, she was re-confronted by Carroll.

'I know I can count on you not to inform Isabella of Captain O'Shea's presence,' he said. 'I am in no mood for one of her scenes.'

Marriage to Isabella, she confirmed. His

superior must have changed his mind about his daughter.

In shock, Hélène removed herself to a nearby salon, thinking of how Carroll and the captain would be sitting by the fire in the library, bargaining over Isabella's future, and drawing up the marriage contract. But why? The captain had informed her in no uncertain terms that he had no desire to marry her cousin. She remembered how frankly he had spoken to her on the day of the duel, and again on the day he had taken leave of them so abruptly.

What am I? she wondered for the thousandth time, looking at her greyed reflection in the tarnished mirror. In betraying Isabella to Carroll, I have only served to deliver her into his hands. The physician remains shut up in the Bastille, she cannot now escape the captain. But what is Carroll, that he should have such power? For all Carroll's wealth, Hélène had noticed the careless disrespect with which the captain treated him. What had changed, that Captain O'Shea should come running, like a little lap dog, at Carroll's command?

'Eibhlín,' said her mother, finding her lost in contemplation of the looking-glass. 'Did you know that Captain O'Shea is with Carroll in the library?'

Hélène turned around, a curious expression on her face. 'If I were to tell you that I needed to speak with him, could you arrange for me to slip away unnoticed, just this once?'

Brighid was surprised, but knew this was no time for confidences. 'That would be difficult,' she said reluctantly, though she was thinking fast. 'The horses are being fed and watered, and the driver is in the kitchen. Perhaps I could get you into his carriage? Then he could drive around, return within the hour for something he forgot, and I could slip you back into the house?'

'*Go raibh míle maiih aqat, a mháthair,*' said Hélène, rising instantly to her feet. It was a reckless, reckless scheme, but why shouldn't she try? After all, she had nothing to lose.

And so it was that the captain found his carriage curtains closed and Hélène awaiting him inside. 'You must forgive me,' she said as smoothly as she could. 'I know how irregular this is.'

'Should I drive on, Monsieur?' the driver called.

'Yes, yes, drive,' he said hastily.

'Thank you,' she smiled. 'I hope you will also overlook my frankness, but we have so little time, and so much to discuss. Have your prospects become so bleak that you must stoop to marrying my cousin?'

The captain sighed. 'Having lived to regret the imprudence of my former confidences to you, I really should profess my admiration for Mademoiselle Carroll's fortune, its distinct merit being the imminence with which it will be placed at my disposal—I have contracted some rather pressing debts I must discharge.'

'Gambling debts?' she asked, her heart pounding. Had she miscalculated?

'I prefer not to play, but on this occasion, it was unavoidable,' he acquiesced. 'It is not a considerable amount, but it is one I don't have, and as I lost it to a superior officer, I must find it as soon as possible.'

'I understand. A handsome dowry would relieve you, not only of this debt, but of awkward social situations in which you feel obliged to play . . . simply to maintain the semblance of having the means to play.'

'In a manner of speaking, yes.' He looked at her, puzzled. 'Though it is not quite that simple. Suffice it to say that my ambitions require some substantial investment.'

'But to succeed at court, you need a compliant wife, and Isabella . . . You spar so constantly, even the bloodiest battlefield would seem a respite from the turmoil of your domestic life.' She paused, needing to force herself to proceed to her next, even more sensitive issue. 'Do you remember the first time you saw me?' she asked nervously. 'You came upon me in the hallway, and, assuming I was Carroll's daughter, you inspected me thoroughly, and I felt, that is, I had the impression that I did not displease you?'

'You know you did not,' he said, though he

turned away. 'But it is foolish to speculate on what might have been.'

Brutal, but honest, thought Hélène. He succeeded only in strengthening her longing for the opportunities that had been withheld from her, and increasing her resentment by his tone. 'Then, at least, tell me, why did Carroll choose you?'

'You would really care to know?' he asked in disbelief at her perseverance. 'Well, then, Carroll did not so much choose me as was chosen for me by my uncle, who looks out for my interests: Carroll wishes to have his petition of nobility granted, but as he has no obvious proof of genealogy, or indeed claim to the old Irish aristocracy, he has turned to my uncle for assistance. My uncle has a certain influence, you understand, but one which comes at a price. So you see, Mademoiselle Ní Fhlathartaigh, how very fortunate you are that you are not Mademoiselle Carroll.'

Her mother had been right. Hélène pondered this a moment. Her mother belonged to the old Irish nobility. What if, what if she were to turn this to her advantage . . .? Hélène's thoughts began to race, but she attempted to still them—if she were to succeed, she must move slowly, prevent confusion and a sense of the enormity of it all from getting the better of her.

'You know that Isabella loves someone else?' she said finally.

He looked troubled. 'That is indeed unfortunate. I had suspected something of the kind, but . . .'

'But what, Captain? Have your suspicions also been aroused by the unseemly haste with which Carroll wishes to marry his daughter?'

The captain looked coy, despite his obvious embarrassment. 'Not unseemly, surely? My uncle has often spoken to him of the match, though he did not appear overly eager till of late . . . Do you mean to imply there are pressing reasons for this union, that the nature of the friendship between Mademoiselle and her physician . . .?' Here he trailed off delicately, and looked at Hélène in such a manner that his meaning could not be mistaken.

Hélène almost laughed at the turn the conversation had taken. 'No! At least, not in the way you imagine. Mademoiselle and her physician occupied themselves solely with politics during their time together. They were working on a pamphlet of some kind, a denunciation of slavery that proved so inflammatory Carroll had the good doctor thrown in the Bastille. Inconsolable brides may well be the norm in Paris, my dear Captain, but surely not brides who seek to undermine the very foundations of the family fortune?'

'I understand you perfectly,' said the Captain, hastily revising all his previous assumptions. 'I should not wish to find myself embroiled in such . . . circumstances. Perhaps it would be best for all concerned if I were to . . . walk away.'

'You would do that?' asked Hélène softly. All that she hoped to attain was in view, if only she could realise it. 'But what of Doctor Connor? He performed a service for you once. Are you content to leave him languishing in the Bastille? My understanding is that Carroll prevailed on a friend of his for the *lettre de cachet*. But you are Captain O'Shea. Surely your influence is greater than his?'

'In a manner of speaking. I feel sure I even know how he did it, but . . .'

Seeing his doubt, Hélène decided to stumble on, lest she lose her courage so close to the end. 'I'll be very blunt, Captain,' she said, not looking at him all the while. 'You have intimated that your uncle wields more influence than Carroll, and Carroll requires his assistance in having his petition granted. No matter how great a sum of money exchanges hands, Carroll will be more beholden to your uncle than your uncle will be to him. That gives your uncle, and by extension you, the upper hand. Now, you find yourself in a situation where you require a bride equipped with Carroll's money. You do not seem overly concerned as to who she is, so I thought . . .' She hesitated here, in need of courage to continue. Glancing at him, she saw he was listening attentively, and with a kind of curiosity, as if she were some creature he had not been expecting.

'The possibilities are endless, Captain. I believe you could present Carroll with a *fait accompli*: first, you would need to secure Doctor Connor's release. Then, he and Isabella could leave Paris together, removing themselves from Carroll's sphere, and leaving him without a daughter to be married. But, if he could somehow be persuaded to make me his 'daughter' in her stead . . .'

'That would be difficult,' exclaimed the Captain with a mixture of pity, admiration, and something else.

'Perhaps,' she admitted. 'But my mother has genuine papers to prove her nobility. They could be made to mean something, could they not? All this would require your uncle's assistance, and even then . . . you would have to want it badly enough to risk . . . being betrothed to me?' she said, appealing to him directly for the first time.

'And what of you, Hélène Ní Fhlathartaigh?' he said at last. 'Do you want it so badly? Knowing as you do what I am, knowing I could not take you without Carroll's money?'

She smiled sadly. 'It is the way of the world, and yet I do not believe you to be so very indifferent to me, Captain O'Shea.'

CHAPTER EIGHT

For all O'Shea's talk of intrigue, much of it had been the product of observation rather than participation. He was, however, sufficiently versed in corruption to know how to set Hélène's intrigue in motion: what words to choose when broaching the subject with his uncle, how best to detach Carroll's contact with a more generous bribe.

Here he was, striding across the drawbridge that separated the Bastille from the petite bourgeoisie of the Faubourg Saint-Antoine. Within a few moments, the doctor would be brought from his cell and delivered into the captain's hands. This is power, he thought, as he stood in the courtyard, surveying the clock with its representation of two chained prisoners. Despite his weariness, the captain savoured the victory, feeling it race through his spirits and go to his head like a few rapid shots of liquor. The swaggering physician, who had commanded Mademoiselle Carroll's attention so effortlessly, who had come to Donnchadh's rescue with such contempt for him, the captain, was now going to be beholden to him for his release. He smiled in smug anticipation, remembering the disdain of a voice full of its own superior medical skill. Then the guards brought Connor out. He looked ill and troubled. The captain's rush of intoxication passed.

'Captain O'Shea. To what do I owe this honour, if it is indeed an honour?'

'Come now, *Monsieur le Docteur.* We are both now fully cognizant of your oddities, but surely even you are capable of viewing your release as something akin to an honour?'

'Speak frankly, Captain,' said Connor. 'As you see, I am unwell, and in no condition for verbal wrangling. Am I being released, and if so, why? I know you are close to Carroll, and demand to know where I stand.'

'If I remind you that you are standing in prison at present, will you have the goodness to defer the matter until we have actually left?' responded the captain in Irish.

It was light outside, and the street was crowded, with more noise than Connor had heard in a number of weeks. The captain indicated his carriage.

'The price of writing such a pamphlet has taken quite a toll,' he said, concerned. 'I wonder if you are fit to travel?'

'It is but a cold,' said Connor dismissively. 'A product of winter, and not the clumsy retribution you imply.'

'You will forgive me for my solicitude, then. Though indeed, it is not every day I come to the rescue of errant, would-be *philosophes.* The plan is simple: late tonight, you leave Paris. It would be distinctly reassuring to know that you will survive the journey.'

'I am to leave Paris, you say. Is there anything else I should be aware of?'

'Allow me to explain,' said the captain, who was becoming exasperated. 'You are very fortunate indeed that I have succeeded in securing your release. You could be facing yet another night in the Bastille while Carroll casts around for a suitable husband for Isabella, but instead, Mademoiselle Hélène and I have arranged your escape, on condition you take it and never return to Paris. Congratulations on your impending marriage, Doctor. I dare say you will wish Hélène and myself the same?'

'What an intrigue,' said Connor, at a loss for words, and too tired to think clearly, though he guessed at what had been left unspoken. 'Dare I ask at what price our freedom?'

'Enough, Doctor. I have read your pamphlet—briefly, it is true, but enough to anticipate your contempt.'

Connor looked curiously at the captain before turning away, struggling to decipher his feelings. 'I am through with Paris, in any case,' he said finally. 'I look out this window, and all I see is the corruption of the rich, the misery of the poor. Nothing more. Not now. What is it you see there that you want so badly?'

'Do you really need to ask? Opportunities unlike any I could have in Ireland.'

'And you accept that, unquestioningly?' Connor persisted.

'I have arranged for your friends to meet

you at this address,' said the captain opaquely, stopping at an inn in a narrow street. 'May your journey proceed safely.'

* * *

Hélène had pleaded indisposition, and had been seated at the window for the most part of the day, awaiting the success or failure of their enterprise. Finally, she saw the captain's uncle's carriage drive slowly past the *hôtel*. She stood up with a mixture of anxiety and elation: this was the sign she had been waiting for.

She found Isabella with Angélique.

'Angélique, my mother needs you downstairs—there seems to be some problem with a delivery of wine?'

Hélène had hit on the Frenchwoman's one weakness. Angélique sprang to her feet immediately, but Isabella glared back at her when she was motioned to follow.

'I'll sit with Isabella, if you like,' said Hélène sweetly. 'My mother says it'll take only a moment or two, anyway.' She sat down beside her cousin, and waited until the sound of Angélique's footsteps had died away. 'Isabella, I know you're angry with me, but what would you say if I were to tell you that Connor was released from the Bastille today?'

'Is this another intrigue, or is it the truth?' asked Isabella, resenting her for arousing a shudder of hopes that had to be immediately repressed, for this cousin was not to be trusted.

'It is perfectly true,' said Hélène. 'Your father knows nothing of it. So what need you care if it is another intrigue or not? He will meet you at this address tonight, and then you will both leave Paris immediately if you have an ounce of prudence left, though I don't imagine you do.'

'Perhaps I possess sufficient prudence to question your word. How have you of all people managed this?' Isabella countered sceptically.

'If it is frankness you ask for, I persuaded Captain O'Shea to do it. We hope to be married once your father has agreed to his uncle's newly revised terms for obtaining letters patent for the supposedly noble House of Carroll.'

Suddenly, it all began to fall into place. 'I think I understand. You are orchestrating my departure so that you can assume the role of daughter,' said Isabella.

Despite her self-professed frankness, Hélène winced at the cold clarity of her cousin's words. 'You speak as though I am stealing your identity, when you have rejected it at every turn. I am merely stepping into your discarded gowns,' she retorted defiantly.

'It hardly dignifies the word "stealing",' said Isabella. 'If it pleases you to marry the captain, then I wish you both well. If you wish to play daughter to my father, then that too is your affair, but what about his fortune?'

Isabella did not know how to continue—a girl who could use Connor's pamphlet against them both obviously didn't care how her father had come by his money, and yet that same girl had risked so much to have Connor released. Who was she, and what made her act as she did?

'What right have you to judge me?' Hélène asked. 'We have never been on an equal footing. You were free to think as you pleased, secure in the knowledge that you would always have someone to run to—your father, your uncle even, the physician . . . But I was alone, shunted from Ireland to a convent to your father's house, like an inconvenient parcel.'

'What a dark picture you paint,' said Isabella, indignant. 'But perhaps the world is darker than either of us can ever know. We will always differ on the particulars.'

'I am marrying for my own establishment, like everyone else,' said Hélène defensively. 'My future is secure. I shudder to think what yours will be. *Adieu*, Isabella.'

'Is this goodbye?' Isabella shook her head with real regret, regret for all the hopes she had carried with her to Paris, and regret that she would never now come to an understanding with this strange, troubled cousin. 'Hélène, I have parted on bad terms with too many of my family not to wish you well. *Adieu*, Cousin. I hope you find happiness somewhere.'

Hélène was moved by the tone of her cousin's voice. *'Slán leat, Isabella. Go n-éirí an tádh leat i gcónaí,'* she said sadly as she heard Angélique's returning footsteps resounding loudly in the corridor.

CHAPTER NINE

One more morning spent watching for a carriage, thought Hélène, who had been studying the skyline since before the break of dawn, watching the subtle changes of the light. The *hôtel* was so quiet and still, Isabella must have crept away as stealthily as the night, not knowing that Brighid had drugged Angélique into a heavy, unbreakable sleep, for which Isabella would be blamed. Soon, fires would be lit, and it would be discovered. Hélène sat, one last morning, listening to the first sounds of the day begin to gather force.

'Are you dressed, Eibhlín?' asked her mother in pre-rehearsed French words. 'Isabella is not with you, is she? She does not seem to be in her room.'

Despite their truce, the look they exchanged was ambiguous. She is playing on my terms, thought Hélène, but only because it is her game, and for all its clarity and simplicity, I do not see that there will be any clear winners and losers.

'Isn't she? Perhaps she rose early. She sometimes does that, I believe.'

The captain's carriage had arrived, and the entire household now knew that Isabella was gone. As arranged, Hélène followed her mother down to the *vestibule* where O'Shea and his uncle were being told that Carroll was not at home.

'But I must speak with him this morning,' the uncle was insisting.

'Come with me,' said Brighid, intervening. 'You have chosen a most inconvenient moment to call, but I will see what I can do.'

'Not inconvenient at all,' said Carroll, who had also seen the carriage, and had come to pre-empt any awkward slips on the part of his servants. He did not want the O'Sheas to know that Isabella could not be found in the house. 'Cousin, won't you go see to that other matter?'

Brighid drifted silently away, while Hélène lingered where she was, at some distance from the other three.

'Carroll! Where is that daughter of yours? You've kept her hidden from me for so long, I decided I must come and see her for myself.'

'Indeed I have, but I regret she is indisposed this morning,' he replied, hastily leading them into the salon, followed at a remove by Hélène.

'Indisposed?' The elder O'Shea raised a sceptical eyebrow. 'When, pray tell, will she be sufficiently recovered to be presented into the company of one of her father's closest friends?'

'If you will excuse me, I really must see to it that the physician has been sent for,' said Carroll hastily. 'My servants are so unreliable. Hélène, would you be so good as to play for these gentlemen in my absence?'

Hélène did as she was bid, though her nerves were straining in anticipation of the next step, thus impeding her covert attempts to observe this uncle who had several fates now in his hands. Within a few moments, Carroll had returned, followed by her mother, who ran in after him with perfectly judged distraction.

'Oh Cousin, what shall we do?' said Brighid, distraught. 'Isabella really is gone! She has taken some of her things and simply disappeared, we cannot find her anywhere!'

'She is gone?' asked the uncle in feigned amazement. 'But what can this mean, Carroll?'

'Angélique is still sleeping and cannot be woken, but I found this in her chamber,' said Brighid, holding out the note Isabella had left behind.

Angrily, Carroll snatched the paper from her and read it quickly. 'It is no matter,' he said evasively. 'I assure you, she will have returned by nightfall.'

'I beg to disagree,' said the captain. 'If Mademoiselle Carroll has run away, that is a very grave matter indeed.'

'But a fortuitous one, perhaps,' added his uncle. 'The truth is, Carroll, I have come on a rather delicate errand. My nephew's affections have been engaged by that pretty little ward of yours, sitting by her harpsichord, so demure and lovely. It would be a tragedy, would it not, to waste that sweetness by insisting that her beloved marry her so unwilling cousin?'

If Carroll was surprised by this, he chose not to display it. 'Hélène, leave us,' he said, his countenance and voice opaque. 'You and your mother go try to wake Angélique.'

Upstairs, Angélique was still sleeping her heavy, drugged sleep. '*Beidh tú ceart go leor i gceann tamaillín*,' said Brighid, addressing the wiry little frame, its aggression all drained away. 'And you'll be fine too, Eibhlín.'

Hélène looked down at Angélique, so effortlessly felled. But will I? she wondered. This uncle has the key to all that Carroll wants today, but Carroll is so slippery, so arbitrary, he could want something different tomorrow, and what then? She shook her head, attempting to quell her doubts. No regrets, she told herself. A large marriage settlement and a comfortable apartment in another part of Paris, and I will be free, won't I? We need only today.

That day was Hélène's, as she had planned it. It took some time, but eventually she and her mother were called back downstairs, where the three Irishmen had concluded their bargaining. Battles waged and fought, they all seemed reasonably content with the outcome.

'Well played, Hélène,' said Carroll dryly. 'I see I have acquired a daughter, and at quite a high price too. To be sure, I had other plans for you, but as you are all so eager to fulfil my nearest wishes, then I will accept the proposition.'

It's done, then, she thought with relief. Over and done with. I have won my place in the world. Now, all that remains is to live it.

* * *

Isabella and Connor had left Paris far behind. From the window of the carriage, Isabella looked out at the countryside she might never see again. By now, Hélène would have secured her captain.

Meanwhile, Isabella and Connor faced uncertainty of their own. First they would go to Dublin, that much was settled. There, they hoped to live life on their own terms, doing all the things they believed in, despite the impediments in their way. In the Bastille, Connor had come to realise that Ireland held considerably more sway over his imagination than he had thought, and he longed to try his hand at it again, now that he had summoned the courage openly to strike out his own path. Isabella found herself agreeing with him in sentiment, and wondering with some amusement what her aunt would say when she learned that her niece had returned to Dublin, married to the physician.